SEVENTEEN STORIES

by
Judit Martin

TERRESTRIUS PRESS LTD.

by Judit Martin
Fiction
Augusta's Daughter: Life in 19th. Century Sweden*
Kajsa, Augusta's Grandaughter*
Swedish Portraits: Five Short Stories*
The Bridge*
Seventeen Stories

Non-fiction
Every Three Hours: Life As A Weather Observer
Swedish Medieval Church Painting

[*published by Penfield Books]

First published in the United States of America in 2020 by
TERRESTRIUS PRESS LTD.
Kula [Maui], Hawaii: 96790
www.terrestriuspress.com

ISBN: 978-1-7357831-5-4

designed by William Scobie-Mitchell
typeface: Garamond
printed in the United States of America

To Penfield Joan
who believed in me

THE STORIES

PART ONE
AMERICAN BEGINNINGS

This collection of short stories begins with semi-autobiographical portrayals of sibling rivalry while growing up in middle class America in the forties and fifties. Eventually this childhood obsession shifted its focus to a place called Europe, which in turn led to a radical change in my life. (Amazingly, seventy-five years later, Erin and Sunny are working together to publish Erin's writing.)

Erin and her beloved Sunny, Easter, 1946

MICKEY

The last stars evaporated, washed out by the gentle lightening of the eastern sky. The storm of the previous day had moved on, leaving in its wake a sea of new-fallen snow. Across the fields and over ditches rose great wind-sculpted drifts, petrified in motion, while smaller waves remained washed up against tree trunks, rocks, fence posts, leaving little gullies on their lee sides. The unblemished whiteness of innocence. A new day.

It was the only day of the year that Erin awoke on her own, inspite of having lain awake long into the night. From her bed she could see the dark snowlined tree limbs skeletoned against the grey sky. She thought about the baby Jesus, whose birthday it was. He must have been cold lying in the manger on a pile of straw, with just a few rags wrapped around him instead of wearing nice warm sleepers. Several years ago when the Sunday school classes presented their yearly Christmas pagent, the teacher had asked her parents if her little brother Sunny could be baby Jesus. He didn't even go to Sunday school yet, but everyone in the village agreed that he was a perfect Jesus with his curly blond hair. The only thing missing was the halo, they said. But Erin knew it was just invisible. Her mother certainly treated him like he was the Holy Child. He played baby Jesus for two years. The third year he was too big for the manger and they had had to use a doll instead.

Erin slipped out of bed, curious to see what was under the Christmas tree. But as soon as she opened her door a crack the old cow bells clanked. She sighed.

"Erin! It's too early to get up. Go back to bed for awhile."
It was her father's voice.

Like every other year, he had tied the cow bells on a string
between her door and theirs so that he would hear when she
tried to sneak downstairs to look under the tree.

"Erin, did you hear me?"

"I was just going to the bathroom," she lied.

"Don't tell stories!" came his reply. No one lied in her
family--they just told stories.

Her anger rose, not for being caught in a lie, but for the
fact that she was being accused of lying, when it could just as
well have been the truth. She pulled up her nightgown,
spread her feet wide apart, and peed on the floor by the door,
then went back to bed.

Her father had so many stupid ideas and rules. Not just
the bells. Names, for example. He wanted to name her
Roberta after himself, but because he was called Bob, she
wouldn't be allowed to be called Bobbie--which, of course, is
what would have happened. Too confusing, he said.
Consequently, his mother-in-law stepped in and she became
Erin, after no one. Then when her brother was born, he was
so glad to have a son that he insisted on giving him his whole
name--Robert Andrew. But instead of calling him Andrew--
or even Andy--they called him Sunny. Most people thought
it was spelled Sonny and was instead of Junior, but actually it
was because of his blond hair and sunny disposition, as her
mother never tired of telling anyone who showed the least bit
of interest. Everytime she heard her mother's words, her
stringy mouse-brown hair became stringier and her already
cloudy disposition took on thunder cloud proportions. Erin
hated Sunny. She always had, ever since the day they brought
him home from the hospital. Her mother carried him around
a lot and often held him on her lap, even when he was no
longer a baby. It was then that Erin realized that it was
possible to sit on her mother's lap without crying first,
although she never figured out how to go about it. To
compensate, she became expert at inflicting subtle tortures

on Sunny when no one was looking. If he was going to get to sit on her mother's lap, he could just as well cry for the priviledge.

Erin must have dozed off, for the low winter sun was pushing its way through the frosty window when the clanking cow bells woke her.

"What's on the floor here?" her mother wanted to know once she had untied the bell string and opened the door.

When Erin didn't answer she shrugged and went into the bathroom for some toilet paper.

"Was this really necessary?" she asked disdainfully when she had finished wiping it up.

"I couldn't wait," was all Erin said.

Down in the living room Christmas was already beginning. Under the tree were piles of presents wrapped in fancy paper and tied with crinkle-tie bows. And around the base of the tree circled an electric train track with a Lionel engine, flat car, box car, and caboose poised on it. Sunny's, of course. He was already squeeling with delight while her father pushed buttons and pulled levers on the transformer to make the train zoom around the tree with its whistle shrieking.

Erin sat down beside a pile of presents with her name on them and opened one. It was a Bobbsey Twins book -- one she had already read. There was also a big flat package -- a Monopoly game. And a number of smaller ones -- bubble bath, a little purse, a necklace, colored pencils and a drawing pad. But nothing to com- pare with Sunny's train. She felt like ripping out handfuls of his golden curls and then kicking his stupid train to kingdom come. In the next instant she felt like crying. Neither her mother nor her father noticed her disappointment, engrossed as they were in Sunny's excitement over his train.

Suddenly her mother jumped up.

"Oh dear!" she exclaimed. "We forgot the candy canes for the tree! Can't you go and get them, Erin? They're in a bag in the laundry room--on top of the freezer."

"OK," she answered, glad to get away from their joyful Christmas.

She pulled the laundry room door open angrily and reached for the bag of candy canes. Behind her something thumped. She jumped, a shiver running down her spine. It thumped again. This time she turned around. On an old blanket over in the corner by the drier lay a black and white puppy looking at her with big brown eyes. His tail thumped again. Around his neck was a half untied red ribbon and under one paw a torn-off tag which said, "Merry Christmas to Erin from Santa."

"Oh!" she gasped, slapping her thigh--a habit she had when words failed her. "Oh!" she cried again. "Oh! Oh! Oh!" Her hand beat on her thigh.

The dog stood up and stretched, assuming that all the thigh-slapping meant he was to come to her. But first he yawned. His long pink tongue curled upward like a scoop, then suddenly disappeared into his mouth again. Then he went to where she was already hunkered down waiting. She slipped her hands up under his floppy ears and scratched gently, whereupon his tongue reappeared and began washing her face--methodically, like a blind person's fingers "seeing" an unknown face. When he was finished, she put her arms around him and buried her face in his baby-soft fur. She could feel her heart thump thump thumping and hear his tail thump thump thumping on the floor at the other end of him. Never had she felt so happy.

Finally she got to her feet and opened the door to the kitchen.

"Come, Mickey," she said. Long ago she had decided that if she ever had a dog, his name would be Mickey. She no longer remembered why. Standing at her side, his back came up to her knee. Whether he was black with white spots or white with black spots was impossible to determine. He was simply black and white, with a semi-bushy tail.

Just as they came into the living room the train was coming out from behind the Christmas tree. Like a cat,

Mickey leaped onto the engine, derailing it. Sunny began to wail.

"You have to train him better than that," remarked her father, as if she had had him for months.

And she did train him better than that. She taught him to sit, sit up on his haunches, lie down, roll over, play dead. She could put a piece of meat on the floor and tell him, "No!" Hours could go by, and the meat would lie there, apparently forgotten. But as soon as she called,"OK!" he rushed from wherever he was and ate it. If she told him to go get his dish, he came with it in his mouth and tossed it at her feet. Should it land upside down, he put his nose against it and drove it into the nearest wall so hard that it flipped into the air and usually landed right side up, after which he set it down in front of her more carefully than he had the first time. If she skied, he leaped through the snow beside her. If she went sledding, he sat on the sled between her legs. If she bicycled, he ran beside. And every day after school he was waiting at the end of the driveway when she came across the field from the bus stop.

He had only one weakness, one area in which he was unable to control himself: He found wild rabbits and the neighbor's chickens irresistable. But he never hurt them. Many times he had been seen on his way home with a chicken in his jaws. But as soon as someone yelled; "Drop it!" his mouth would open, as if the words had pushed a button, and the chicken would more or less hop to the ground, ruffle its feathers in disgust, and head for home. As for rabbits, his preference was for babies, which he carried in his mouth, tenderly as if they were his own. Since it was impossible to know where he had found them, Erin took care of them until they were big enough to take care of themselves. Sometimes there were three or four at one time. When she let them out onto the lawn to eat and play, Mickey made sure that they stayed close together, as if he were some sort of rabbit herder. And he also saw to it that they were kept clean, licking each one all over the face, between the ears, then between the back legs and up under the tail. And if he could manage to keep it on its back long enough, he washed the stomach.

For the first time in her life, she felt important. The rabbits needed her; without her they would die. And for the first time in her life, she felt that someone really cared about her--and just her. That Mickey was only a dog didn't matter. Or perhaps she didn't even remember that he was a dog. He was her best friend. Her only friend. She played with other children in school, but she avoided going home with any of them when invited and never invited them to her house. She preferred to play alone. She lived in her own private world, where she was part of another family who lived far away. She was the only child and those parents adored her. And she didn't have a brother named Sunny or a father with a lot of stupid rules, nor did she need to wonder how it would be to sit on her mother's lap just for the fun of it. Mickey fit into that family perfectly. No one got angry if he went number two in the front yard or came in the house with muddy feet. They loved him anyway.

However, having Mickey didn't make her hate Sunny less. She took great delight in smacking him with the dog brush when she found him brushing Mickey one day. Another day, when she came home and found him throwing a ball for him to chase, she grabbed the ball out of his hand, purposely bending his fingers back so far that he cried. When her mother came out with the weeping Sunny in her arms and asked why she had bent his fingers, she replied that she had only taken the ball away and that he was just telling stories. Any time he wanted to do something with Mickey she automatically said no. Sunny had her mother and she had Mickey. There was no sharing.

Much of the summer was spent by the creek down in the valley behind the house. Other summers she had only waded in the shal- low gravely places, but Mickey quickly tired of wading and enticed her into the deeper pools, where the bottom was sandy and water spiders skimmed over the surface. She had always been scared to go into places where she couldn't see the bottom, even though it wasn't over her head. But with Mickey splashing ahead of her, she forgot to be afraid. But most of all, she talked to him. Everytime she felt slighted or unfairly treated by her parents, she took her tears and rages to him. He would cock his head this way and that and raise his ears so he could listen properly, then lick away her tears. They were inseparable. At night he slept stretched out on the bed beside her, his head beside hers on the pillow. He ignored the rest of the family.

Usually Erin looked forward to school starting, for she enjoyed learning--and especially reading about other people and places. It gave her another sort of fantasy world in which to live. Besides, she was one of the best in the class and won the teacher's praise without having to try. She set herself apart from the rest of the pupils by always doing something different, better, more creative than the rest of them. Even if her parents took no special notice of her individuality, it was seen and praised in school. But after her summer with Mickey she no longer cared about school. It was just a block of time she must sit through before she could go home to him again.

One day when she came across the field from the school bus he wasn't waiting at the end of the driveway. For a second she couldn't breathe. She ran for the house.

"Mother! Where's Mickey?" she cried.

"I don't know. Wasn't he waiting there?" she said, as if she had asked if the newspaper had come.

"Where's Sunny?"

"He's out in the sand pile."

Erin hurried out to where Sunny was driving a little metal dump truck up and down hilly roads of hard packed sand, his lips vibrating with his special motor sound.

"Where's Mickey?" she demanded.

"I donno," he answered nonchantly.

She snatched the truck out of his hand. "You better tell me before I pull out every one of your ugly curls!" she threatened.

He looked up at her, his under lip already beginning to quiver. "I donno," he repeated nervously.

She squatted down, blocking her mother's view of him in case she was watching from the window. Gently, she put her right hand around his leg just above his knee. He tried to jerk free, but she was already starting to squeeze.

"You better tell me where he is before I break your leg off, do you hear?" Slowly her grip tightened..

"I said I donno," he sniffed, trying not to cry. Once he started crying she would make it hurt even more for being a cry baby.

She squeezed as hard as she could for a few seconds, then let go.

"You better not go tattling, either," she warned him. "Understand?"

He nodded, wiping his eyes.

She waited until he stopped sniffling, then tossed the truck to him and walked away, making sure to dig her heals into his roads.

The rest of the afternoon she searched the neighborhood, knocking on doors and asking if anyone had seen Mickey, and calling his name until her throat was sore. That night she cried herself to sleep.

In the beginning she was certain he would turn up again. Maybe he had just chased a rabbit and gotten lost. Or maybe someone had thought he was lost and had adopted him, in which case he would run home the first chance he got. Then again, something could have happened to him in the woods--he could have gotten his foot caught somehow or hooked his collar on something. Instead of getting on the school bus in the mornings, she took her lunch box and hid in the bushes by the bus stop until it had driven past, then went down into the woods and searched until it was time for the bus to bring her home.   After a few days the teacher   phoned and wondered why she hadn't been in school.

"I don't like school anymore," she said when her father questioned her about her absence. She always made a point of being as evasive to his questions as possible.

"Where have you been, though?"

"Down in the woods."

"Is it Mickey?" he continued.

She nodded slightly, against her will.

"He probably just ran away. It happens all the time, you know. We can get you another dog."

She just shook her head.

She began praying to God every night, begging him to bring Mickey back. When that didn't help, she began to bargain with Him. If He would give Mickey back to her she would help her mother at dinner time without having to be told. She would keep her room clean. She would even stop being mean to Sunny. The latter was the hardest to offer as a bargain, because often she had no control over the things she did to him. When nothing happened, she began keeping her promises ahead of time, just in case God didn't trust her to keep her word. She implored Him to prove that he was the nice God they talked about in Sunday school.   Nothing helped. And every time she asked her parents if they knew what could have happened to Mickey, they always said the same thing--that dogs ran away all the time. But she knew he would never run away from her.

One day towards the end of October her grandmother came to visit. Erin ran out to greet her.

"Do you know what's happened to Mickey?" she asked hopefully when they had finished hugging.

Her grandmother held her at arm's length and looked straight into her eyes.

"I thought he got run over just after school started," she said.

"R-run over?"

"Didn't your mother and father tell you?" she asked, clearly surprised. She pulled Erin to her, wrapping her arms around her securely. "I'm sorry," she said softly. "I thought you knew...."

When her crying had subsided somewhat, they walked toward the house, Granny's arm still around her. Inside the front door Erin broke away and started upstairs to her room to be alone. From the kitchen she heard her grandmother's angry voice.

"Alice, do you mean to tell me that you two never told her the truth?"

Just as she reached the top of the stairs she saw Sunny's train in his room. She plucked the Lionel engine off the tracks, walked back downstairs, put on her jacket and went outside. A raw wind twisted her hair across her face and forced its way through the thin jacket, but she was oblivious to everything but the rage and hurt burning inside her. Reaching the creek, she laid the engine on its side on a big rock beside the water and smashed it over and over and over with a stone. She hated her parents who had let her hope so long, she hated God for not being the nice Sunday school God she'd been taught to believe in, and she hated Sunny because he was Sunny. She could not cry hard enough to make her hurt go away. When she finally stopped smashing the engine it was nothing but a pile of broken metal. No one could have guessed what it had once been. Pulling out the front of her sweatshirt, she scraped the pieces into it and walked slowly up the hill again, sowing handfuls of metal to the right and left as she walked. By the top of the hill her sweatshirt was empty.

When she was later asked if she knew what had happened to the engine to Sunny's train, she answered only, "Maybe it ran away." That was all she ever said, no matter how many times they asked her.

[previously published in Scotland]

GOLDILOCKS

Erin sat up in bed and rubbed her eyes. The winter sun, which usually lightened her room to grey when it was time to get up, must have still been sleeping, for she couldn't see anything. Not even the hall light shone in under her door, nor could she hear any voices or footsteps. Sighing, she fell back against the pillow and closed her eyes again. The cat at the foot of her bed yawned, then moved up to the pillow and recurled itself beside her cheek. But in spite of its lulling spinning in her ear, she was too excited to go back to sleep. Today was her birthday. At last she had gone from being six-going-on-seven- -which was so complicated to say--to being all the way seven. And she and her mother were going downtown to Detroit to go shopping for her birthday present at Hudson's Department Store. Actually it wasn't necessary to go shopping, for the only thing she really wanted was a Mickey Mouse watch. But it would be fun to look at other things, too, just in case she saw something she would rather have. But best of all, they were going to take the train. Not a dinky little open train like at the zoo. A real train.

To Erin, trains were magical. The closest she had ever been to one was at her aunt and uncle's house, where the railroad went past on an embankment right at the end of their block. When they went to visit them, she was always put to bed in the back bedroom while the big people talked and laughed all evening. But rather than going to sleep, she would lie awake in the darkness listening. Sooner or later a rhythmic chugging emerged out of the night, growing louder and louder until the enormous beam of the headlight swept through the window and across the bed. Just as it disappeared, the whistle wailed a long drawn-out good-bye and she could hear the sharpness of the wheels clickety-clacking against the rails as it passed at the end of the street before fading into the distance. In her mind she could see the thick trail of white smoke from the engine getting thinner and thinner as it waved gloriously along the tops of the cars. As long as she could remember, it had been her dream to go somewhere on the train.

She was also looking forward to going downtown with her mother, just the two of them. She didn't like going places with her little brother Sunny. He was only three and got to sit on her mother's lap all the time and she had to hold his hand. And people were forever saying how cute he was and what beautiful curly hair he had. She wished they didn't have him. She had never asked for a little brother in the first place.

Slowly the sky began to lighten outside her window. Erin turned on her bedside lamp. Hanging over her desk chair was her red dress with small blue and yellow embroidered flowers across the chest. It was referred to as her "good dress" and was reserved for Sunday school and birthday parties. She hated dresses. If she had her way, she would only wear blue jeans. Yet this morning she pulled it over her head without a second thought. She knew it was the ticket for the train ride and she gladly paid the price.

She studied her reflection in the bathroom mirror. Her stringy mouse-brown hair, dishwater grey eyes, and toothlessness wouldn't have been quite so bad above a sweatshirt and blue jeans, but the contrast of her good dress made her look worse than usual. She snapped her mouth shut. Even if all seven year olds had a few teeth missing, she didn't see why she had to look like a Halloween pumpkin.

"Hurry up, Erin!" her mother called from the kitchen. "You don't want to miss the train, do you?"

The sound of her name made her cringe. She couldn't stand the way her mother said it, short and hard, like a slap, whereas she always sung out Sunny's name gently, stretching the Sun part before swinging into the rest of it. Yet she had the feeling that her name suited her somehow, just as Sunny's suited him.

In the kitchen Sunny had already finished breakfast and was being dressed in his sailor suit.

"Why're you putting his good clothes on him?" she asked suspiciously. "He's not going too, is he?"

"Of course he is," her mother answered. "What shall he other- wise do?"

"But I thought..." she began, "I thought it was going to be just us on my birthday. Can't Daddy take care of him?"

"You know he works on Saturdays."

She sighed and picked up the already cold piece of toast and jam on her plate. The glow had begun to fade from her excitement. She watched her mother brush Sunny's thick blond curls and wipe the jam off his face. He still had all his teeth and people said he looked like a little angel. Secretly she hoped someone would kidnap him on their way downtown.

"Come on, we have to hurry," her mother said a little sharply as she handed Erin the leggings to her good coat.

"Do I have to wear them?"

"Yes. It's cold out."

Reluctantly she stuck her bare legs into them, feeling the prickly wool grab at her skin as they slid down. They were so tight that they had to have zippers from the knees to the ankles in order for her feet to get through and there was no room to tuck in her skirt, so it had to hang out for everyone to see. Nor did she like the matching coat any better, for its slippery lining made her arms cold. But worst of all was the wide-brimmed hat which tied under her chin and had a silky ribbon hanging down her back like a tail. If she were a mother, she would never make her kid dress up in such clothes!

Her discomfort was forgotten once they got to the station.

"Can I hold my own ticket?" Erin asked hesitantly, after her mother had paid the man in the window and been given their tickets. "I won't loose it. I'm seven now."

Much to her surprise, her mother handed it to her. Erin pulled it out of the cellophane envelope and read it. One child under 12. Round trip B'ham-Det. $1.27. Nov. 29, 1945. Up in the right hand corner was a picture of an engine with smoke coming out of its smoke stack. It made her heart flutter. Carefully she slid it back into the envelope and tucked it into her pocket.

Outside an icy wind rushed down the track from the north and across the open platform. Her mother and Sunny huddled against the leeward wall of the station house, while Erin stood bravely in the middle of the platform, several yards from the tracks. She had waited so long for a chance to wave to the engineer that even the freezing wind forcing its way through her coat couldn't drive her away. Presently there was a low rumbling and then she saw it way at the end of the tracks, surrounded by clouds of smoke. The headlight was aimed right at her. She held her breath and got ready to wave. But to her surprise, the engine got bigger and bigger the closer it came. In no time it was larger than the one at the end of her aunt and uncle's street. And still it kept on growing, like a great black monster. It didn't clickety-clack, it roared and screeched as it rushed towards her and the gigantic wheels seemed eager to suck her in between them. Never had she been so frightened! She tried to back away, to run to her mother, but her feet were glued to the wooden platform. She wished her father were there. He would have been standing beside her holding her hand, rather than hiding against the station wall. Suddenly whirls of loose snow and smoke blew her hat off, inspite of its chin string, whipping strands of hair across her eyes. She stood paralyzed, her hand frozen on its way up to a wave. Then with a loud hiss the wheels ceased their menacing turning and the train came to a halt. Everything was suddenly silent, except for the wild thumping of her heart against her ribs. She closed her eyes, sick and dizzy from her fright, no longer knowing where she was.

"Come on, Missy," a strange voice called. "All aboard!"

Someone grasped her half-raised waving hand and tugged gently, tipping her off balance. One foot took a step to follow, but her knee buckled as if it were made of rubber.

"Here, let me help you," the voice continued.

She felt herself being swung through the air and set down again. A door closed heavily behind her. Before she could open her eyes, there was a jerk and she lost her balance again, falling against the owner of the voice.

"Are you coming, Erin?" she heard her mother call.

"I'll help her," the voice replied. "You go ahead an' find seats."

By now the floor was bouncing rhythmically under her feet, faster and faster, until the clickety-clacking joined in. She opened her eyes, relieved.

"This your first train ride, Missy?" asked the voice connected to her hand.

Nodding, she looked up at the man beside her. He had on a black coat with two rows of shiny brass buttons and a little brass engine, like the one on her ticket, pinned on his pocket. Perched on his head was a funny round hat. He was different from anyone she had ever seen.

"Why's your skin all brown?" she asked curiously.

"'Cuz I was born that way. Hasn't you never seen a Negro before?"

"Uh-uh," she answered. "It's a nice color."

He laughed, showing a row of ivory white teeth with gold edges.

"Engines is nothin' to be scared of, as long as you don't stan' on the tracks," he told her. "They jus' make a lot a steam an' noise."

He led her down the aisle to where her mother already sat, with Sunny on her lap. Guiding her into the window seat facing them, he dropped her hand.

"Tickets, please," he said turning to her mother.

"I have my own ticket," she told him proudly. "It's my birthday and we're going all the way downtown."

"Oh my!" he exclaimed. "How old are you?"

"All the way seven."

"Well, well," he said.

She watched as his brown fingers fumbled with the brass engine on his pocket, and the next thing she knew, they were fastening it onto her coat.

"Happy birthday!" he said, bowing low before her.

"Oh, thank you!" she cried. She crinked her neck to admire it. "What's your name?"

"Sam. What's yours?"

"Erin."

"You have a good time downtown, Erin," he concluded and picked up his ticket punch from the empty seat beside her.

"I will. An' thanks for the nice present, Sam."

Sam continued down the aisle and Erin turned toward the window, pretending she was traveling all alone. She listened to his "Tickets please" as long as she could hear him, but he never once stopped and talked to anyone else.

Presently the train stopped at a station and a woman in a fur coat entered their car carrying two suitcases. Just as she reached their seats she set the suitcases down to catch her breath. Straightening up, her gaze fell on Sunny.

"Why look at that hair!" she declared.

Sunny smiled at her, blinking his large sky-blue eyes with their long girlish lashes.

"Yes, isn't it lovely," her mother agreed, running her finger tips through the soft ringlets.

The woman looked over at Erin.

"Don't you wish you had your brother's beautiful curls?" she gushed.

Erin glared at her.

"No, I don't!" she stated flatly. "I wish he was dead!"

The woman took a step backwards, as if Erin had shoved her.

"Oh!" she gasped feebly. "What a thing to say!"

But Erin had already turned toward the window again, her forehead resting against the cool glass. One after the other the telephone poles flicked past faster and faster, dark lines against the snow.

With an indignant huff, the woman continued on her way, dragging her suitcases after her.

"You shouldn't say such awful things," her mother scolded once she had disappeared. "Don't you like your little brother?"

"No. I hate him," Erin replied matter of factly, still looking out the window.

"Don't be silly. Why should you hate him?"

"Because of how he is."

"What do you mean by that?"

Erin looked at her mother holding Sunny, his head jiggling gently against her chest. She shrugged her shoulders. There were no words for how he was, just pictures which only she herself could see. Like now, the way he was snuggled in her arms. Or the way other people smiled at him, called him an angel, made a fuss over him. Sam was the only person she knew who had not noticed Sunny. Her fingers sought the brass pin, caressing it lightly. Just thinking about his big brown hands pinning it on her coat made her feel warm inside, as long as she kept looking out the window.

Stepping out of the slowly turning circular door onto the main floor of Hudson's Department Store was like entering a fairytale world. The Christmas season had just begun and everything shimmered and glittered. Erin had never imagined there were so many different things to buy. And straight ahead of them was a moving stairway.

"Oh, can I ride on it?" she begged.

"Of course," her mother answered.

"No ride!" Sunny whined. "Sunny hungry."

"I know, dear," her mother told him. "Let's ride the stairs all the way to the top and get some lunch in the cafeteria before we start shopping."

Standing on tip-toe, Erin hung over the escalator's hand rail so she could take in as much as possible of what each floor had to offer as they glided past.

"Oh, toys!" she cried when they stepped off onto the third floor. "Can't we just look for a minute?" Without waiting for an answer, she dashed toward a shelf full of stuffed animals. Her mother hurried after her, pulling Sunny by the hand.

"No look!" he shouted, stamping his foot determinedly as soon as they caught up with her.

Erin heard snickering laughter behind her.

"Isn't he priceless!" someone burst out.

25

"Sunny no look!" he cried, stamping his foot once more, accompanied by more laughter.

"Erin, let's go and eat first," her mother suggested.

"OK," she sighed. It was always the same. Sunny stamped his foot, people laughed, and he got his own way. The one time she had tried stamping her foot, all she got was a swat on her bottom.

In the cafeteria her mother bought lunch for the three of them, loading everything on one tray. On their way to an empty table a woman in a black dress and white apron and cap rushed up to them.

"Would the little gentleman like a high chair?" she inquired of Sunny.

"Yes, thank you," her mother answered for him.

Before they even sat down she was back with the chair. She lifted Sunny up and set him in it.

"I hope you enjoy your lunch," she said, patting him lightly on the head.

Just as Erin opened her mouth to inform the woman that it was, in fact, her birthday, not his, she saw their reflections in the wall of mirrors beside their table: A stringy-haired scarecrow beside the baby Jesus. She looked down quickly and began picking at her food.

"Well, have you decided what you want for your birthday?" her mother asked after they had spent over an hour examining every toy and game on the entire third floor.

"Oh, yes," Erin replied. "Come."

She led her mother from a shelf full of teddy bears over to a counter displaying children's watches.

"There," she pointed. "A Mickey Mouse watch."

The saleswoman pulled out the tray of watches and set it on the counter. Erin picked up the Mickey Mouse one and held it up for inspection, while her mother picked up one of the ordinary watches.

"Wouldn't it be better to get one like this, instead?" she said. "When you're a little older, you won't want to wear a Mickey Mouse watch. This one you can have for many years."

"I won't get tired of Mickey Mouse," Erin replied, already sensing that it was a lost cause.

"Of course you will," her mother told her. "You're not going to be a child forever."

"I can have it when I'm big, too," she argued.

"Look at these others here and see if there is one you like," her mother insisted, holding out the one she had chosen.

"But I really only want a ...." she began, but her mother had turned around and wasn't listening.

"Sun-n-n-ny," she called out. "Sun-n-n-ny. Where are you? Oh my God, he's gone!"

She dropped the watch and rushed back the way they had just come. Erin lay the Mickey Mouse watch back on the counter carefully and went after her. But by the time she reached the teddy bears, her mother was nowhere in sight.

"Sunny's lost," she mused half aloud.

She sat down beside a big teddy bear, elbows on her knees and chin in her hands. She could hear her mother's voice echoing in the distance, but it had lost its sing-song tone and was pleading tearfully.

Erin began to consider the situation. Think if Sunny was really gone, if she no longer had a little brother. No golden curls for people to comment on, no more priceless foot stamping causing laughter, no one occupying her mother's lap and attention. Life without Sunny would be better than any old Mickey Mouse watch! Then it wouldn't matter if she looked like a pumpkin. People would see her anyway. Even her mother would have to. She closed her eyes as tight as she could and wished, even though she had nothing magic to hold at the same time.

"Don't get found. Don't get found. Be someone else's Goldilocks," she whispered over and over to herself.

"Excuse us," a woman's voice interrupted finally. "Are you Erin?"

She jumped. In front of her stood two women in long black robes which reached down to the floor. Even their heads were draped in black cloth, with white ruffles around their faces. Witches! Shaking her head, she pressed herself back against the teddy bear to get away from them.

"Aren't you the little girl whose brother is lost?"

She was just about to say no when she noticed they had heavy crosses dangling from a strings of beads amongst the folds of their robes. Then she understood. They had come to tell her that Sunny was dead.

"We found him and took him to the Lost and Found," one of them told her. "Come with us. Your mother is there with him now." She held out her hand to Erin.

No longer afraid, she jumped to her feet and took the offered hand. Neither of them had said anything about his hair or how cute he was, so she knew for sure he was dead. She'd never seen anyone who was dead before.

When the cluster of women in the middle of the Lost and Found office separated to let them through, instead of finding her brother lying dead as she had expected, she found him standing on a chair sucking on a candy cane, as well as sucking up attention. She burst out crying!

"Look how glad your sister is to see you safe and sound," someone said to him.

Only the woman holding her hand seemed to understand and comforted her with a little hug around her shoulders.

Her mother thanked the gathering of women and picked up Sunny so as not to loose him again.

"Come on, Erin," she called. "We mustn't miss the train."

"The watch..." Erin said as they neared the counter.

"Oh, that's right!"

Shifting Sunny to her other hip, she asked the saleswoman to wrap up the watch she herself had chosen.

"Can't I have the Mickey Mouse one?" Erin pleaded.

"You wait and see. You'll be glad you got this one instead," her mother assured her.

Without saying thank you, she thrust the prettily wrapped box into her coat pocket. It wasn't a watch she had wanted; it was a Mickey Mouse watch.

Erin had hoped to see Sam on the train. His pinning the engine on her coat had been the only nice thing that had happened the entire day. But the man who punched her ticket was just an ordinary man without brown skin.

When the train finally stopped at their station, her mother stepped out into the aisle ahead of her, still carrying Sunny.

"Go ahead. I'm coming," Erin told her. She stood up, pulling the still-wrapped watch from her coat pocket, and dropped it onto the seat behind her, then followed her mother down the aisle and out into the bitter cold evening. She wished she was still six-going-on-seven.

PETER RABBIT

Erin lay stretched out on the porch swing, sweating in the humid July heat. She had on her first store-bought dress, a patriotic red, white and blue cotton pinafore with a big ruffle-edged collar. It had been purchased to celebrate the end of what her parents, as long as she could remember, referred to as "Hitler's war." Just what that was, she wasn't quite sure, except that it was far away from America. Something to do with the radio program her mother and father listened to every night at dinner time and during which she was not allowed to talk.

In spite of the heat, most of her stomach and chest were covered by an enormous white rabbit. Along the entire length of his backbone ran a single black stripe, ending in a perfectly round black spot just above his tail like a giant exclamation mark. His back legs hung down limply on either side of her hips, while his front paws appeared to be joined in prayer on her chest. Both ears stood straight up, as though he were listening intently while she read the pictures in a Donald Duck comic book aloud to him. But his real interest was in the ruffled edge around the collar of her dress that he was chewing with rapid little rabbit bites. This she ignored, caring only that he was paying attention to the story. All the while her toes were shoving the swing back and forth from one end to the other. Each time the metal of the frame hit the fender-shaped armrests at her head and feet it made a sharp-edged clanking noise. She was riding on a train; the rhythmic clanking and jerking were taking her far, far away. The hard horsehair-filled cushions were like the ones on the only train she had ever ridden, except that the green and black striped material covering them was scratchy rather than fuzzy. It smelled just like the neighbor girl's army surplus tent. She wished she could have a tent of her own, but her parents said she wasn't big enough to sleep outside alone at night. After all, they reminded her, she was only seven. The discussion always ended there. They never heard her when she explained that she mostly wanted a tent to play house in. Maybe they understood that she wanted it so she could pretend she lived somewhere else. At any rate, she knew from experience that it was useless to argue or beg. Instead, she asked if she could sleep on the porch swing. In the darkness, surrounded by the smell of the cushions, she could easily pretend she was in a tent. But the answer was no, the reason being that she had a perfectly good bed to sleep in. If she had three wishes, she would use the first one to turn her father into a little boy, the second to turn her mother into a little girl, and the third to make herself into a grown up. Then they could see what it was like to be children and continually told no, for no good reason, whenever they wanted to do anything that was fun.

They had also said no when she had wanted a rabbit, but when her grandmother brought her Peter as an Easter present, there was nothing they could do. He was already full grown and came with his own cage. It was called a self-feeder because it could be set directly on the lawn, letting the grass stick up through the chicken wire bottom. But of course her father refused to have it destroying his lawn, not to mention the droppings which would foul the grass. Consequently, the cage stood on a square of cement beside the garbage can, leaving Erin to pull grass and weeds for him from the field across the road. However, when her father was at work, she let Peter loose on the front lawn so he could eat as much as he wished. She even taught him to sit up on his haunches and beg for dandelions or fresh carrots she pulled from the garden. And when he was finished eating, she pushed him around in her doll buggy while he slept. She loved him more than anyone else in the family; certainly more than she loved her little brothers.

She stopped reading and closed her eyes, listening to the sound of his munching. Suddenly the opening of the top of the Dutch door cut into her solitude like a knife.

"Can't you stop making that God-forsaken clanking noise with the swing!" her mother declared, annoyed. A second later she caught sight of Peter's busy mouth and her annoyance turned to anger.

"How many times have I told not to let that smelly rabbit lie on you and eat your clothes! That dress is brand new!"

"I don't like dresses," Erin answered simply.

"I'm not interested in whether you like them or not. That's what little girls wear."

"No it's not! Why can't I wear blue jeans like other kids?"

"Because your father and I don't like seeing you in blue jeans. You can wear your shorts around the house in the summer time."

"Yeah, but I only have one pair and whenever I want to wear them you won't let me 'cause they're dirty. But you never wash them."

"Put the rabbit back in his cage and go out and play."

"There's no one to play with. Besides, I'm reading to him."

Her mother sighed in exasperation, as she always did in such exchanges, and disappeared from the doorway as abruptly as she had appeared.

"Don't feel bad," she told Peter. "She doesn't like you 'cause you're a rabbit and she doesn't like me 'cause I'm not a real girl. But I don't care. You like me and I know you'd let me wear blue jeans if you could talk. And don't pay attention to her when she calls you a smelly rabbit. I think you smell nice. Besides, my grandmother likes us."

Erin knew her mother was disappointed in her because she didn't like to wear dresses, but she couldn't help it. If only she had been born a boy, she was sure her mother would have liked her better. As it was, they were always arguing about her clothes or the fact that little girls mustn't go without shirts or sit so that people could see their underpants. When she wanted to know why, she was told it was "not nice." To her further, "Why not?" she was told, "It just isn't." Such illusive answers were rather mystifying and set her imagination to work. But when her father wouldn't let her go without shoes because she dragged so much dirt into the house on her bare feet, she realized that he made rules just for the sake of making rules. Shoes were hardly any cleaner. And it was unfair that her brothers spent the whole summer running barefoot and shirtless, not to mention that they peed behind the garage. No one yelled at them or complained about how they were dressed. She could see that her mother liked them just as they were.

"Don't watch when she smiles at the boys," she told Peter. "It'll just make you sad."

As was their custom, the whole family went to the state fair in September. Erin had always found the exhibits of farm animals boring, preferring the midway with its rides and carnival atmosphere. But this year it was nearly impossible to drag her away from the rabbit exhibits. It was the first time she had had a chance to see how Peter compared with other rabbits. When she realized that there were others bigger than him, she turned her attention to their markings, concentrating on the pure white ones. So far as she could tell, not one of them had a black stripe along its backbone, nor a black spot above the tail. Next year she would enter him in the fair. Think if he could win a blue ribbon--or even just a red one!

Finally her mother took her by the hand and pulled her into the next tent where canaries, hamsters, gold fish, turtles and other house pets were for sale. Her two younger brothers were gaping at the hamsters.

"Can't we have one?" they begged. "Please.... Erin has a rabbit so why can't we have a hamster?"

Her parents looked at each other.

"Under one condition," her father said. "It has to live in the basement. And, of course, you have to feed it yourselves and keep the cage clean."

"We will! We will!" they promised.

"OK. Which one do you want?"

They began pointing and arguing immediately.

"Hold it!" he declared. "I guess you should each have your own so there won't be any fighting."

Erin watched while they made their choices and a cage was picked out. To her, hamsters were disgusting with their big bottoms sticking out behind them. She would rather not have a pet at all than have a hamster.

Autumn came and school started. The grass stopped growing and the dandelions and weeds turned brown and died. Peter had to eat hay instead. He didn't seem to mind, but Erin could see that he was lonely after their long summer days together. Nor was it so much fun to play with him outside on cold afternoons after school.

"Can I take Peter up to my room and read to him for awhile?" she asked one day. "It's too cold and windy to play outside. Besides, the boys have their hamsters in the house."

"Rabbits don't belong in the house," her mother answered. "It's enough that your clothes smell after you've been playing with him."

"He doesn't smell."

"That's because you don't notice it since you smell the same way yourself," she was told.

"But he's lonely," she protested.

"He's not a house pet. I don't want his darn droppings all over."

"He doesn't go to the bathroom when I'm playing with him," she retorted. "Besides, I'll clean it up if he has an accident. And I won't let him nibble on my clothes."

"I'll bet," her mother scoffed. "Your father has said no, and that's all there is to it."

Finally one day she approached her father on the matter.

"Please can I play with Peter up in my room? It's no fun playing with him outside now. It's too cold."

"No," he answered simply.

"Why not? The hamsters are in the house."

"It makes extra work for your mother."

"But she doesn't have to do anything. I'll take care of him myself and if he has an accident, I'll clean it up."

"The answer is still no," he said absently.

"Buy why? " she asked, trying to hold back her tears.

"I've told you why." He opened his newspaper and she knew the matter was closed. It was always like that.

The same discussion took place numerous times, with only slight variations, until one day when Erin went into her brothers' room unexpectedly. They were sitting face to face on one of the beds, their spread legs straight out in front of them, feet sole to sole. Between their ankles was a little pile of broken graham crackers. Each held his hamster by its stubby tail while it struggled to get free and run down the leg-formed runway between them to the graham crackers.

"One, two, three, go!" called the older brother.

They both let go and the hamsters rushed to the food.

"Mine won!" cried the younger brother, whose legs made a shorter runway. They had obviously been playing for some time, for she saw small number two's here and there on the bedspread, as well as a yellow stain. She ran down stairs in a rage.

"Why can't I take Peter up to my room when they can have their hamsters up there? There's even pee and shit all over the bedspread!"

"Erin! Shame on you!" her mother snapped, at the same time as her hand slapped across Erin's mouth. "Such language is forbidden in this house! Go up to your room!"

She lay on her bed crying and mulling over her parents' unfairness. She could find no reason for it except that she was a girl. Yet she knew her mother wanted a girl; it was just that she wasn't a real girl. Or maybe they just didn't like her. But she didn't know what to do to make them like her better.

"Guess what?" her mother said by way of greeting when she came home from school the next day. "We've found a home for your rabbit where he won't be lonely."

Erin just stared at her.

"What?" she asked finally, sure that she had heard wrong.

"The Schmidts have taken him. They have lots of rabbits, so he'll have company."

Erin's bottom lip began to quiver. The Schmidts lived on the other side of the village, somewhere out past the cider mill. She would never be able to go and see him.
"N-n-no," she cried. "No!"

She ran out to his cage, not even bothering to put on her jacket. It was empty. She was devastated! She hadn't even gotten a chance to explain to him or tell him good-bye. He must think she didn't love him anymore. How could her parents be so cruel? She sank onto the big stone beside the cage, leaned her head against its wire wall, and cried until her shivering overtook her tears and she was forced to go in.

She sat at the dinner table in a daze, hardly able to eat.

"Can't you smile a bit?" her father said from the head of the table.

She glared at him.

"It's not the end of the world," her mother added..

She hated them! They couldn't be her real parents. She must have been adopted. She wished they were dead, both of them.

"Just ignore the way she's acting," she heard her father say to her mother after she had been excused from the table. "She'll soon forget all about him."

But she didn't forget. All fall and winter she dreamed about how she would get him back in the spring. She figured out new tricks she would teach him and how she would enter him in the state fair. She was sure he would win a ribbon. And a prize rabbit certainly would be able to come in the house now and then.

Christmas and New Year's passed uneventfully, as well as the first part of January. Presently Erin began looking forward to the annual village potluck dinner the week before Valentine's Day. Her class was going to give a skit in which she had the leading part. But the night before the dinner both her brothers came down with chicken pox. She was so upset by the thought of missing the evening that her mother finally phoned the neighbors and asked if Erin could go with them.

The skit went perfectly. The enthusiastic applause warmed Erin, making her feel good in a way she had never experienced before. In the midst of her second bow she noticed Mrs. Schmidt sitting at a table to the right of the stage. As soon as the curtain closed, she hurried through the maze of tables and chairs in the emptying town hall in order to catch up with her. She wanted to hear how Peter was doing. Along the way she snatched a large carrot for him from one of the uncleared tables, rubbing it briskly in her hands so he would recognize her smell and know it had come from her.

Out in the cloak room Erin found Mrs. Schmidt chatting with a couple of other women. She stood a little ways away, waiting for a chance to interrupt them without being impolite. But before the chance presented itself, Mrs. Schmidt pulled a white fur jacket from its hanger and slung it around her shoulders, cape-like. Erin realized they were leaving and took a step towards her.

"It's stunning," she heard one of the women say. "But where do you...."

"We're Germans, you know," Mrs. Schmidt answered, anti- cipating the question. "We raise them ourselves. To eat."

She laughed and turned toward the door without noticing Erin. Down the middle of the jacket's back ran a single black stripe, ending in a perfect black spot!

A grotesque series of pictures flew through Erin's mind like a speeded-up movie. Her mouth fell open. But instead of screaming, she vomited up her entire dinner, then slumped to the floor still clutching the carrot. The next thing she knew, she was being carried out into the cold of the night.

"Give her some air!" someone shouted.

"She must have eaten something which didn't agree with her," someone else suggested. "She'll be OK in a minute."

The carrot dropped unnoticed into the snow. She knew she would never be OK. She could never forgive her parents. Never! It was so awful that she couldn't even cry.

The neighbors took her home and explained to her mother that she had been sick to her stomach after the skit.

"It was probably too much excitement," her mother concluded.

Erin heard them talking, but it was as if she were half asleep or dreaming. Then the neighbors left and she was led up to bed.

That night was one long nightmare. Every time she closed her eyes the pictures came: Peter's throat being cut, his head being chopped off, his neck being broken, his struggles, the blood on his fur, his skin being pulled off, Peter being cut up, cooked, and eaten. The next day she was delirious. The doctor diagnosed it as influenza.

After a few days she was able to make herself think about something else when the pictures came. But she could still feel them like a shadow behind her back. Finally one afternoon she got out of bed and, taking out her dresses one at a time, cut off every collar which Peter had decorated with his nibblings. The real lace collar on her Sunday dress she smoothed out and laid in her spelling book. The others she took into the bathroom, along with the only three photographs she had of Peter. Without looking at them, she cut the pictures into tiny pieces over the toilet bowl. When the last bits fluttered down onto the surface of the water, she dropped the collars on top of them, then flushed the toilet. She watched while the water swirled into a whirlpool, sucking down the contents. Then she closed the seat and cried at last.

That night she came downstairs to dinner, eating in silence. The next morning she went to school, but spoke only when the teacher asked her a direct question. Everyone attributed her be- havior to the fact that she had been ill and she was left in peace, both at home and at school.

Valentine's Day came several days later, and with it the spring term's open house at school. The morning was spent cleaning desks and then cutting and pasting Valentine cards for the parents. After lunch the pupils had their own party, with candy and the opening of the big valentine box. All the cards they had made or bought for each other were delivered, with much giggling over the unsigned ones, mostly declarations of secret love from girls to boys. Erin sat by herself, ignoring the others.

After the party, like everyone else, she propped her name card in the pencil tray so her parents could find her seat that evening, then set out examples of her work on her desk. Lastly she took out the valentine she had made for them. It was not like everyone else's red hearts decorated with white paper lace and sweet words. It consisted of a large black heart with half-chewed real lace around the edge. Pasted haphazardly across the middle of it was a strip of white paper on which was scrawled "I hate you!" in heavy black crayon, with "from Erin" in smaller letters underneath. She set it on top of her school work, backed away a couple of feet and squinted, then moved it a fraction of an inch to the left. Satisfied that it was exactly in the middle of her desk, she hurried out to catch the school bus.

JOSEPH

Snow had been falling from the heavy sky for days; big chunky flakes that piled up quickly, transforming the little library on the edge of the village green into a fairytale picture, with thick snow rolls stretching off the edge of its low roof towards the windowsill-deep snow below. But in spite of the weather, a thin whiff of smoke wandered skyward from the half buried chimney and the path to the door was freshly shoveled. Miss Bauer, the librarian, took her one open day a week seriously, letting nothing stand in its way.

Erin skied down the hill from school, straining to catch sight of the library window, which was always lit on open days. Even though she feared Miss Bauer's old fashioned strictness, she loved the library itself. It was the oldest house in the village, nothing more than a cottage really. It sat directly on the ground, with no steps up to the door, and had the mustiness of a shut-up summer cabin. And the walls of its single room were lined with books. Erin had been there several times simply out of curiosity, but this time she had a purpose.

That autumn a new family had moved into the village. They came from Europe, on the other side of the ocean, and were called refugees. One of the boys was in her third grade class. She was fascinated by him. He was very quiet and shy, and when he did speak, he sounded like her little brother.

"I called Horst," he would say. Or, "I know not," when asked a question.

But at recess he and his big brother sat by themselves, chattering like magpies. Often Erin found some excuse to go near their bench in hopes of hearing what they were talking about, but their way of speaking made no sense to her. When she asked her mother about them, she was told that they were "just Germans." That was the end of the conversation, but not the end of Erin's curiosity.

One day she waited until everyone had gone out to recess, then approached the teacher.

"What's Europe like?" she asked shyly.

"Well, it's hard for me to say, since I have never been there myself," she replied. "People are much poorer than here. And they speak a lot of different languages...."

"But how does it look?" she persisted.

"Every country is different. Why don't you go to the library and ask Miss Bauer if she has any books with pictures?"

And thus it was that Erin set out on that snowy afternoon.

In answer to her inquiry, Miss Bauer led her to a bottom shelf for oversized books and pulled out one.

"This is the only book we have with pictures." she said. "Unfortunately, it's rather out of date. Much of Europe was destroyed in the war."

Erin thanked her and sat down at the table in the middle of the room. She could tell that the book was old, for the leather along the spine creaked slightly as she opened the thick black cover. Inside it smelled like her grandmother's attic. Skipping the text at the beginning, she went directly to the pictures at the back, where each page contained a single black and white photograph. Carefully she turned page after page. There were mountain scenes, pastures of grazing cows, farmers plowing with teams of horses, small churches and great cathedrals, sailing ships, cobble-stoned streets with houses lined tightly against narrow sidewalks, tiny straw-roofed cottages. She turned yet another page, but before she could let go of it, her hand began to tremble. In the center of the picture was an unpainted two storey house at the top of a low hill. The triangle between the upstairs window and the peek of the roof was decorated with a cut-out wooden design in the shape of a fanned peacock tail, or perhaps the rays of a rising sun. In the distance behind the house a snowcapped mountain stood guard, its broad rounded summit like a protective bosom. Erin's eyes followed a path from the front door of the house, down the hill through a field dotted with racks of drying hay, to where it disappeared into a clump of trees at the bottom right hand corner of the picture. Suddenly she saw him, a man half hidden by the trees. He was looking straight at her, waiting.

"I'm coming," she called aloud.

"Hush! No talking in the library!" Miss Bauer snapped.

Erin jumped, nearly knocking the book to the floor. The man went on staring at her expectantly.

"Wait," she whispered, closing the book.

She put on her jacket, pulled up the hood, wound her scarf around her neck a couple of times, and went to the librarian's desk with the book.

"May I borrow this?" she asked breathlessly.

"Do you have a library card?"

"N-n-no. Do you have to have one?"

Miss Bauer slid a paper across to her.

"Have your parents fill this in. It costs $2.00."

She whisked the book out of Erin's hand and onto a little cart behind her chair.

Much to Erin's disappointment, her parents refused to pay two dollars just so she could borrow a few books.

"But there's a book I have to borrow," she protested. "It has lots of pictures."

"You can just as easily look at it there," she was told.

The next week she pulled the book from its shelf and, opening the back cover, leafed forward through the pictures she had never gotten to the previous week. And once again, when she came to the house on the hill, the man was still standing in the clump of trees staring at her. No matter which way she moved, his eyes followed her, as if he were trying to tell her something. Erin studied every detail of the picture, yet her attention was constantly interrupted by the power of his gaze. She couldn't take her eyes from him. What did he want? He made her feel funny, as though she was in a dream.

"It's time to go home," a voice informed her suddenly.

"I am home," she replied without thinking.

"Don't get sassy!"

Miss Bauer was beside the table pulling the man away from her, while his eyes held hers almost pleadingly. Only the closing of the cover broke the spell.

"Did your parents fill in the form for a library card?" she inquired curtly.

Erin shook her head. She watched the book disappear into the shelf, then hurried out into the darkness of the evening. Quickly she jammed her feet into her ski bindings. When she leaned over to fasten them, instead of feeling the tears she had been pressing back, the photograph appeared on the backs of her eyelids. And with it, a sense of urgency.

"I'm coming," she called in a hissing whisper.

Straightening up, she grabbed her ski poles and lunged forward, then stopped short. She had no idea how to reach him.

In the week that followed he possessed not only her waking thoughts, but also her dreams. She could hear him talking to her when she was alone, but couldn't understand what he was saying. At night she understood his words, but in the morning they were gone. She could feel him near her, she knew him, but his name remained always just out of reach. Finally, she gave him a name—Joseph—and he became even more real.

The days crept past more slowly than those before Christmas. By the time she skied to the library again she had made up her mind. Instead of taking off her jacket, she merely unzipped it. Pulling the book from its shelf, she went to a little table on the far side of the room. She could almost feel Miss Bauer's eyes following her, reading her intentions. She moved the chair a bit to one side, so as to hide the book with her body. Then, with a quick glance around the room, she opened it at random. There in front of her was Joseph's face, bathed in a ray of sunlight from the nearby window. He was smiling.

Erin's heart beat as though she had been running for miles. Nervously her fingers fumbled with the corner of the page, trying to separate it from the others. But once she had it in her grasp she hesitated, her desire to possess the picture playing itself against her fear of Miss Bauer. She tried to calm her anxiety by looking at the other pictures, but it didn't help. Her cheeks and ears were burning and the hair at the back of her neck was damp with sweat. It was like standing on a high diving board, trying to get up the nerve to jump. Then, when she was about to chicken out, she heard Miss Bauer go into the lavatory in the little back room. Now! Holding her breath, she quickly tore the picture from the book and slid it between the pages of her spelling book. In her haste the last part of the tear had taken a short cut across the corner of the picture, leaving a bit still fastened in the book. She tugged at it with her thumb and forefinger. Just as it began to loosen, the toilet flushed. Erin grabbed her school books and fled. The lavatory door clicked open as the library door clicked shut behind her.

Once home, she hurried up to her room, closed the door, and pulled out the picture. Flopping onto her bed, she propped the it against the pillow. Joseph looked at her questioningly.

"What do you want?" she whispered.

She already knew, could see it in his face. He was calling her.

"Where are you?" she asked him. "How can I find you?"

But before he could answer, the bedroom door opened and her father was standing giant-like above her.

"Is that the picture you ripped out of the library book?" he demanded.

Erin's heart stopped beating and her mouth became desert dry. When she failed to answer, he snatched it from the pillow.

"No! Don't!" she cried.

"Put your snowsuit on and get yourself down to the library immediately, before it closes. Miss Bauer is waiting for you.

44

And take this with you." He dropped the photograph onto the bed. "We'll discuss it when you get back."

Erin was paralyzed. How had Miss Bauer found out? How could she face her and, worst of all, give the picture back? She looked at Joseph. He didn't seem upset. It was as if he were telling her, "You don't need the picture. You'll never forget me." But she wanted it anyway.

The distance to the library had increased hundredfold in the hour since she had last skied it. She could just as well have gone without a jacket, for her blood was like ice, freezing her from the inside. More than anything she had ever had to do in her life, she dreaded facing Miss Bauer. Beyond that point she was too scared to even speculate.

Miss Bauer was sitting stiffly at her desk with the book open in front of her when Erin came in. Without a word, she laid the picture on the blotter.

"Whatever possessed you to destroy a perfectly good book?" she implored, her words sharp and quick, like the little strokes her mother used when chopping onions.

As always when she was in trouble with grownups, Erin didn't answer. She knew they were powerless to make her speak. Instead, she stared at her feet.

"Your father says you have no money to pay for the book, but he has promised to punish you himself. And you are no longer welcome in the library."

With a lump in her throat, she watched Joseph disappear forever between the pages of the book.

"How could you do such a thing?" her father raged when she returned home.

She didn't answer.

"Miss Bauer said you've been coming in for some weeks, looking at the same picture all the time, even talking to the man in it as if you knew him...."

"I do," she interjected unthinkingly, but he was too engrossed in his speech to hear her.

"....and that today you left the book on the table, with a torn corner of the picture sticking out. Can you tell me what this is all about?"

"I had to have the picture of Joseph an' you wouldn't let me have a library card."

"You can't go around stealing everything your mother and I won't let you have!" he exclaimed. "And who is this Joseph?"

Suddenly she realized she didn't know who Joseph was, that she couldn't explain him to anyone. He was her secret. She shrugged her shoulders and hung her head. Holding the image of the picture on the backs of her eyelids, she let her father preach at her—his usual form of punishment.

Time passed. Joseph had been right. The picture was unnecessary. He remained vivid, forever a mystery, until her teens when she let him slowly slip into the background, becoming like an uncle or a cousin one belongs to yet never meets.

When Erin was 25, she finally went to Europe, the fulfillment of the dream she had had ever since she used to eavesdrop on Horst and his brother in third grade. She traveled aimlessly, driven by a restlessness which nagged her up and down and back and forth over the European continent, as though she were searching for something, but she didn't know what. Eventually she bought an old house in Sweden, a country which, during her travels, had held little appeal. Why Sweden? she often wondered. It made no sense.

The years went by. Bit by bit she put down roots in the coun- tryside and her restlessness faded. It was as if she had come home.

The summer she turned forty a couple of good friends suggested she celebrate by going up north with them to their cottage.

"Oh, I'd love to! I've always wanted to go to the north of Sweden," she blurted spontaneously. Actually, the thought had never occurred to her.

"It's really beautiful," Stefan told her.

"When I was a kid, I used to spend my summers up there on my grandparents' farm," Frida explained.

"Are they still living?"

"Oh no. My grandfather's oldest son has the farm now. But we have a little house on the edge of one of the fields that we use as a summer cottage. You'll love it."

The journey was long, through endless miles and hours of pine forest, until late afternoon when they suddenly emerged from the trees into open rolling farmland along the shores of a huge lake. Presently they turned off onto a dirt road, drove up a hill, and onto a grassy track through a little wooded area on the edge of a meadow. Ahead of them she could see the cottage. They got out and stretched, travel-weary.

"Hello!" a voice called from the distance.

"Oh, that's my uncle," Frida said. "Come, let's go and say hello before we unload the car."

She led them along a pine needle covered path through the trees. Coming down the sloping meadow towards them was Frida's uncle. The four of them met in a grove of tall fir trees.

"Hello, Frida! Hello, Stefan!" he greeted. Frida held out her arms to hug him, but he had already turned to Erin. "Welcome!" he cried heartily.

"Uncle Elias, this is our friend Erin," Frida explained.

"Yes, yes," he exclaimed, reaching eagerly for her offered hand.

As their hands met, it was as if a bolt of lightning passed between them. It was so strong that even Frida and Stefan felt it. All four of them stood motionless, staring at each other. After what seemed like an eternity, Erin's gaze continued beyond them, up the path to the unpainted two storey house with the fanned peacock tail/rising sun decoration, and then to the rounded mountain top behind it. This time the picture was not on the insides of her eyelids, and the man was no longer alone in the clump of trees at the bottom right hand corner.

At last Frida broke the silence.

"I'm sorry we're so late," she apologized.

"Better late than never," Elias mumbled, still smiling at Erin, her hand clutched in both of his.

"We have to go and unpack the car, Uncle Elias," Frida told him. "We'll come up and see you when we're finished."

With a little squeeze, he let Erin's hand slip out of his, then winked at her as if they shared a great secret.

"I'll put the coffee pot on the fire," he told them gaily.

Suddenly Erin's legs were so rubbery that she could hardly stand up.

"Wow, I've never seen him so happy," Frida remarked on their way back to the car.

"Why? What's with him?" Erin tried to ask casually, coughing lightly to cover the shaking in her voice.

"Actually, I don't know so very much," Frida told her. "Just that many, many years ago his wife died in childbirth. According to the story, a storm prevented him from going after the midwife. Apparently he sort of flipped out. The next day he waded through hip-deep snow down to the village with the baby in his arms, going from door to door in search of a wet-nurse. But the child was already dead. He never re-married, claiming that his wife was coming back soon. For a while he was regarded as a sort of village idiot, but in every other respect he's completely normal, so people finally quit talking about him. But even now out of a clear blue sky he can say, 'I can feel her getting closer.'"

By now they had reached the car. Stefan pulled out a couple of rucksacks and went to unlock the cabin, while Frida followed with a load of groceries.

"Are you coming?" she called from the porch.

But Erin didn't hear her. In a daze, she clung to the little rain gutter around the edge of the car roof, gazing at the figure of Elias hurrying up the path towards the house.

THE LAST SUMMER

The little Evenrude outboard sputtered to life on the second try, coughed unwillingly, then evened out to a smooth whirring. Erin's father swung the wooden boat around in such a tight half circle that the bilge sloshed up between the floorboards and across her bare feet. When the bow was pointed towards land, he gave it full throttle. Erin sat on the rowing seat with her back to him, holding tightly to its wooden edge as the boat splashed through the waves. Each time it smacked down, a fine spray showered her face, washing away her salty tears.

Her father sat sideways in the stern, steering somewhat gingerly. His head was turned at an awkward angle, as though he were trying to look at the back of his shoulder, and held securely in place by a large green and yellow striped lure. One of its triple hooks was fastened in his cheek, the other into the back of his neck. Her fishing pole stuck up beside him like a radio antenna, the line drooping between the last eyelet and the lure.

She had cast the way he had shown her, expecting to see the lure sail out across the water. Instead she had felt it snag, as if she had a bite. Her father's unexpected cry had made her jump. Turning, she saw his fingers fumbling around the lure warily, like a blind man's, smearing trails of blood across his face and neck. Finally, he had pulled his hand away, glanced at it, then rinsed it in the lake.

"Hang on," was all he had said, as he gave the start rope an awkward jerk.

She couldn't tell if he was angry or just in pain. Numbly she had turned around and held on.

All spring she had been looking forward to her 10th birthday, when her father had promised to take her camping. Just the two of them, without her mother, who hated camping, or her little brother Sunny tagging along. And she would be able to wear her "ghastly baseball jacket" night and day if she wanted to, or go shirtless in the sun, without being nagged about how she was dressed. She had gotten her birthday presents the day before they left, a sleeping bag with a poncho that snapped around it and an army surplus knapsack. And the knife.

She thought back to the previous day's long drive up north....

The setting sun flickered through the endless pine trees, gradually sinking out of sight while dragging the remaining daylight along in its wake. Finally only blackness remained, sliced in half by the narrow beams of the headlights. With nothing more to look at, Erin slouched in the big front seat, the fuzzy cloth upholstery warm against the backs of her bare legs. Even though the '49 De Soto was several months old, it still had that wonderful new smell. And a radio, its dial glowing green in the dark. They had listened to it most of the way, first the Tigers-White Sox double header, then the news, and finally Jack Benny. She had been glad for the distraction, for she always felt a bit shy when she and her father were alone together and not doing anything which steered their conversation. At the same time, there was a sort of silent closeness between them. She liked him better than her mother and she knew she was his favorite. Sometimes he helped her make models or they played catch and he taught her how to bat. In the summer they went fishing now and

51

then, in the winter to hockey games, if they weren't on school nights. Occasionally she could see that her mother was jealous, but she couldn't help that she didn't like girlish things. Besides, no matter how hard she tried, she could never seem to get her mother to like her the way she liked her brother Sunny.

Suddenly Jack Benny said good night and the studio audience broke into applause. Her father switched the radio off, then leaned over and opened the glove compartment.

"Hold out your hand," he said. "I have a present for you. I didn't wrap it because it's not new. Your grandmother bought it for me in Switzerland when she was there right after the war."

She felt the weight of his Swiss army knife on the palm of her hand.

"Then, if you remember, my father gave me one for Christmas. I think you should have one of them."

She closed her fingers around it slowly, afraid to believe it was true. She had often looked at the two jack knives lying side by side in the top drawer of his dresser. Sometimes when no one was home she even took them out and opened all the blades and tools, always careful to put them back exactly as she had found them. She had simply assumed one of them would eventually end up in Sunny's pocket.

"Oh, thank you!" she said softy. "I've always wished I could have one!"

"I know. You've been looking at them often enough," he laughed.

Erin felt her face turn hot, but said nothing, thankful for the darkness. She was both embarrassed about having been caught in the act and happy that he had noticed and understood her longing.

And now everything was ruined.

The sun had been so warm while they were fishing that she had taken off her shirt. Now she sat hunched over, shivering in the wind and chilly spray.

"Erin," her father called, his voice half blown away on the wind, "come and sit back here with me. Please."

She wiped her eyes and, without looking up, stepped over the open tackle box and slumped down beside him. He took his jacket, which he had been using as a cushion, and wrapped it around her. The loop of fishing line blew between them. Still sniffling, she fumbled in her pocket after the Swiss army knife, opened the scissors and snipped off the line several inches from the lure. It was the first time she had used it.

"Don't cry," he said, pulling her tight against his side to warm her. "It's nothing serious. Accidents happen now and then."

There was no one at the boat livery when they tied up at the dock. A note on the door said, "Back at 4". Her father got into the car and strained to look at himself in the rear view mirror.

"Aren't we going to a hospital?" she asked when he got out again.

"No, it's too far away. Besides, I think we can take care of it ourselves."

He sat down on the dock and told her to get the first aid kit out of his knapsack and the wire cutters from the tackle box.

"Wash around the hooks with antiseptic," he said.

Cautiously she dabbed at his cheek. She had never touched him like that before. It felt strange and unnatural. It was always he who took out her slivers or rubbed Vicks on her chest when she had a cold. She had never taken care of him.

"OK," she said finally. "All the blood is gone and it looks clean."

"Now take the wire cutters and get a good bite on the shaft of one of the hooks," he instructed.

She slid the nose of the cutters between the hook and his cheek as gently as she could. When she had a good grip, he put his hand over hers and squeezed. With a pop, the wire snapped in two, allowing him to straighten his head.

"Now take a hold of the hook end and pull it out," he said.

Holding her breath, she grasped the hook between her thumb and forefinger and slowly drew it out of his skin. It was easier than she had expected. But when she looked at the one in the back of his neck, her stomach went queasy. The barb had gone through his skin, but the tip of the hook had not come out again.

"Cut it so the shaft is as long as possible," he told her. "Then we'll see what we can do."

That done, he handed her a cork out of the tackle box and explained how she should wiggle the hook a little so she could see where the tip was under his skin, hold the cork against it, and then slowly press the hook into it as hard as she could.

"I can't!" she cried.

"Of course you can," he told her. "Just pretend you're Florence Nightingale and you've been taking care of bloody battle-wounded soldiers all day. To push a little hook though a thin layer of skin will seem like nothing by comparison."

Still she hesitated.

"If you hold the cork in the right place, maybe I can do it myself," he said.

She placed the cork over the bump the tip of the hook made in his skin. His hands reached up to replace hers.

"Never mind," she heard herself say. "I can do it."

She felt her two hands pressing the hook and the cork together, as though they didn't belong to her. It was like trying to stick a fork into a tomato; first there was resistance and then suddenly the skin gave way with a tiny pop that she felt rather than heard. When she pulled the cork away the hook followed and it was over.

Digging through the first aid kit, he handed her a tube of his favorite cure-all ointment. She hated the stuff. It looked like mashed prunes and smelled worse. He was always gooping it on cuts and stubborn slivers against her will. With a certain gholish delight, she squeezed out a gob and rubbed it on his wounds, expecting him to react with disgust, as she always did. But all he said was, "Ah, that feels good!"

Ignoring him, she pulled out her knife, opened the scissors for the second time, and cut two gauze pads which she taped to his cheek and neck.

When they set off across the lake again, Erin sat shirtless in the wind and spray once more, warmed by an inner pride.

Late in the afternoon they set up camp in a secluded little cove. Just above the beach the sandy soil was covered with sparce short grass, beyond which a half circle of low trees offered protection from the weather. While her father took care of the boat and cleaned the few fish they had caught, Erin made a fireplace in the clearing with some large stones and gathered a pile of dry wood. When her father came up from the shore he had their empty lunch bags with him.

"Here's some paper to start the fire with," he said.

"I don't need any. Look here," she said pointing proudly. She had made a tepee of tiny dry sticks, with a log cabin construction of larger sticks surrounding it. In the very center were a few thin sheets of birch bark. She struck a match and set fire to a bit of bark she had left sticking out on one side. It crackled a little, then suddenly the whole tepee blazed up.

"Where on earth did you learn that?" he asked, surprised.

Glancing up at him she saw he wasn't pretending. He was genuinely impressed.

"Girl Scouts," was all she said.

Having eaten and washed their dishes in the lake, they hurried to roll out their sleeping bags before the dew fell. The fire had burned down to a pile of glowing coals, occasionally sending up little tongues of flame into the night. In the darkness the birds called their last good nights to one another, the wind stilled, and the lake ceased its lapping at the shore. It was as if the whole world had gone to sleep. Presently Erin looked up from fire. The moonless sky was covered with millions of stars.

"Do you know where the north star is?" she asked, breaking the silence. She had read somewhere that in the old days people used to follow it if they were lost, but she couldn't imagine how they knew which one it was.

"Do you see the big dipper?"

"Yeah."

"Go from the star at the bottom front edge of the bowl to the lip star and then straight out. It's the next big star," he told her.

"Oh, there!" she said. "But what about the little dipper?"

"The north star is the last star in the handle of the little dipper," he explained. "The little one is upside down and pours into the big one."

By now they were both lying on their backs, their fingers jabbing at the sky. He pointed out more constellations-- Cassiopia's crown, lyra, the northern cross, Leo major and minor--and told her the myths connected with them. She listened spellbound. It had never occurred to her that her father ever even looked at the sky.

"Did God really create all that?" she asked him.

"I don't know, but I would like to think so."

"What about heaven? Is that up there too?" she wondered, waving her hand at the sky.

He didn't answer right away.

"I don't really know, to be honest," he said finally.

Something in his hesitation encouraged her.

"I don't think people go to heaven when they die," she said daringly. "Not to hell, either."

"You mean you believe they just die and that's it?" he asked, surprised.

"No. I think that you get born again somewhere else."

"Hm-m-m," he replied curiously. "What makes you think that?"

"Because I feel like I've lived other places long ago," she answered. She had never told anyone that before.

"Perhaps you have," he mused. "Millions of people in India believe the same thing."

"Oh," was all she could think of to say. She had always assumed it was her own private belief, nor was she sure she liked all the company.

"If I were you, I wouldn't say anything to your mother. Her way of looking at religion doesn't leave room for such beliefs."

"Why doesn't she like me?" Erin asked suddenly. It was a question she had wanted to ask for so long, but had never found the right opportunity.

"What makes you think she doesn't like you?" he asked. She could hear in his voice that he was stalling because he didn't want to answer.

"Because nothing I do pleases her. I can't explain it exactly. You just knew when someone doesn't like you. It's like she doesn't approve of me."

"Your mother was very unhappy when she was a child," he said. "Maybe she is jealous of you because you're happy. I think she expected you to be like a doll that she could dress up in pretty clothes, rather than a person with a mind of your own."

"I can't help it..." she began, but a shooting star across the dippers cut her off. "Wow! Did you see that?" she cried. "That was the brightest one I've ever seen! It wasn't a star from the big dipper, was it?"

"No. Those stars are always there, like the sun and the moon." He paused a few seconds. "You know," he went on, "when you get older and move away from home, wherever you are, we can always meet at the star on the lip of the dipper. It'll always be there."

"Oh, what a nice idea," she remarked. It made her feel warm and secure.

Far into the night Erin lay awake in her sleeping bag, gazing at the stars while thinking about their conversation. For the first time in her life she felt special. She knew that her father saw her as a real person, not just a kid under foot, and that he liked her just as she was. And she knew her grandmother liked her as she was, also. Whether or not her mother approved of her didn't matter so much any more.

By the time they made the long drive home several days later Erin no longer felt shy with her father. They had so many things to talk about that neither of them even thought about turning on the radio. And best of all, they had already decided where they were going to go camping the next summer.

For Erin, coming home was like being put back in a cage. She longed for the smell of the pine forest, the sound of waves slapping against the side of the boat and on the rocks along the shore, and the friendly warmth of a campfire. But most of all she longed to lie in her sleeping bag and talk about things with her father before falling asleep under the stars. Every time she looked at the green and yellow lure she had hung from her desk lamp memories from the summer enveloped her like the warmth of his jacket on her shivering back.

All too soon summer cooled into autumn and school started again. Suddenly her life became dominated by that which she had most dreaded. It had already happened to several girls in her class, so she knew her turn was coming. To stall for time, she resolved not to look at herself when she got dressed or undressed. She didn't want to know. But even if she didn't see what was happening, others did.

One day at recess a couple of boys started pointing at her chest and laughing. Automatically she glanced down to see what was so funny. Two little bumps poked out under her t-shirt. Her hand flew up to cover them and she ran to the toilet. In her horror, she forgot her resolve. Up went her shirt in front of the mirror. To her shock, they stuck out a good half inch. Out of curiosity she touched one lightly with her fingertip. It was swollen and soft. She pushed it in, but it popped out again. She pushed the other one a little harder and held it in.

"Please go away," she begged aloud, even though she knew it was no use. It made her sad to think that she could never again go without a shirt. She didn't want to grow up. Grown ups had to have jobs and babies and cook and iron and clean. Her mother never had any fun, she just worried about things. Erin didn't want to be like her. She never wanted to become an adult.

However, Erin's body had its own plans regarding adulthood. And it seemed to be in a hurry to get there. Although her parents said nothing, she knew they had noticed. Especially her father. For her mother, bodies hardly existed. One simply kept them hidden under proper clothing. Thus Erin did her best to hide her body from herself and others under layers of too-loose clothes.

Like every winter, colds and the flu made their rounds of the school. Erin was not immune. One night she woke up coughing uncontrollably. Presently the hall light went on and her father appeared in her doorway. In one hand he had a jar of Vicks and in the other his standard cough syrup concoction--a mixture of whisky, lemon, and honey. She had learned years ago that it was a waste of time to protest. Besides, as much as she hated to admit it, the cure actually helped.

She sat up and took a swallow of the cough syrup, then lay back against the pillow. Unbuttoning the top button of her pajamas, he smeared Vicks on her neck and upper chest. Before she realized what was happening, his hand slid across one of her budding breasts, cupping it ever so slightly, and then over the other. She saw that his eyes were closed.

"Not there," she said, squirming out from under his touch.

His eyes opened and he removed his hand.

It wasn't until after he had gone that she understood what he had done. At first she didn't know what to think. It was confusing and somehow unpleasant. Finally she told herself he was simply rubbing Vicks on her, as he had always done. The fact that he had never before put it on that part of her chest was somehow forgotten.

With the onset of spring the earth slowly awoke from its winter sleep. Small buds formed on trees and bushes and flowers. Erin took out her baseball jacket from where she had hidden it when her mother had wanted to wash it. Pressing her nose into the dirty material, she took a deep breath. It was like sitting in front of a campfire again. The whole summer came rushing back to her and with it the longing.

That evening her mother went up to put Sunny to bed after dinner, leaving Erin and her father to do the dishes.

"We're still going camping, aren't we?" she asked.

"You bet!" he answered. "That is, if you still want to."

"I've been waiting ever since we came home last summer," she replied. "My baseball jacket still smells like smoke."

"You'd still smell like smoke yourself, if you'd had your way!" he laughed.

And thus their plans, which had been asleep all winter, awoke like the spring. Erin, too, came alive with expectation.

The dishes finished, she hung up the wet dish towel and turned to kiss her father good night. But instead of giving her his usual little dry peck on the lips, he put his arms around her, pulling her to him. He pressed his half open lips to her mouth. They were soft and warm and slightly wet. Something hard moved against her stomach. Instinctively she knew what it was. As she hastily backed out of his embrace, he let his hands slide around her sides and up over her breasts, pausing to feel their growing fullness. Jerking away, she rushed upstairs to her room. The first thing she saw was the green and yellow lure dangling innocently from her lamp. She ripped it down and stuffed it into her pencil case. Then she grabbed her jacket and threw it into the dirty clothes hamper. That night she cried herself to sleep.

The next day after school she went down the basement and pulled her father's tackle box out from under the work bench. After scooping all the hooks, sinkers, and small lures out of the top tray and dumping them into the bottom of the box,

60

she lay the green and yellow lure belly up in the biggest compartment, then slid the box back under the work bench.

From then on, as much as possible, she avoided being alone with her father. She tried not to think about the coming summer.

The weeks passed. One evening she again found herself alone in the kitchen with him, dish towel in hand.

"I was thinking that maybe we should have a little tent when we go camping this summer," he remarked.

"I don't feel like going any more," she forced herself to say, then glanced up at him to make sure he understood what she meant.

She would have hated him less if he had apologized. Had he begged and promised, she might even have changed her mind.

Instead he said, "I guess Sunny's old enough to go instead. He can use your sleeping bag and knapsack."

She couldn't believe she had heard right. It was as if he had knocked her down and then kicked her all over. It hurt so much she couldn't even cry.

That night she lay in bed hating her father for his weakness and insensitivity and hating her own body for having come between them, while at the same time trying to protect the memory of the last summer from also being twisted into hate. Finally she got up and unrolled her sleeping bag on the bedroom floor and opened her Swiss army knife. It was not really made for the job, but with a combination of the scissors, the largest knife blade, and the saw, she succeeded in turning the sleeping bag into a pile of cloth scraps and cotton wadding clumps, all of which she stuffed back into the waterproof carrying bag. Then she cut her knapsack and poncho into large squares and piled them together neatly. Finished at last, she returned everything to its storage place on the top shelf of her closet and went to bed.

But it was many years before she could look at the big dipper without a lump rising in her throat.

DEAR JOE

February 1999

Dear Joe,

If it were possible to go backwards in time and spend a single hour with just one person out of all the thousands of people I have known throughout my almost 60 years, without a second thought I would choose you. In spite of the fact that our paths followed the same track for less than 12 hours. So many times I've wished that I could drop a letter into the mail box and that it would, in some magical way, find its way to you. Idle dreams! You must be old now—at least in your middle 70's—or perhaps you are no longer living. Yet, for me, you will live as long as I live.

On the desk in front of me lies a faded yellow seat ticket with three holes punched neatly through the cardboard: One over February's F, another over 13 for the date, and the last over W for west. At the bottom is the Chicago Northwestern Railroad symbol. Only the year is missing. But it's not necessary. It was 1960, when I was 20 years old and in my junior year at university....

She paused and laid down her pen, remembering....

Erin slipped her arms out of her navy duffel coat, then pulled it up around her shoulders before leaning her forehead against the cold glass of the train window. The flat Michigan farmland flicking past was neither speckled with sunshine nor accented by shadows, for the sun hadn't bothered to make its appearance that day. The world was like a black and white film; white snow, black tree skeletons, and buildings in various shades of gray. She had made the same journey numerous times, but the scenery was always uninspiring, regardless of the time of year. Bored, she leaned back in the seat and closed her eyes. She might as well sleep until she had to change trains in Chicago. From there on everything would be new and different, for she had never been further west. The prospect excited her. At the same time, she felt a strange uneasiness, as if she were rushing headlong into something totally unknown, in spite of the fact that her future was neatly mapped out in front of her. Or rather, for her and Ralph, who would be waiting for her when she reached her destination.

She thought back to when they had gotten engaged the previous summer. It had seemed romantic, parked by a lighthouse on the shore of Lake Michigan in the moonlight. In a year and a half, when Ralph had his master's degree and she her bachelor's, they would get married. He planned to teach in a small college, eventually reaching the rank of professor, and she would teach grade school for a couple of years, stop when they had children, and return once they were grown. To be a college professor's wife seemed rather exotic, at least compared to her ordinary middle-class upbringing. And Ralph was, as her mother put it, "good husband material." He was conscientious, a hard worker who would provide well for his family, as well as being easy going, sensible, intelligent, and kind. No, there was no reason to feel uneasy.

The train was late when it reached La Salle Street Station, leaving Erin barely half an hour to get across town to Union Station. Dragging her two huge overweight suitcases, she rushed out into the street to find a cab. By now it was dark and Chicago's eternal wind stung her face with tiny ice pellets. Rush hour traffic was crawling past at a snail's pace. Finally, a Checkered cab pulled up beside her wildly waving arm and she jumped in. The apprehension she had felt earlier in the afternoon returned, but this time she knew it was because she might miss the train. Actually, it wouldn't matter that much. She could always go out to Ralph's parents' house for the night. They would love to have her, she knew. But the urgency to make the train dominated all else.

"Can't you drive a little faster?" she prodded the driver. "My train leaves for the West Coast at 5:35."

"I'm doing the best I can, Ma'am," he told her. "I can't drive over the cars in front of me."

"I'm sorry," she replied. "It's just that I have to make that train," she continued, wondering why she was being so pushy when it really didn't matter.

It was 5:30 when the cab let her off in front of Union Station. Lifting her suitcases as high as she could, she began to run. Just as she came out onto the platform, one of them was grabbed out of her hand from behind.

"Come on!" a man's voice called. He opened the door to the last car and helped her up the steps with her luggage, then climbed up after her and pulled the door shut. The train began to move.

Erin sat down on her suitcase and leaned back against the wall to catch her breath, while the man half slumped against the opposite wall.

"Thanks," she panted.

"It was nothing. I was running for it myself."

When she had recovered sufficiently, he helped her move her things through several cars to her reserved seat.

"Thanks again for all your help," she told him. She sat down in the aisle seat and pulled a book out of her bag, making it clear she didn't want further company. He was friendly, but many strangers were friendly. She didn't feel like getting involved in a conversation. He nodded and continued down the aisle. As soon as he was out of sight, Erin took her bag and walked to the back of the car where she had seen stairs going up to the dome. One of the things she had most looked forward to on this trip was riding in a glass-covered dome car, where one could see in all directions. There wouldn't be much to see at night, nor was the landscape particularly exciting between Chicago and Minneapolis-St. Paul. But even the sense of rushing through the night attracted her. And she could look at the stars if the sky cleared.

To her surprise, the dome car was dark and empty. She took the front seat. Presently she heard someone coming along the aisle behind her. She knew, without turning around, who it was. In spite of her lack of desire to talk with anyone, she found herself welcoming his approach. He stopped beside her.

"May I sit down?" he asked. "I don't bite."

Erin felt her face redden. Quickly she removed her bag from the empty seat and moved over.

"I'm sorry," she told him. "I didn't mean to be so stand-offish. I guess I'm a bit wary of strangers."

"That's OK. I like your honesty."

She looked down at her lap, glad he couldn't see her embarrassment in the dark.

"Where are you headed?" he continued.

"Washington State. And you?"

"Only St. Paul. 7:00 o'clock tomorrow morning. So, you have a couple of days to sit here and enjoy the scenery. It should be quite beautiful once you get out into the Rockies, especially with all the snow. I envy you. What are you going to do in Washington?" "Finish university. And you?"

"I'm a professor at the University of Minnesota. Philosophy. I was at a conference in Chicago. I was supposed to be there one more day, but quite suddenly I could no longer abide the stiffness of the atmosphere and decided to go home tonight instead. I had to rush like mad to make the train. There must be some reason behind it."

"What do you mean?"

"I don't think things just happen at random. They happen for reasons, although often we don't realize it at the time. Like now. For some unbeknownst reason, I suddenly got the urge to go home. And, like you, I nearly missed the train. If only one of us had had to run for the train, our paths would never have crossed. Why they crossed remains to be seen."

Erin was surprised by his words. Her girl friends could talk about things happening for a reason, but she had never known a man to say such a thing.

Neither of them spoke for a while. The gentle rocking of the train lulled her into a sense of familiarity with this strange man. Without looking at him, she knew his head was tipped back and that he was staring through the dome at the sky. She looked up. The storm clouds were gone and the Milky Way had taken possession of the heavens.

"It is so peaceful looking at the stars," he mused finally. "It never fails to bring me back to a reasonable sense of proportion about myself and my importance in the universe. Think if everyone were required to gaze at the stars for half an hour every night. Alone. With no one to talk to. Just look and contemplate."

"Yeah," she laughed lightly, awed by such a thought.

Once again they were silent, a comfortable silence which didn't need to be filled with words. It was as if they were old friends.

"What do you want out of life?" he asked at last, turning part way around in his seat to face her. She could feel his eyes searching her face through the darkness, as if they were seeking a doorway into her.

I want to be happy," she answered spontaneously.

"There is certainly nothing wrong with that!" he exclaimed.

"I don't know. I have always gotten the impression from my parents and teachers that happiness is not the 'right' goal in life. That other things are more important. A career. A good marriage. Success. Security. Money. I know I should care about those things, but I don't, even though I try to."

"Rubbish! Those are other people's values. If those things aren't important to you, they certainly won't bring you happiness. Ignore them and go your own way. No one, and nothing outside of yourself, can give you happiness; you have to find it within yourself."

He leaned back in his seat again and looked up at the sky.

"But why Washington?" he asked.

"My fiancé is in graduate school there."

"And when he's finished?" he continued.

"We're going to get married and I'll work for a couple of years before we have kids." She realized too late that her tone of voice had sounded rather unenthusiastic.

"You sound a little hesitant," he concluded. "Is that what you really want?"

"Not exactly," Erin admitted. "But...."

"What do you dream of doing?" he probed.

"Do you really want to know? It's a bit crazy."

"I wouldn't have asked otherwise," he replied.

"I would like to live somewhere else," she told him, her voice becoming lighter. "I have always felt that I was born in the wrong country--well, even in the wrong century. I would like to live in an old house out in the countryside somewhere in Europe."

"That's not impossible."

"The thing is, Ralph wants to teach at a small college and eventually become a professor. Success is important to him. He's not interested in living in Europe--and certainly not in an old house. He says we can go on a European tour after he's retired. And my parents keep telling me I should quit my silly daydreaming and think of the future, that Ralph will make a wonderful husband, that he's dependable and can offer me a secure and stimulating life on some college campus."

"It sounds like Ralph doesn't really fit in with your dream."

"It was just a dream. Girls always have unrealistic dreams, but they give them up when they meet the right man. I gave mine up the night Ralph proposed," Erin said, waving her left hand in the darkness. "I realized that it was time to be realistic. Besides, how could I say no, when he had driven 300 miles and picked a beautiful spot by a lighthouse in which to ask for my hand and put a diamond ring on it? Suddenly I was at a point of no return, without even realizing it."

"Death is the only point of no return," he remarked.

"What do you mean by that?" she asked, taken aback.

"It's never too late to change direction. To follow your dream instead."

"But...."

"As we grew up we were taught to conform to society's rules: To think rationally, make decisions based on reason, plan for the future, work hard, save, invest, sacrifice for others. The list is endless. Life's 'shoulds'. If we follow society's rules everything will turn out OK--as long as we are content to exist in that tight little box, where dreams remain nothing more than dreams."

"But how...." Erin interjected.

"Create your life the way you want it. If you want to live in Europe, make up your mind to do it. If you want to badly enough, you will find a way to make it a reality. Never mind what other people might say. It's your life and no one else's. It's possible to follow your heart instead of following other people's 'shoulds'--if you dare to do so."

"But what about Ralph though? And our plans?"

"Can you be happy living his dream and denying your own? Are you being honest with yourself--and with Ralph?"

She said nothing, for she had no answers. Such thoughts had never crossed her mind.

The train slowed as it neared a town. The gates were down across the streets and warning bells dinged, but there were no cars to warn at that hour of the night. The engine let out a single shrill whistle and from the car in front of them a large mail sack was tossed onto the platform. Then they picked up speed again and the town fell away behind them.

"There is something nice about delivering the mail bag in the middle of the night when everything else is asleep," the man remarked.

"Funny, I was thinking the very same thing," Erin laughed.

"Sometimes I wonder whatever possessed me to become a professor," he mused. "I should have had a more romantic sort of job. One summer I worked as a forest ranger in a fire tower perched on top of a mountain. Early in the morning the valleys were bedded in fog. It was like being in heaven, surrounded by clouds. Then the sun would slowly burn it off, exposing the valley floors as if by magic. It was unforgettable!"

She could hear by his voice that the fog was evaporating before his eyes as he spoke.

They fell silent once more. It was as if there was nothing more to say. Presently he covered her hand with his own, wrapping his fingers around it. They talked a bit, quietly, about life and dreams and values. The train passed through small towns, sometimes stopping, other times simply slowing to get rid of a mail bag. Red lights blinked at crossings, green ones along the tracks, and the whistle echoed into the night. When they ran out of words, their hands kept them connected. Finally Erin yawned, scrunching down in the seat to get more comfortable.

"You can put your head on my shoulder," he told her.

"Tell me your name first," she replied.

"Joe. What's yours?"

"Erin."

She moved so that she could rest her head against the shoulder of his tweed jacket. Her eyes closed and she fell into a light sleep, conscious of each time the train altered its rhythm, conscious of Joe's cheek resting against her head. Never in her life had she lived to totally in the present. There was no past and no future. Only now.

As they neared the Twin Cities the sky began to lighten behind them. Joe squeezed her hand slightly to wake her. At first she thought the night had only been one long dream, yet she knew that something important had happened to her during the night. Although neither of them spoke, he continued to hold her hand. When the train pulled into the St. Paul station, he led her down the stairs to the little platform between the cars. Suddenly he dropped her hand and hugged her, pressing her face against his neck.

"Always follow your heart, Erin," he said softly.

Releasing her, he held her at arms' length, then kissed her

on the forehead, gave her a quick hug, and stepped off the train. She watched as he disappeared into the stream of morning commuters....

She picked up her pen again.

....Joe, I cannot imagine that you remember that night long ago, for it was my life which was changed, not yours. When I boarded that train in Chicago, my future lay before me, straight and narrow as a prairie highway: Finish school, get married, teach a couple of years, buy a house, have two kids two years apart, and live happily ever after. It wasn't what I wanted, but it was all I knew. My dreams would never be more than just that: Dreams. I had no map for reaching what I really wanted in life, no bridge to connect my dreams to reality. You showed me another road and handed me a map.

By the time the train got to Washington, I knew my life had turned off the straight and narrow onto a twisty hilly road with no signposts or guard rails. A road where Ralph could never follow. He had plans, but he had no dreams. Nor could he understand that you had simply showed me that it was possible to travel a different road. If he had understood that, we might have had a chance. But the idea of ending a relationship simply to remain true to oneself and one's dreams was incomprehensible to him. He was convinced it was you I wanted. Ironic. He was a chemistry major, but he failed to understand the function of a catalyst!

After that my life took a new direction and four years later I was on my way to Europe, never to return. Since then I have been living my dreams. And I long ago found the one thing I wanted in life: Happiness. You were right, it can only come from within. And when it exists, it is possible to survive anything. Over the years I have come to many forks in the road and each time your words have come back to me: "Follow your heart." Often the road has been rough, but never without rewards. And infinitely richer than the straight and narrow road across the prairie.

Thank you again, Joe.
Erin

THE BET

Erin could hear her telephone ringing urgently as soon as she came out of the shower room at the far end of the dormitory corridor. Clutching a towel tightly around her dripping body, she half-ran towards her room, hoping to get there before whoever it was hung up. A ringing telephone meant only one thing: a date. She hadn't had a date in ages; not since she had backed out of a relationship with the first guy she had gone to bed with. She had liked him well enough, even loved him perhaps, but he wasn't husband material. In America in the early sixties girls didn't necessarily go to college with a career in mind. At least not a permanent career. Most got married, worked for a couple of years and then settled down in the kitchen to raise children. An unattached senior girl had cause to be somewhat anxious, for once she graduated and left the campus it was much more difficult to find a husband. Of course, one could also remain single, but that had to be out of choice, not an act of fate.

Closing the door with her butt, she grabbed the receiver off the wall.

"Hello?" she said breathlessly.

"Hello," came a male voice.

Silence.

"Ah, who is it?" she asked a little impolitely. She didn't like it when people made her guess who she was talking to.

"Irving," he said simply.

"Irving?" she repeated. The name meant nothing to her. "Irving who?"

"Irving Bahzahonk," came the answer, as if that automatically cleared up the matter.

"Irving Bahzahonk?" she repeated. "I don't know any Irving Bahzahonk."

"Don't you remember? We met at Cosmopolitan Club. You know, where all the foreign students hang out."

"Are you a foreign student?"

"No. I'm an art student."

"Oh." Erin's mind was beginning to clear and out of its haze she could make out a half-bald guy with a beard, a gap between his two front teeth, and eyes that had bored into hers like laser beams. And a name tag which had said Irving something-or-other.

"Yeah, now I remember," she said hesitantly.

"Good. I was wondering if you would like to go out on Friday night? I'm not rich, but we could take in a flick. Or else maybe you feel like posing for me."

"Posing for you?"

"Yeah. So I could draw you. They don't have much in the way of models in the art department, so some of us find our own."

"In the nude?"

"Well, that's up to you."

"How 'bout a movie instead?" she suggested.

"OK." she could hear the disappointment in his voice. But modeling nude, or any other way, for that matter was not her thing.

"By the way, what is your real name?" she asked.

"I told you. Irving Bahzahonk."

"I don't believe you."

"You can call me Irv, if you don't like Irving—as long as my mother doesn't hear you."

"But Bahzahonk?" she pressed. "Where does that come from?"

"Bahzahonk was a count in Transylvania," he replied. "We go back hundreds of years."

Erin was at a loss as to what to believe, so she let the matter drop. But she was anything but convinced. At the same time, he sounded more interesting than a lot of guys she had dated. And certainly mysterious.

That Friday night they went to a foreign film at the student union which, as she later discovered, hadn't cost Irving a dime since he was alternate evening manager of the union building. In those days, going to foreign films topped the list of things to do if one wanted to be cultured. (Or at least second to reading Kierkegaard, at which she had failed miserably.) The fact that she couldn't keep up with the subtitles was beside the point. She wouldn't have understood Fellini's *La Dolce Vita* even if it had been dubbed in English. But at least she could say she had seen it.

When Irving (she couldn't bring myself to call him Irv—it was too much like Urp) walked her back to the dorm, he bowed low before her, kissed her hand, and asked if he could have the pleasure of her company on Sunday evening.

"That would be lovely," she told him in the same tone in which he'd asked.

"Great. Would you like to see my paintings?"

"Sure," she replied. At the same time, she wondered what she was getting herself in for. She knew nothing about painting and would probably quickly expose her ignorance. But the thought of going out with an art student was certainly appealing. She had always felt an attraction for the 'starving artists' who lived in tiny Parisian garrets.

Erin was already starting to like this guy. He was unlike anyone she had ever dated. Exciting was probably the best word to describe him at that point. She felt like she was stepping into a world whose door she had always longed to enter.

His paintings were abstract and the most she could say about them was that they spoke to her or they didn't speak to her. Fortunately, most of them did.

"But what do you need a model for when you paint abstractly?" she asked him.

"I don't really. I just said that to see how you would react," he said, while his eyes pierced hers. "But I would certainly like to draw you sometime, just for fun and because I find you attractive. So any time you feel so inclined, you know where my studio is."

She actually began to give it some thought. To model fit with the whole image of the type of life she was being introduced to. The struggling artist's model. So one cold winter evening several days later she put on a pair of tights and a leotard and went to his studio. When she took off her coat she could see the pleasure on his face. Little did he know that, as a baggy-clothes dresser, it was a huge step for her to appear in a skin-tight outfit. Worse than that, she quickly discovered that standing absolutely still in an unnatural pose was sheer torture. But it was all part of the adventure.

Erin soon learned that Irving, which he stubbornly maintained was the name his mother had given him, was a modern-day starving artist. He and his roommate Lyle shared a graduate student apart- ment and ate what they could scrounge up: bushels of apples from Lyle's family's orchard, potatoes from Irving's family's backyard, day-old bread from the local bakery. Before long she was smuggling hard boiled eggs, cheese, fruit and whatever else she could stuff into her pockets from the dormitory dining room to supplement their monotonous diet.

Things were moving fast in this whirl-wind relationship. Erin was being wined and dined, even if there was no wine or dining. And although he refrained from whispering sweet nothings in her ear, he did let her know that she was the most fascinating girl he had ever taken out, that he had never seen such wonderfully blue eyes as hers, that he'd never enjoyed himself so much with a girl. Some evenings they stopped off at his place on their way back from the art department, but more often than not there was a white t-shirt hanging outside on the door knob to indicate that Lyle was already there with a girl. Now and then, when they were early enough, they got to hang out the t-shirt themselves. But most of the time they inhabited the only private place on campus that was warm that bitter cold winter: the heating tunnels. It was just a matter of finding a manhole in a poorly lit stretch of sidewalk, lifting the cover and jumping down a few feet onto the sandy floor, and letting the cover drop back into place above them. They could walk under the entire campus beside the giant heating pipes or spread out a blanket in a wide place. It wasn't quite like parking under the stars on a hilltop above a city of twinkling lights, but it served its pur- pose. It was different and exciting, which suited her just fine. By this time she was blindly in love and it wouldn't have mattered where she was, as long as she was with Irving.

One night, three weeks after their first date, Irving came to pick her up in Lyle's VW beetle. Lyle was sitting in the driver's seat. It struck her as strange, since they had never double dated before. Even stranger was the fact that Lyle didn't even have a date. He was their chauffeur, simply. Irving explained that Lyle thought it would be cool to drive around while they necked in the back seat. No one said anything, but there was a tension in the air as he drove. After about a quarter of an hour he suddenly pulled up to the curb, got out, and walked away.

"What's the matter with him?" Erin asked.

"Ah, he's angry at me," Irving began in a small voice.

"Why?"

"Because of something I haven't told you."

"What?"

He took a deep breath and let it out slowly.

"Ah, well, I have a confession to make." He waited, but she didn't know what she was supposed to say, so she said nothing.

"Ah, I have a confession to make," he repeated. "First of all, my name is Jon, not Irving." He waited again, but she said nothing.

"That's the least important part of my confession," he said finally. "Well, it's like this." He began talking fast, as if to get it out as quickly as possible. "I bet Lyle that I could take out any senior girl and get her to fall in love with me within two weeks. We drew up a list of ten candidates, threw a dart at it, and you won. The only problem is that it backfired on me and I have fallen in love with you."

Erin was stunned. It was one thing to hear that he had fallen in love with her, but there was a whole lot more to it that had a nasty taste in her mouth.

"Can you say that all again?" she said finally.

He repeated what he had said, word for word.

"We can quit the whole thing here and now if you want," he offered. "It's up to you."

"I don't know," she replied in a shaky voice. "Maybe you should take me back to the dorm so I can digest all this."

"Alright," he said, climbing up into the driver's seat and starting the car. Erin huddled in the far corner of the back seat feeling like a naïve fool, with the whirlwind of the past three weeks lying in ashes around her.

Back in the dorm, she collapsed on her bed in a daze. So the past three weeks had been nothing but a sham. A great experiment. He had simply been playing a game with her emotions in order to win a bet. Yet he had said it had backfired and that he had fallen in love with her. Had he suddenly become sincere after that? She began examining his every word and every gesture, wondering which had been honest and which had been purely for effect. She quickly realized that she had no idea, that she doubted everything he had said and done.

The next evening he came over with a dozen red roses, apologizing profusely. She looked at him, then at the roses, which certainly had set his budget spinning, and a feeling of bitterness welled up inside her.

"You destroyed something by playing your game," she told him. "I trusted your sincerity when it wasn't real. How can I know if this is real or just a new game?"

He was taken aback by the tone of her voice.

"Can't you give me a chance to prove my sincerity, to show how I feel about you?" he asked meekly.

"I don't know," she replied, for she honestly did not know how she felt. "Call me in a week and we can see."

During the week that followed, Erin received three or four hand-drawn cards with cartoons lampooning the stupidity which had caused him to lose the only girl he had ever cared about, and with promises to reform. She didn't know if she was beginning to take pity on him, whether or not she believed his sincerity, or whether she loved him in spite of what had gone down. But bit by bit she found herself drawn to him once more. She missed him. She missed the times we had spent together.

In her diary her wrote: "You have fooled me once, but I shall never let you close enough to do it again. You have destroyed something by playing your game. I look at you now with a cynical eye and question your sincerity, for once I trusted it when it wasn't real. How am I to know if it is real or if this is a new game?"

Too many questions. Had it all been for effect? At what point did he begin to fall in love? Did he become sincere then? How could she ever trust him? Never mind that it had backfired. What if it hadn't? As hard as she tried to get past their false start, Erin never quite succeeded in trusting his sincerity again. Not even after five years of marriage.

When she by chance met Lyle again years later, she asked him about Jon's bet, but he didn't seem to remember such a thing; not even after she refreshed his memory with the details. And thirty-some years after their divorce, when they had become friends once more, she asked Jon what ever had possessed him to do such a thing. To her surprise, he claimed he had no idea what she was talking about. Nor did a refresher course improve his memory. With two out of the three of them having no recollection of the event, she should have begun to wonder if it was all a figment of her imagination. But she didn't. She had written it all down in her diary that long ago night when she had returned to the dorm after hearing Irving's confession. And she still had the diary.

PART TWO
PERSONAL WORLD

Although I found my roots at last, life did not automatically become all roses, as can be seen in the first two of these stories. Love is a very powerful force, and when it degenerates into domestic violence, it leaves deep psychological, emotional and physical scars that never completely heal.

The third story was in response to a friend who had asked how I went about writing a novel.

THE LETTER

A single letter lay in the bottom of the mail box. Even before her fingers grasped it, she knew. She'd been expecting it for years. Or had she been longing for it? She wasn't sure. Certainly not fearing it, at any rate. She slipped her thumb under the flap, which had gone soft and started to unstick from lying in the rain-dampened box. It opened neatly, without tearing. She slid out the two tightly-written pages and unfolded them. "Dear Erin," it began. "I'm sorry to have to be the bearer of this message. Paul is dead." She didn't bother to read further. She didn't want or need to know. It was enough that he was dead. That it was over.

Instead of going back into the house, she stuffed the letter into her jacket pocket and walked down the road. It was soft and muddy under her boots, with deep cloudy puddles which hadn't had time to clear after the mailman's car. On both sides of her the forest smelled of pine. If a love could have a smell, theirs would have been pine. Their first two months together had been spent wandering in the pine forests of northern Sweden. She had never been so happy as she was that summer. Paul had been her life's passion; later its greatest love. But not her first love. Before him she had been engaged to one, given her virginity to another, and married a third. Yet all the while some part of her had always been searching. Waiting. Then giving up. But when she met Paul she knew it was he she had been searching for. Whether or not to leave

81

her husband was never a question. The question was only how to do it as painlessly as possible.

Unexpectedly, her actions, although condemned by her father, drew her and her mother together for a few brief moments, the only in their lifelong alienation from one another. Like lighting a match in the darkness, it was intense, but short-lived. Was it really a touching between mother and daughter? Or was it just an unhappy woman, who had never found the courage to right the mistake made years before, who was trying to warm herself in the glow of her daughter's strength? Rhetorical questions. And in the meantime, the matchlight fizzled out into nothingness again. Old patterns are etched in indelible ink. Erin was raised on disappointment and no longer noticed it. Nor cared.

Besides, that was an aside from her and Paul. It didn't matter. They had each other. It was enough. Full to overflowing. They were lovers and they were best friends-- soul mates, in today's jargon. As Paul used to say, they were bound by unbreakable iron bonds. They shared all that could be shared and knew each other as deeply as it was possible to know another person. Together they built dream castles in the air and, unlike most people, succeeded in bring them down to earth, making them real, and giving them life. That Paul was a wounded warrior was a knowledge shared between them. It was Paul's cross and her challenge. They were both convinced that love had the power to heal.

When she first knew him--in the days before she loved him--he would brag to her husband about his conquests with women. And the more he bragged, the louder the little voice inside her whispered "thirty year old virgin." Later, when they were finally together and night after night his body refused to "perform" he was forced to admit the truth she had suspected. But she had succeeded in talking and caressing him out of his humiliation. But for Paul, her help and understanding gave her a power over him which he found belittling. As far as he was concerned, life had already belittled him sufficiently, thanks to his parents. His mother and step-father should have gotten themselves a dog to blame and beat for their unhappiness, instead of using Paul.

The first time his violence showed itself to her was in Amsterdam. He had spilled a bottle of milk on the floor of the camper and she had begun wiping it up. When he'd told her, firmly, that he would do it himself, she had gotten out of the camper and walked along the sidewalk looking in shop windows, waiting for him to finish. Suddenly she was tackled from behind and thrown to the ground.

"Get back in the car!" was all he said.

Somewhat shocked, she had obeyed, wondering what had happened. Later he told her he had thought she was leaving him.

"But I came after you, didn't I?" he declared, as proof of his love.

To her it was a strange sort of proof, but then everything was strange and new at that point.

She hadn't known it at the time, but she had just climbed into the front seat of the roller-coaster car which was to carry her through life with him. The bar was fastened securely across them, locking them together, and it started to climb. (Roller-coasters always begin with a climb.) They quickly reached new heights together and the low country around Amsterdam was forgotten.

They began to play music together, guitars and banjo, notes and chords tossed back and forth between them, a musical conversation, playing on each other, intertwining and braiding together. They sang and laughed, riding high on a wave of song.

At those times Paul's hatred of women was kept at bay or, at worst, aimed at his mother. Then gradually things began to change. Suddenly, without warning, the roller-coaster could take a nose dive and she would find herself swimming in the same detestable pot of soup as his mother. A pot labeled "women." All women. No exceptions. They were all trying to control and destroy him and he couldn't trust or tolerate any of them. Often when she tried to pull herself up out of the muck he would let her get her fingers over the edge, then crush them under his heal and watch her fall back down again. But when she now and then managed to find a way to pull herself out of the pot, he would then set her up on a pedestal to dry. Then he worshiped her. At those times he never inquired as to how she happened to have been in the soup. Bygones were bygones and all that mattered was now.

And while she was on the pedestal they journeyed to greater heights. They reached sexual glories which neither of them had imagined possible. They were inside each other's heads, com- municating without speaking. And the dream came to life again and took on new form. They would have children, a real family -- which neither of them had ever really had -- in an old house out in the country, have animals, grow vegetables. They would work and play together and their children would be loved and happy. And while they were waiting and saving, he went to a shrink to clear away the past and make way for the new.

And then it happened, as if the stage had been set for them and all they had to do was walk onto it and live their lines. They found their house in the country, in a foreign country where they didn't even speak the language. They moved in and planted seeds for their family and their food. Paul built their furniture--a table, chairs, cradle--and she sewed baby clothes, as well as Paul's and her own clothes. Their goats gave birth and then milk. And their music floated on the night. It was too good to be true. Literally.

And as her stomach grew so, too, grew Paul's fear, his jealousy. But he gave it another name: Erin's craziness. And thus began a whole new vocabulary of experiences. At the head of the list should have been "projection," but it was an unknown in her dictionary of possibilities at that time. It came afterwards, when it was too late. Instead, the list was headed with "fear of being abandoned." In his early years Paul had been abandoned by his mother and two foster mothers.

(That his mother later reclaimed him only gave him a target for his hatred.) When he and Erin were first together he had understood the implications of his fear. But now it had grown so large that it ate him up and so he could no longer see it because he was inside it. He knew Erin was going to abandon him as soon as the baby was born, so he set out to drive her away in order to be in control of the situation. He lost his grip on himself and reality and beat her for everything and nothing. He claimed she was sick, evil, one gigantic ego. "I love you so much that I'm going to kill your sick ego, even if I have to kill your body to do it," he would declare. "You're not fit to be a mother!"

And, living as they were, in their own little world together, strangers in a strange land, where there was no one to create a third point of reference, she came to believe him. Physical and psy-chological violence, as every torturer knows, does wonders towards breaking down even the strongest.

In those years she had been on her way out the door countless times, out of fear, desperation, even madness. But each time she was about to reach out for the latch Paul somehow, deep inside, seemed to sense it and, with no explanation for past behavior, returned to his old self again. Once more the dream became reality. They loved and shared, watched the children grow and made music. The meadows blossomed and the forests came alive with birdsong. That part of Paul could never believe he had given her a black eye or that his fists had broken her ribs. Gradually she began to realize that, indeed, it was not that Paul who had stood behind her with the butcher knife pressed across her throat. There was another Paul, a Paul whose eyes were black with hate. Hate for himself and for her because she loved him. To accept that love led him to the edge of a psychological jungle that he was deathly afraid to step into, much less try to find his way through. It was easier to hate and be unworthy of love. That he was used to. The road was straight and direct, with no surprises along the way. No risks, either. When you have nothing, you have nothing to loose.

With time that Paul grew stronger and developed new tactics, dominating the tender, sensitive Paul. Perhaps it would have been better if she could have stopped loving him, taken away the necessity to hate. But one does not turn love on and off like a water faucet. Besides, the iron bands, in spite of everything, were still intact. She knew him too deeply, she knew his pain. She could see it behind his blazing black eyes, the crying child, the adult gazing out between the bars of the prison of himself, hopelessly trapped. Sentenced to life imprisonment.

At some unknown point in their relationship the fissure within him had widened and then split completely, forming two separate beings. For all practical purposes there were no bridges between the two Pauls. Now and then, on an unusually good day, she had been able to get the loving Paul to take a quick glimpse across the chasm and acknowledge that there was a violent being on the other side, spewing hate, a being who was taking over, stealing his life away from him. She had hoped that the awareness of this other being would encourage him to seek help. But it only encouraged his black side to take stronger control in order to protect itself from possible obliteration Slowly she began to realize that his ego would never permit him to look at the dance of destruction he had perpetrated during the seven years they had been together. There was too much to see. It was too overwhelming. Yet she knew that the other part of him was desperate, yet too desperate to play his last hope. For if therapy didn't help, what then? The only thing which kept that part of him going was knowing that he still had the option of going to a shrink--tomorrow. One Paul was too weak to kill himself, the other Paul too arrogant. Besides, both parts of him thrived on misery.

In the end she had had no choice but to leave. His hate was beginning to maim and destroy the two children they had created to stand in the center of their dream. To stay was to say, "I accept the way you are. It's OK to be a hateful, demanding, destructive tyrant when it suits you." It wasn't OK. Perhaps her greatest act of love towards him was in playing her last card and leaving, even though it meant breaking her resolve to never put herself on his list of women who had abandoned him. She could only hope he would wake up and get help. And when he had one day appeared unexpectedly and demanded to know why she had left, she told him the truth, that sometimes love is greater than what you can see happening in the present moment. It cost her an eardrum.

"Don't ever say the word love to me again!" he had screamed, slapping her across the side of the head with the flat of his hand. "And don't forget that neither of us can break the iron bands!"

And she never did.

Somewhere along the road her footsteps had turned her around and she found herself walking up the driveway. A little puff of wind tried to push its way through the big old oak tree, turning over leaves, which in turn dumped their collected pearls of rain water down onto her jacket. Paul would have appreciated the grandeur of the oak and its mate on the other side of the driveway. He loved trees.

Once indoors, she shook off her jacket and hung it to dry in front of the potbellied iron stove in the hall, shoved a couple sticks of wood into the kitchen stove, and slid the kettle over onto the hottest place. Then she sat down in front of it to warm herself and wait.

Once again she remembered how, many years ago, a complete stranger had remarked that she was filled with sadness. She had laughed. She had actually felt quite happy. But the remark had popped into her head now and again ever since. Finally she had realized it was true. She was sad.

It had taken some years after leaving Paul to disentangle herself from him, to discover what was really her and what was only the shroud of the evil bitch image in which he had swaddled her. Once she had worked her way through that reoccurring nightmare of brambles she reached a state of peace within herself. Then came the sadness. The years had passed--more than twenty of them--but the dream she and Paul had shared never faded. True, it changed form a bit. The children grew up and moved away from home. But the underlying foundation, the way of seeing and living, remained the same. It was only that she lived it alone. Not out of choice, but because she had never met anyone with whom she could share it, no one she felt so close to as Paul. If a relationship couldn't surpass the depth and closeness she had had with him, then she wasn't interested. It only accentuated her aloneness.

She had pulled her life together as best she could. The children had grown up knowing the truth about their father, and that she still loved him. She had sold the house where they had lived together and moved far away from her memories, met other people, started a new life. Although her new friends knew about Paul, none of them had met him. To them he was simply a name, the father of her kids, a man who was mentally deranged and had beaten her. He was part of her past, nothing more. None of them knew that he still lived with her, walked beside her through her daily life. Even her children were shocked when she had recently remarked that not a day went by when she didn't think about him. She had absolutely no desire to meet him or renew the contact she had worked so hard to clip off, for she knew having even the slightest contact meant taking the whole package. The only part of Paul she longed to touch was the part she had fallen in love with in the first place. The Paul of the shared dream. But, according to people who knew him, that Paul hardly existed anymore. That she continued to share her life with him was something over which she had no control. He was just there, beside her, connected by the iron bands. (Funny, it had been years since she had thought about his words for expressing it--"iron bands".)

Yes, the sadness was there and probably always would be. But it was mostly for Paul, for the life he had missed, the family he had missed, the love he had missed. Her own sadness was for what could have been, but wasn't. So many times she had mused over what it was that had prevented him from breaking out of his prison. Was he too weak? Possessed? Was it his unseen karma? She would never know. But one thing she did know: He would have been otherwise if he could have been.

The splattering of boiling water onto the hot stove from the overfilled kettle snapped her back to the present. She put a spoonful of loose tea into the strainer, set it in her mug, and poured the water over it. While waiting for it to steep she took the letter from her jacket pocket and smoothed it out on the table. She began to read, ready to know now.

"Dear Erin," it began. "I'm sorry to have to be the bearer of this message. Paul is dead. As you know, his mental health had deteriorated greatly over the past years. He never sought any form of help and thus was never diagnosed, but it is clear that he was a multiple personality. Apparently he could no longer handle it. His death was not by 'natrual causes,' but whether he acted in a moment of lucidness or complete madness is impossible to determine. He left no note, only one of his weird drawings. It is of a pair of iron shackles. The rings are solid, but the chain between them is broken in two. Underneath he had written, 'The iron bands are broken--at last. Go in peace'....

She folded the letter and slid it back into its envelope without reading the rest, then lifted the strainer out of her mug. The warm tea dripped from it, like raindrops from the oak tree.

THE ROVING GYPSY

The humid June air pressed down on the night, without a single breath of wind to offer relief. Even the heat lightning in the southern sky was fading, moving in the wrong direction, abandoning the town to its fate. Erin meandered along the still-warm sidewalk, going no place in particular. She was simply restless, and a bit lonely.

All at once her feet steered her across the street unexpectedly. At first she wondered why. Then she heard it--guitar music seeping out through the half open window of a coffee house. A couple of paces past the door she stopped and retraced her steps. Something in the music was calling her, like a pied piper or the proverbial roving gypsy. She went in and ordered a beer. Automatically her eyes swept around the crowded room. At the far end sat the guitarist on a low platform, playing and singing into a single microphone, even though most people were too busy talking and laughing to pay much attention. Erin threaded her way between tables and chairs to an empty table directly in front of him. Turning her back on the rest of the room, she hunched over her glass to make herself as inconspicuous as possible. She didn't want anyone to start talking to her. She always felt extremely self-conscious when forced to carry on a conversation, as though she had no contact with her real self. She closed her eyes and listened, swaying to the music. The rest of the room and its occupants ceased to exist and it seemed as if he was singing just to her. Some of the texts contained strange images which she didn't fully understand, but it didn't matter. His voice was soft and mellow, leading her to a quiet place inside herself, where words were unnecessary. A place she hadn't been in years.

When he finally stopped singing there was scattered applause and then people went on with their conversations. She felt his eyes on her and looked up. He smiled.

"Did you like it?" he asked bending toward her slightly.

"It was wonderful," she said quietly. Embarrassed, she looked down again and took a swallow of beer.

A few minutes later he appeared at her table, guitar case in one hand and a small knapsack hanging from his shoulder.

"Did you really like it?" he asked.

"Yeah, I did," she told him.

"Then it was worthwhile," he concluded.

There was a silence.

"Sit down, if you want," she said shyly.

"Can't we go outside instead? It's so noisy in here. Besides, I have to catch a train in a while."

"OK," she agreed, while at the same time reluctant. She had only come in to listen to the music. The old feeling of insecurity swept over her, but she couldn't very well tell him that she was afraid to talk to people. Besides, something about him made it impossible to refuse. She stood up and they made their way through the crowd Indian file and out into the heat of the night.

"By the way, my name's Kjell," he informed her.

"Erin," she reciprocated.

They walked side by side toward the station, neither of them speaking. When they came to a playground, Kjell led her over to the merry-go-round. He sat down on the wooden seat with the guitar case standing up between his legs, his arms crossed loosely over the top of it. It was then that Erin noticed the gold wedding band on his left hand. She relaxed a bit.

"Don't worry," he said, taking in her relief. "If I'd had less than honorable intentions, I would have taken it off."

"I'm glad you didn't. I've been fucked over enough for this lifetime. I even find friendship difficult."

"Then why'd you come with me?" he asked, laughing lightly.

"I couldn't help myself. Why'd you ask me?"

"Because you were the only person in the whole room who seemed to like my songs."

"I didn't just 'seem to'," she protested. "They touched me in a way that I haven't been touched in years."

"How do you mean?"

"It's a long story." Already she had said too much and could hear her ex-husband Mike's snide remarks about what an egotistical, sympathy-seeking bitch she was. She regretted that she had gone outside with him.

"My train doesn't go till midnight," Kjell said.

She fidgeted, smoothing her skirt over her knees, not wanting to go into it, yet wanting to.

"Can't you tell me?" he continued. "I'm a pretty good listener." The sincerity in his voice pulled her along.

"Well," she began slowly. Then suddenly the words rushed out, tripping over each other. "Well, if you open your innermost self to someone you love and they not only betray your trust, but also twist your words and throw them back in your face, mocking and deriding you, calling you crazy and evil day after day, year after year, well, in order to survive, you have to withdraw into yourself like a snail and turn off your feelings. Close and lock all your doors, batten down the hatches around yourself. And afterwards you dis- cover you no longer have the key to get out of your protective prison. So you go through the motions of living, yet you are dead inside, unable to feel anything, neither love nor hate, joy nor pain." She stopped short, covering her face with her hands. "I'm sorry. I didn't mean to tell you all my troubles," she apologized.

"You said my songs touched you in a way you hadn't been touched in years. But how could I understand, if you didn't tell me?" he remarked.

"Well, what I started to say was that your songs somehow pushed their way in through the key hole."

"I'm glad. But you don't have to go around like the walking dead, you know. Change your way of thinking. Instead of telling yourself, 'I'm dead inside,' start telling yourself, 'I'm alive! I'm free to grow and blossom which ever way I wish.' It is your attitude which steers your life, and you choose it yourself."

"I guess you're right," she said humbly. "I never thought of it that way."

He looked at his watch.

"Can't you walk with me to the station?"

"Of course."

They walked slowly, having plenty of time. Strangely, she felt completely at ease with him, something she hadn't felt with anyone, male or female, since Mike had worked her over body and soul. Unlike most men, Kjell showed a softness and sensitivity, rather than a protective shell, creating an aura of calmness and inner strength which let her feel safe. They chatted along the way, about the child he and his wife were expecting, her own children, his first record which was coming out in a couple of weeks, and about how she was trying to get back on her feet after her years with Mike and his violent schizophrenic mood swings. By now they were sitting on a bench outside the train station. He listened attentively, without the 'oh's' and 'ah's' and 'how awful's' she was used to hearing from people when she mentioned how she had been physically, emotionally and psychologically battered. When she finally stopped talking, he touched her arm lightly, so that she turned and looked at him.

"You have been through something which can make you strong," he said. "But first you have to let go of it. Leave it behind you. Go beyond it. Then turn it into something positive. And start to live again."

Just then the train swept into the station, bringing the first cool breeze of the evening. They got up and walked towards it.

"As I said earlier, I'll send you a list of when and where I'll be singing this summer," he assured her. "I do hope you will come and listen when you can."

Suddenly he hugged her with his free arm.

"See you again soon," he yelled into her ear over the screeching brakes.

Before she could utter a word, he released her and ran to catch the last coach, which had stopped a ways past them. He turned in the doorway and waved. As she lifted her arm to wave back, she realized she had stood like a pillar when he'd hugged her. She was thankful he couldn't see her embarrassment from the already moving train.

She retraced the past hour on her way back through town, going over Kjell's words, his gestures, his songs. She was glad he was married, making it unnecessary to keep her guard up. The one thing she feared most of all was being faced with the possibility of physical contact. Mike could shove her away when she hugged him, accusing her of giving off bad vibrations or, in the middle making love, suddenly kick her out of bed violently, yelling about how she was trying to castrate him. Since then, it had been impossible for her to touch or let herself be touched. But Kjell offered something she longed for, a safe platonic relationship, where the conversation lay on a deeper level than social niceties and the weather.

As promised, he wrote to let her know where he would be playing the rest of the summer, saying that they had had a baby girl whom they had named Lisa, and adding that he hoped to see her face in the audience again soon. Since he had put his return address on the envelope, she wrote back, addressing it to both him and his wife, congratulating them and sending a little nightgown she had made with Lisa's name embroidered on the collar. His wife Elizabeth wrote back, thanking her, and added that Kjell was pleased that she liked his songs.

Kjell led a gypsy's life that summer, going from town to town with his guitar and his songs. Erin followed in his path, attending all of his concerts and coffee house performances that were within a day's drive of where she lived. And even though he was becoming more and more popular, with larger and larger crowds gathering around him afterwards, he always managed to shake them off rather quickly and make his way to where she sat by herself. And each time his attention surprised her, for Mike had convinced her that she wasn't worth anyone's attention, not to mention that she was a nobody, while Kjell was rapidly becoming a somebody. Yet he seemed to enjoy her company. Mostly they just walked and talked about everything from life and death to Eastern religion, philosophy, society, the state of the world, their children, music, the unhealed scars from her relationship with Mike. Sometimes it was a little too much about Mike, yet he always listened, unjudgingly, and his advice was positive, uplifting, aimed at showing her how to take control of her life rather than letting it pull her down. And each time she met him she came away refreshed, as if she had had a long cool drink from a deep well on a hot summer day. Invigorated and inspired. Filled with energy. Thanks to his encouragement, she started to write seriously and even got a couple of her stories published. But most of all, her emotions began to stir, sending out tiny fragile tentacles, like wild flowers peeping cautiously out from under dead leaves in the spring to see if winter had gone. And the deadness which had encased her for so long slowly gave way to a reawakening. By the end of the summer she realized she was in love with Kjell, that she had been almost from the beginning. Yet it was a sort of love she had never experienced before, for she didn't want him, she only wanted the feeling she got from knowing he existed and was her friend. That was more than enough. Between their meetings she held mental conversations with him. Wherever she went, whatever she did, she took him with her, felt him by her side. He was her muse and mentor. But she was careful to keep her feelings well hidden when they met.

Their friendship continued in this manner over the next few years, growing and deepening. She attended the majority of his concerts and they met afterwards, always finding some place they could sit and talk. With time their parting hugs became warmer and more intense, yet never reaching beyond the bounds of friendship. For Erin they were tremendous charges of energy, which kept her flying high for weeks afterwards. And during the winters they exchanged letters, hers always written to both him and his wife. Often Elizabeth wrote also, and eventually they visited each other. Yet the importance of Kjell's role never lessened. Unknowingly, he was the healing potion in her life, with his encouragement and advice, philosophy and caring.

At the end of the fourth summer Klell was again singing in the coffee house where they had first met. Rather than catching the late train home afterwards, he asked if he could spend the night at her place. On the way there they lost themselves in the depths of a conversation which continued far into the night over her kitchen table. When they finally exchanged their usual parting hugs he held her a long time, with his cheek resting on the top of her head.

"Erin," he murmured finally.

She lifted her head automatically, thinking he was going to say something, but to her surprise, he kissed her instead. A little shyly at first, then more and more intensely. Without stopping to think, she responded, in a way she never thought possible. Ordinarily she would have backed away when his hands crept up under her sweat- ter. But instead, she followed his lead, caressing the smoothness of his back, touching his face, sliding her fingers into the softness of his hair. Suddenly she wanted to devour him, be devoured by him.

"Come to bed with me," he whispered.

"Kjell, I would like nothing better," she told him, realizing as she said it that she was actually free within herself to do so, and consequently, also free to choose not to, "but what about Elizabeth? I can't do that to her."

Also she knew that she could not make love with him without exposing her true feelings and risking the friendship, a friendship which meant too much to her to trade for a night in bed.

"I've never been unfaithful to Elizabeth before," he said.

"Then it's no idea to start now, and especially not with me," she told him.

He hugged her tighter, swaying slightly.

"Maybe you're right," he sighed. "It's good that one of us can keep a straight head."

But some time after they had gone to their respective beds, he came into her room and slipped under the covers beside her.

"I'll be faithful," he assured her. "I just want to lie next to you."

And thus they spent the night, lying close together, touching, kissing, sharing a tenderness which was the end in itself, rather than just a step on the way to something else.

Erin relived that night over and over for weeks afterwards, while at the same time wondering what she actually meant to Kjell. If they instead had just had a good fuck, she could have passed it off as one of those late night things which happens between people. But it hadn't been that at all. His hands, his mouth, his eyes had all shown her something beyond "a good fuck." But what?

Then one day she received a post card from Elizabeth-- "just to say hello" from the west coast, where she and Lisa were visiting her parents for a few weeks. Seeing her opportunity, Erin wrote a letter addressed only to Kjell, requesting that he burn after he had read it. In it she tried to explain the role he had played in her return to life, as well as the deep love she felt for him, making clear that, in all the years she had known him, she had never felt the need to act upon that love, nor did she now. It was only that she wondered what lay behind their night together from his side. Whatever it was, it would change nothing.

When his answer came, it was evasive. The next time they met, his eyes, too, were evasive, as well as his words. She saw that he was uncomfortable, nervous, afraid. Closed. And keeping his distance. It was as if they hardly knew each other. Indeed, they were more like strangers than the first evening they had talked.

She never discovered what it was that had caused Kjell's rather extreme reaction, for their friendship, the one thing she had wanted to keep, dissolved with his evasiveness. At the same time, she realized that he had led her out of her fear, handed her the key to unlock her feelings, and set her free. She no longer needed him in order to feel alive.

THE NOVEL

A warm summer breeze leafed through the open notebook as if searching for something. But the pages were blank, waiting for the story which was to fill them. Erin picked it up from the little round lawn table, closing the black and red cover against the wind's intrusion, and cradled it in her lap while she scooted her chair into the sun. Then, hoisting her feet onto the chair in front of her, she let the palm of one hand slide meditatively over the book's glossy surface. Her life had been moving toward this moment for as long as she could remember. All she had ever wanted to do was write, but something had always come in the way: jobs, lack of confidence, the absence of encouragement, a violent marriage, fifteen years of single parenthood in a foreign country. Yet she had continually reassured herself that, when the children were grown, she would pick up her pen and at last fulfill her dream. But now, when both of her daughters had recently moved away from home, she was no longer quite so sure of herself, or her dream. She had bought the notebook, but just what was to happen next was still rather abstract.

Sighing, she opened the cover and stared at the empty page, suddenly afraid to mar it with her pen. Where should she start? What should she write? In the same instant she knew. She would write a novel about a single woman who, like herself, was a weather observer in Sweden. She called her Claire.

Excitedly she reached for her pen, curious to learn more about Claire's life. To her surprise, she discovered that she had taken a job as a substitute observer at a weather station in the mountains of northern Sweden. The reason? To isolate herself so she could spend her time writing.

At once Erin's interest was aroused and she began searching detailed maps to figure out where this weather station could be. Nor did it take her long to pin-point it, for her gaze constantly sought out a hump-shaped bit of Sweden which pressed itself into Norway, an area to which she had for years felt drawn. Although she had never been to just that particular place, she loved the surrounding countryside. It was there, ten years earlier, she had met Elias. The first time they had shaken hands the shock of recognition had passed between them like a bolt of lightning, startling not only the two of them, but also her friends who had introduced them. But she had quickly disentangled herself from the love affair which budded between them. Not only was he a good 15 years older than she, but their backgrounds were too different; she a product of middle class America and he from old-fashioned Swedish peasant stock. Nor could she tolerate his suffocating possessiveness. Yet he played a very important role in her life. Ever since childhood she had felt that she had lived in other times and places--especially Norway--before becoming Erin, and for her, he was the proof. There was no other reason why she should find herself so strongly attracted to this man with whom she had absolutely nothing in common. The only thing that didn't fit was that he lived in Sweden instead of Norway.

From the beginning the novel took on a life of its own, over which Erin had little control. It was Claire's story and she, Erin, was just as curious about the twists and turns it was going to take as any other reader would be. However, there was one thing both Erin and Claire had forgotten in their desire for isolation: In reality, every weather observer must have a relief observer who is required to do a certain number of observations each week. Erin remembered it first and created him. Claire realized it when he showed up at the door. His name was Anton. In an attempt to still give Claire her isolation, Erin made him into a shy, grubby character who rarely spoke and had no use for women. They had every reason to dislike each other. But Claire didn't follow her lines. She became inquisitive about the observer she was replacing and asked Anton who he was and what had happened to him. She was informed that he was an old woodsman who had been crushed by a falling limb while cutting trees in the forest. At the moment he was in the hospital, paralyzed, hanging between life and death. Erin liked the idea of 'an old woodsman' and immediately thought of Elias, who had once told her he could smell a fox's tracks in the forest. So she called him Elias and gave him similar qualities.

Over the days and months and years which followed, Erin read Claire's story as it flowed from her pen. She watched her and Anton take care of Elias at home, feeding hope by massaging his degenerating body day after day. She watched the story of Claire's and Elias's love grow out of the bolt of recognition which had passed between herself and the real Elias years before. And she watched Claire and Anton, in spite of their efforts to avoid it, come to care deeply for each other. And in the process Erin, too, fell in love with both Elias and Anton.

One day Erin suddenly found herself wondering about the real Elias. She was lying in bed with the flu and his presence became so overwhelming that she finally got up and phoned his niece, who had introduced them in the first place.

"He's not in very good shape," she told Erin. "Half a year ago they discovered he has Parkinson's. When I saw him recently, he could hardly walk or talk. For the time being he is still at home, but someone has to come in and fix his meals, as well as feed him, since he has difficulty holding a knife and fork. Buttoning his clothes and tying his shoes are out of the question. So it is simply a matter of time...."

Erin had ceased to listen. She was frightened. She had created a person, named him after Elias, and then paralyzed him, leaving him no hope of recovery. And now the real Elias-

-the fox-smelling woodsman who just ten years earlier had participated in a 150 mile bicycle race--was on his way to becoming as good as paralyzed, with no hope of recovery! Had her writing performed some sort of voo-doo? She hung up the phone and, on shaking legs, went back up to bed. That night was filled with dreams she didn't care to remember.

The next day she phoned Elias. His niece was right; he could hardly talk and she was reduced to asking him questions which he could only answer with yes or no. It was hardly an informative conversation. Finally she asked if she could come and visit him. He didn't answer. Understanding that he might not want to see her, or to be seen by her in his present condition, she asked him to think about it, saying that she would call back. But the decision had already been made, although not by either of them.

She drove the 400 miles non-stop, arriving late in the afternoon. The door was unlocked, as was the custom in northern villages, so she let herself in.

"Elias," she called from the hallway. "Elias? Are you here?"

She was answered by a soft shuffling sound as he made his way through the kitchen, skating slowly over the linoleum floor in his slippers. The hall door opened a crack and a little man peeked out. A flicker of recognition crossed his face.

"I hope you aren't angry at me for coming," she said, praying he hadn't seen her shock at the old man he had become. "I just felt I had to see you."

He lowered himself onto a kitchen chair and his shaky hand motioned her to sit down across the table from him. For what seemed an eternity he just stared at her. She didn't know what to say; even less what to do. He was in worse condition than she had expected and obviously barely able to care for himself. On top of that, his whole personality seemed to have dissolved into noth- ingness. It was as if he were already dead. She wondered what had driven her to visit him. She couldn't make him well. Nor could she just walk out on him and drive home again. Then she remembered how Claire and Anton had massaged the fictitious Elias every day. They hadn't made him well either, but they had made him feel better. It was the least she could do.

During the week that she stayed with him, she massaged his entire body for an hour each day--from his scalp down to his toes and out to his fingertips. To her shock, his physical condition improved tremendously, his eyes came to life, and his mind woke up. He even began to talk a bit.

"What did you think when I phoned you?" she asked him one day.

"T'was no surprise. I-I-I've been waiting so long--knew one day you'd come."

Erin's breath caught in her throat. That was exactly what the fictitious Elias had told Claire! She could feel the goose bumps rise on her arms.

There was still one piece of the puzzle she had yet to find: How Norway played into it all. However, it was quickly solved when Erin found an old historical atlas in the book case one afternoon while Elias was napping. Her fingers flipped through the pages, pausing here and there at various maps showing the changes in Scandinavia's borders throughout history. When she came to one from the 1500's she nodded to herself, not even surprised. At that time, the area of Sweden where Elias lived, and to which she always felt such a strong attraction, had been a part of Norway. At last her obsessions with Elias and Norway fit together.

By the end of her visit Erin knew she couldn't leave him, so she invited him to come and stay with her. He accepted.

A month of daily massage transformed Elias. Once again he could walk and talk, climb the stairs and run, and even button his buttons and tie his shoelaces. Together he and Erin dug her vegetable gar- den, cut and split her firewood, and went for walks. They laughed and loved, overjoyed for the miracle which was taking place.

At the same time, there was an element of tragedy lying close beneath the surface, which was growing like a cancer. Elias still had one overpowering trait to which he stubbornly clung: his pos- sessiveness. It was what had ended their budding relationship when they had met years earlier. Like a two year old, he refused to let Erin out of his sight. When she talked on the phone he sat beside her, angry if she spoke English, her mother tongue, and complaining loudly if she talked more than five minutes. He was scornful of her friends, whom he found an intrusion. The few times she went somewhere without him, he sulked and then yelled at her when she returned. Nor could she sleep properly because he pressed her up to the wall, his arms and legs entwined around her like an octopus's. He never left her alone for a minute, not even when she went to the toilet. But most of all, he was openly jealous of her daughters, whom he ignored totally. He couldn't abide her doing anything alone with them and the fact that they spoke English together infuriated him.

All her love and caring and massages had brought to life a monster who was devouring her. Nor could she succeed in getting him to understand what was happening. When he had been living at her house for a month, Erin had to admit defeat. She still loved the soul of this strange man, but a dislike for his behavior was taking over. The day he accused her of spoiling her children, who had been rudely pushed into the back seat by him, she exploded. The next day she drove him home.

Driving south again through endless miles of monotonous forestland, Erin tried to find some meaning behind all that had happened. It seemed so cruel to have brought Elias back to life, given him a taste of that for which he had waited so long, and then snatched it away again. Yet she had fully intended to make a permanent place for him in her life. It was he who had refused to accept that place which was offered, greedily demanding to have her exclusively to himself, without granting her time for her kids or her friends or any sort of life of her own. It was all or nothing. He would never be satisfied with only a part of her.

Shortly after Elias got home, he phoned to tell Erin that the doctors had been shocked by his improvement and concluded that he didn't have Parkinson's after all. He wanted to know when he could come down to her house again. With a guilty conscience, she put him off, and continued to do so each time he rang. His possessiveness had come between them twice already and she could still feel him trying to grasp her through the telephone. She couldn't stand it. Hard heartedly she set about to wean him.

Once again Erin took up her pen and slipped into Claire's skin, transferring her love to the fictitious Elias, who was anything but possessive. And when he died shortly thereafter, she missed him as if he had actually existed in the flesh. And, as Claire, she let herself love and be loved by Anton, until he became as real as other men she had once loved. And thus she realized that there was no difference between fantasy and the past. They both only existed in her mind.

It was not without pangs of guilt that, a year later, Erin learned from Elias's niece that he had regressed and had to be moved to a nursing home.

"The doctors can't understand the strange remission his illness went into last year," she said. "For awhile there, he had no symptoms of Parkinson's whatsoever. I wonder what happened."

"Yeah," was all that Erin could manage to say.

"Anyway, bit by bit it came back. And now he's even worse than before."

Erin's first reaction was to want to rescue him again, to give him the love and care he needed. But a voice inside her screamed, "No!" This was where her life differed from Claire's

106

life. Her Elias differed from Erin's Elias. Never would he allow her the breathing space she needed. She had to admit to herself that she really had no desire to offer her love and care only to be devoured by a tyrant who could never get enough. That was her first step out of the novel.

For Erin, the process of disentanglement was a long and painful one. It took her months of nit-picking and polishing before she considered the novel to be finished. During that time, she circulated it amongst her closest friends, asking for their opinions and criticisms. And then, at long last, she sent it to her agent. There was nothing left but to wait.

It wasn't the waiting that was long and painful. It was the 'nothing left' part. For years she had lived with and in the novel. She knew Claire and Elias and Anton intimately: they were her closest friends, her loves, and her lovers. Elias's cabin was her home, the weather station her work place. She knew every hill and dale and path of the surrounding area as though she had always lived there. The novel had been her life. And now it was finished. Over. Nothing left.

Her friends all reacted positively, as did her agent, but none of the ten or twelve publishers to whom it had been sent were willing to take the risk.

"It certainly is an unusual story," more than one of them concluded.

"Not half as unusual as the reality surrounding it," Erin invariably replied aloud to such rejection letters, while filing them into the wastebasket.

Time passed. Elias died, at last freeing Erin from her guilty con- science, which more than once had played with the thought of again taking him into her life. Now there were no more decisions to make, nothing left to make amends for. It was a closed book.

And on her shelf lay another closed book--dusty, but not forgotten. One day years later, just out of curiosity, Erin blew the dust off and opened it. As she read she felt a chilling anxiety creeping over her. For the first time, she saw the novel for what it was--her own innermost dreams, innocently revealed to her closest friends, as well as to a few strangers. It was as if she had let people read her most intimate private diary. She shivered, deeply embarrassed at having exposed herself so completely. And very thankful that it had never been published!

PART THREE
SWEDEN

Up until the middle of the 1950s, life for those
living in the Swedish countryside was much
the same as it had been for centuries. Not only
did the poor live under primitive material
conditions, but their treatment, by those
considered to be their superiors, was often
inhumane—especially when it came to
children, who were often merely looked upon
as a source of free labor and incapable of
having feelings. But life had always been so
and few had higher expectations. They made
the most of the situations in which they found
themselves. The following five stories are
inspired by the lives of people I have known,
or known about, who lived under the shadow
of their superiors.

INGEMAR

Winter arrived early that year, skipping its warning fanfare of frosty October nights and crisp clear days. It simply blew into the little Swedish village in the middle of the night, dumping its baggage on the ground while everyone slept. That, in itself, was not unheard of. What was unusual was the temperature's failure to rise again and melt the foot of snow pressing like a heavy foot on autumn's lingering vegetation. That people were caught unaware only in- creased their usual complaints about the arrival of winter, which, in one form or another, never failed to invade those northern latitudes. And ultimately there was nothing to do but accept reality, leave the last leaves unraked, and take out snow shovels instead.

The still-white snow crunched cheerfully under the tires as Erin drove cautiously down the steep hill to the village. For several hundred feet rabbit tracks kept pace with the car along the edge of the road in the unmarred snow before suddenly veering off into the forest, only to be replaced by dainty deer prints. In front of her, snow diamonds sparkled in the midday sun, emphasizing the chill of the motionless air.

Near the bottom of the hill she came upon Ingemar leading his ancient bicycle up the road toward her. For once the earflaps on the hat that he wore year round were down and flapping gently with the movement of his steps. The condensation of his breath had caused icicles to drip from his mustache into his ragged gray beard. Erin raised her index finger from the steering wheel and nodded slightly, the customary greeting between acquaintances in the Swedish countryside. Ingemar raised the tip of one thickly mittened hand a few degrees in return. From his expressionless face and slightly vacant eyes, she knew he had been drinking, even though the tracks trailing behind him were relatively straight.

Nearly every day he walked or cycled up to the little house which had belonged to Erin's neighbor Rolf. Regardless of the weather. When she first knew him years ago, his greeting had taken the form of a smile and a full salute, but since then his life had degenerated steadily, until he had turned into a taciturn old bum who cared for nothing but his bottle. The label of "village drunk" had become so tightly wrapped around him that people no longer saw behind it.

She thought back to when she had first met him, nearly twenty years earlier. At that time he was tentatively re-rooting himself in the place from which he had come and from which he had spent most of his life trying to escape. Erin was new to the area then, single and a foreigner. Like every other bachelor in the little mining community, he eventually made his way up to her door to inquire as to whether she needed help with anything. But unlike the others, he dared to come without the support of half a bottle of brännvin, the workingman's rotgut, in his head. So he and his somewhat older sidekick Rolf cut her firewood that year. But of course the wood was only an excuse. As an unattached female, she was a commodity, fair game in a market in which she had no interest. She paid them for their help and thereafter avoided Ingemar. Some years later, Rolf's life was, without warning, cut short by a heart attack. And Ingemar's life sunk into the bottle.

By now Erin had reached the grocery store and other thoughts pushed Ingemar's fate from her mind.

While everyone awaited a thaw, the weather defiantly remained cold and clear, without so much as a breath of wind. As in children's drawings, the smoke from chimneys stood straight up. It was as if the whole world were frozen solid, lifeless.

Erin found such winter weather exhilarating and the first couple of days took long walks deep into the forest, looking for moose and lynx tracks. Then one day she walked along the road instead, checking on a couple of summer cottages, as was her habit. Just past the little roadway in to Rolf's house, something caused her to turn around and retrace her steps a few paces. But all she saw were the still clear prints from Ingemar's boots, edged by the slightly weaving bicycle track. Puzzled, she continued down the hill. It wasn't until she came to the roadway on her way back that she suddenly understood what was strange: There were no tracks coming back out to the road again. She was immediately apprehensive. As far as she knew, Ingemar never spent the night in Rolf's house. Nor had she seen any light twinkling through the forest when she had driven past the previous night. She followed the footsteps.

As the house came fully into view, Erin noticed the side door was standing open. Coming closer she could see two sets of footprints on the steps, one going into the house and one coming out. Rather than walking straight into the house without knocking, as country Swedes do, she called through the doorway.

"Ingemar? Ingemar, are you here?"

When she got no answer, she stepped into the kitchen.

She was greeted by the silence of a still-life painting: Ingemar's plaid jacket hung over the back of a kitchen chair with an empty brännvin bottle on the table in front of it. Thinking that he had perhaps "gone around the corner of the house," as men do instead of going to the outhouse, she followed his footprints to the back yard. There she found him, lying spread-eagled on the ground in his shirtsleeves, his frost-covered hat beside another empty bottle.

In the village Ingemar's death was dismissed with a shrug. He had long been a recluse, a friendless old drunk. Perhaps. But he had not always been so. In the early days of the century Ingemar had been a child. And, like everyone else, he had started life with a mother and a father. It was shortly after that, however, that things seemed to turn against him. As a teenager he finally fled to sea, traversing the world in search of all that he had never had. But wherever he went, he found himself face to face with his traveling companion, a little boy called Ingemar, who carried with him a pocket full of memories.

One of the earliest of his memories was from a gray rainy day just after he had turned six. He had been in the forest all day, following Flora, the family's cow, while she grazed, to make sure she didn't get lost. And to protect her from wolves. The drizzling rain had long since made its way through his clothes, but he hadn't dared go home early in case his father should be there. Flora was to be in the forest between the morning and evening milkings. To bring her home earlier was to risk a beating. Many hours had passed since Ingemar had devoured the cold potato and bitter black coffee which comprised his lunch. Dusk was falling rapidly.

He hurried the cow along the path in front of him, slapping her rump with a stick every time she stopped to eat the soggy mushrooms that grew in abundance during the autumn. The wet sweater plastered to his back made him shiver and his bare feet were so cold that he didn't notice when he stubbed his toes on the roots criss-crossing the path.

As soon as the barn come into sight, Flora broke into a trot, with Ingemar running close behind. After the constant fear of the unseen dangers lurking in the forest, he longed for the security of the barn, where his mother would be waiting with the empty milk pail. But this particular day it was his oldest sister who was waiting instead.

"Hurry up!" she snapped from just inside the open door.

"Where's Mamma?" he wanted to know.

"Just help me tie Flora," she ordered. "Then go and get her water."

He obeyed without questioning further. Experience had taught him not to cross either of his older sisters.

He had never been allowed to draw up water before, but he knew that he must hold on to the end of the rope tightly to keep it from following the pail into the well. He slid the stone weight aside and opened the wooden cover. Grasping the rope firmly, he dropped the tin pail into the darkness of the hole. But when he pulled it up, it was empty. His second try was no more successful. Then suddenly his sister was beside him, grabbing the rope out of his hand and shoving him aside.

"You've to drop the pail upside down, dumb head!" she declared.

When she turned her back, he ran for the house and his mother. In the kitchen the wood stove was blazing, sending clouds of steam billowing to the ceiling from the kettle and several copper pans on its surface. But the room was empty, save for his father half sprawled over the kitchen table, surrounded by the stink of brännvin. Then he heard his mother's voice from behind the door to the best room. Quietly, so as not to disturb his father's stupor, he lifted the latch and pulled the door open a crack. She lay in the sofa, which had been pulled out to make a bed. All but her head and shoulders were blocked from view by the body of a large unfamiliar woman standing beside her. For some reason, the atmosphere frightened him and he closed the door again quickly. Shivering, he hunkered in front of the stove, out of his father's line of vision in case he should he sit up.

What was his mother doing in the sofa bed in the best room? As far as he could remember, the only time they had used that room was when his grandmother 'went away.' They had carried her downstairs from the tiny attic room, where she had lain in bed for as long as he could remember, and put her on the lid to the sofa bed, which was trestled between two straight-backed chairs in the best room. For once he was not sent out of the room when his mother and a neighbor woman washed her, for they were too taken up with their task to notice him standing in the corner. Always before Granny had complained in her squeaky voice when they tried to wash her, but his time she didn't say a word. When they were finished they dressed her in her Sunday clothes, instead of a clean nightgown, and left her lying, uncovered, on the hard lid, all alone in the cold dark best room.

But even stranger was the next day when they put her to bed in a wooden box and set it out by the gate. He watched through the kitchen window as people paused and spoke to her on their way to and from the village, but Granny didn't pay any attention to them. The following day they got all dressed up and took her to church. After the service, to his horror, they nailed a top on the box and buried it in a big hole. Afterwards all the neighbors came home with them and had coffee and cake in the best room. The children, of course, had to stay in the kitchen and be satisfied with a little juice. Ingemar had hoped for a taste of the cake once the others had left, but when his mother had carried out the cake plate, it was empty.

After that, no one went into the best room. All nine of them lived and slept in the kitchen, as always. His parents and baby sister slept in a box bed that pulled out from the bench by the kitchen table, while his four older brothers and sisters slept head-to-foot like sardines in a similar box bed in the corner of the room. Ingemar and his eight year old brother Hugo shared the kitchen rug, which did little to insulate them from the draft coming up between the wooden floor boards. They spent the long winter nights huddled together under a single blanket, sucking what warmth they could from each other. When Hugo complained once, their father bellowed that if that didn't suit them, they could sleep in the shed.

Now Ingemar wished his mother would come out into the kitchen. It was always safer to be near her when his father smelled bad. The closed door between them made him anxious. He tried to make sense of the noises coming from behind the door. Sometimes it sounded like someone was all out of breath from running, then came groaning noises and little whimperings. It reminded him of how his parents sometimes played in bed when they thought everyone else was asleep.

Suddenly a long drawn-out inhuman scream seared the air. His father sat up abruptly. Petrified, Ingemar flung open the door to the best room and rushed in. His mother was lying in the bed, her naked legs drawn up and spread wide apart, with a mass of blood and what looked like animal insides soaking the bed between them.

"Get that child out of here!" yelled the strange woman.

In the next instant his father had him by the ear and was dragging him out of the room, slamming the door behind them. But rather than being let go, he was propelled, screaming with pain, through the kitchen, into the tiny entranceway, and out across the yard, so fast that his feet could hardly keep up with the rest of his body. His father had such a hard grip on his ear that, should he stumble and fall, it would surely have been ripped from his head. Then, with one last thrust, he was cast into the woodshed and the door was shut and hooked after him. It wasn't until bedtime that he was remembered.

The next day his mother was still in the best room. But now she was lying on the lid to the sofa bed, which was again trestled between two chairs. The blood was gone and she had on her Sunday dress. Ingemar was beside himself. All he could think about was how they were going to put her in a box and bury her. He refused to look at her while she lay in the best room. He refused to tell her good-bye. And, most of all, he refused to go with them to bury her. This last refusal, however, was overridden by his father, who threatened to "make him pay" if he disgraced the family by his behavior. Thus he was forced to watch while the lid was closed over her sleeping face and she was lowered into the hole in the ground, pictures he was never able to eradicate from his mind.

The next day he took Flora into the forest as usual. But that evening she came home alone.

116

A week later Ingemar was caught stealing apples in a neighboring parish. After several days' incarceration in the local old people's home, which also served as a work house for the poor, a foster home was found. He was supplied with a slightly too small change of clothes from a boy who had recently died of pneumonia, as well as a piece of brown paper and a length of string with which to wrap them. Then a large important-looking man accompanied him to his new home, to make sure he didn't "get lost" along the way.

A young girl opened the door of the house to which he was taken. Sunlight streamed through large curtain-framed windows, falling on several children around his own age playing on the floor. They stared up at him curiously. But Ingemar's answering stare was even more curious. Rather than playing with pine cones or primitive figures made from rag-clad sticks, they were marching brightly colored tin soldiers and delicately carved horses across the rug. It was the first time he had seen real toys.

A few moments later a tall woman swept into the room, her long dress whispering like the wind in the trees.

"Good day, Herr Andersson," she said, offering her hand to the man with a slight curtsy.

"My pleasure, Fru Blom," his escort replied.

"And this is little Ingemar, I assume," she continued.

Ingemar stood spellbound, unable to take his eyes from her face. Never had he seen anyone so beautiful.

Herr Andersson gave him a shove from behind.

"Are you totally without manners, boy?" he growled.

Red with shame, Ingemar looked down at his battered wooden shoes while holding out his hand. Fru Blom took it gently. Her fingers were almost as small as his own, as smooth as his were rough.

"Welcome, Ingemar," she said.

He bowed his head like his mother had taught him.

"Thank you, Ma'am," he mumbled, aware only of the warmth of her grasp.

Then her hand slid out of his and came to rest on his head.

"You can sit over there while I speak with Herr Andersson," she told him, giving his head a slight turn toward the corner of the room.

From where he sat on the edge of a low stool Fru Blom appeared to be surrounded by a halo of sunlight. She looked like Jesus's mother. That she was going to be his new mother filled him with joy. Time stood still in her presence and he was unaware of Herr Andersson's departure.

Suddenly the girl who had opened the door to him less than an hour before was handing him the package with his change of clothes.

"Come with me," she said. "I'm supposed to show you where you're to sleep."

Puzzled, he followed her outside and across a patch of grass to the barn. She led him along a double row of cows, past a pair of enormous work horses, and into a tiny enclosure at the far end of the building. In the middle of the floor stood a small table, with box beds fastened to the walls on each side of it. One bed contained a lumpy mattress covered with a blanket, the other a large empty cloth bag folded on top of a blanket. Two wooden clothes pegs stuck out of the wall on each side of the door.

"You can take straw from the loft for your mattress," the girl said, indicating the cloth bag. Then she was gone.

Ingemar was still lying face down on the blanket and empty straw bag when a young man came in and threw himself onto the other bed.

"Some help you're gonna be!" he snorted when Ingemar sat up.

"Why can't I live in the house an' have Fru Blom for my mother an' play with the toys?" he sniffled.

The man laughed. "'Cause you ain't kin with 'em. You're just a 'parish urchin.'"

"What's that?"

"It means ya' got no parents, so the parish pays the Bloms to take ya' in. You have to earn your keep, like any other farm hand."

Farm hand. Dräng. The very sound of the word was like being pulled down into the mud, into helplessness.

Since he was too young to begin school, Ingemar was constantly at his master's beck and call. His existence no longer consisted of wandering through the forest with a cow and a head full of dreams. It became filled with dung from fifteen cows, as well as two horses, to be shoveled out twice a day. And water to be carried to them, as well as to those who lived in the house. And there was firewood to split and carry. And turnips to thin and weed, potatoes to plant and dig up, and grain to be threshed with a wooden club. His pay at the end of the year was to be a pair of pants, a shirt, and a pair of wooden shoes. That such a life was normal for a 'parish urchin' offered no solace.

After a couple of months his misery and longing for his brother Hugo caused him to run away. But when he finally found his way home the house was abandoned, save for his brännvin-saturated father. The older children had left home to work as maids and farm hands, the younger ones to foster homes. He never saw any of them again.

A year later, just after his seventh birthday, he was auctioned off to another farmer, who had bid the least amount of money from the parish for his upkeep. The conditions were the same, the only difference being that he was allowed to go to school during the winter months when there was less work to be done. And in this way, Ingemar's childhood passed, with a different bed in a different barn each year. And with each move came the childish hope of finding a mother and a family. A hope which was never fulfilled.

At the age of 14, like everyone else, he was confirmed and henceforth considered an adult. He gave up his dream of a mother and a family and went to sea.

One autumn the freighter on which he had been working for several years was forced to dock for repairs at a port along the Australian coast. The crew were given a week's leave. Thus far Ingemar had managed to avoid being dragged into whore houses with the others when they were in port. The thought of going in to such a place frightened him, for he was ashamed to admit that he had no idea of what to do with a woman. Luckily, port calls had been few and far between, shore leave short. And as a last resort, he had always been able to save himself by quickly passing out from a few whiskies on an empty stomach. But a week? He decided to go off exploring on his own, far from the waterfront.

The little café he went into the first evening was full of people, all being served by a single waitress. His eyes followed her as she moved gracefully between tables, chatting and laughing while her pencil flew over the order pad. He was fascinated, even aroused.

The next day he returned at lunch time. The café was empty. She smiled playfully at him when he asked for a "hamburier."

"Where're you from, anyway?" she asked.

"Sveeden," he replied in his best seaman's English.

She laughed, but not mockingly. Gaily.

When she returned with his food, he asked her to sit down since there were no other customers. They exchanged names—Ingemar, Margaret—and talked of ordinary things. The weather, their jobs, the places he had been.

The rest of the week he never strayed far from the café, where he took all his meals, and its waitress, with whom he spent all of her free time.

"Where're all your mates?" she asked him one evening. "You always come here alone."

"They like the whore houses," he told her.

"And you don't?"

"I donno. I've never been."

"Have you ever done it with a girl?" she probed.

Ingemar felt his face and ears get hot. He looked down.

"Well? Have you?" she persisted.

He shook his head.

"Come on," she said and grabbed his hand. "It's no good for a sailor to be a virgin."

She led him up a narrow staircase at the back of the café. His only reaction was that the steps seemed well-worn. Perhaps she, too, was a whore. He was both frightened and excited, but most of all, embarrassed over his ignorance.

"This is where I live," she said, opening the door to a room at the end of the hall.

It was immaculately clean, with a bright spread over the bed and lace curtains at the window. She closed the door behind them and pulled him down onto the bed beside her. Kissing came easily enough, once he got started. And eventually his hands even found their way up under her clothes. He began to relax.

"You have too many clothes on," she whispered.

Ingemar stood up and, with his back to her, undressed awkwardly. Margaret, too, squirmed out of the little she still had on.

"Come," she said. "I'm waiting."

He turned around slowly. She was lying on her back, naked, with her legs drawn up and spread wide a part. But rather than seeing a young woman eager to receive him, Ingemar saw his mother with a bloody mass of guts between her legs and death in her eyes. Gagging, he rushed out into the hall and threw up.

Ever afterwards, even the thought of a naked woman repulsed him.

Time passed. Eventually life at sea proved to be too much for Ingemar. He had long ago given up searching, if, indeed, he even remembered he had been searching for something. Alcohol not only helped him avoid women, but it also served to dull his loneliness, his longing. In the end, it was alcohol which set him ashore, for he had become a hazard on board.

Feeling more lost than ever, he returned to the village where he was born, on the slight hope that he might find Hugo. But, instead of Hugo, he found Rolf, one of the "big boys" he had looked up to during his childhood. Rolf had cared for an ailing mother and alcoholic father long into his own middle age. When they finally died he had been a bachelor for so long that the thought of marriage never occurred to him. But he was lonely. And when Ingemar started to come up to his place, Rolf welcomed him. But he never drank from the bottle Ingemar placed on the table between them.

One spring afternoon they sat as usual at Rolf's kitchen table. A warm breeze laced with the fragrance of both pine sap and lilac slipped through the open window, playing gently with the curtains on its way. Outside the air was thick with birdsong. Rolf gazed out across the yard to the forest beyond, trying to penetrate its thickness with his eyes. On the other side of the table a bottle clinked clumsily against the edge of a glass. Rolf whirled around.

"Damn it, Ingemar!" he bellowed, sweeping the newly-filled glass across the room with the back of his hand. "Must you make love to that fucking bottle all the time? I've been sitting here day in and day out, for years on end, putting up with my alcoholic father. I'm not going to start putting up with you now! Take your bottle and get the hell out of here!"

Ingemar stood up unsteadily, grasped his bottle around the neck, and made his way out the door. Rolf turned back to the window with a sigh.

On his way out to the road, much to his own surprise, Ingemar began to cry. Lifting his hand to wipe away his tears, he suddenly found the forgotten half-full bottle waving in front of his face. He flung it, with all the force he could muster, against a rock.

Two days later, cold sober, he walked back up the hill to Rolf's house.

"I'm sorry," he said hesitantly from the doorway.

Rolf took a cup and saucer from the cupboard, filled it from the coffee pot at the back of the wood stove, and set it on the table. He nodded toward the empty chair. Then he poured out a bit of coffee from his own cup onto the saucer, placed a sugar cube between his front teeth, and sucked the hot coffee through it. When he had finished, he turned his empty cup upside down on the saucer and leaned back.

"Shall we take the binoculars and go out in the forest and check the bird houses?" he suggested.

And thus it began; a friendship which gave Ingemar the strength to live in an unclouded reality—most of the time, at least. And when the old demons overpowered him he kept to himself, for he could not risk loosing Rolf. They never talked about his problem. It was his and he fought his demons alone. But Rolf always knew when he was in their grip and was unable to sleep until Ingemar returned to his door, sober once more.

"Do you still have your driver's license?" he asked one day. Ingemar nodded. "Let's pool our resources, then, an' get us a car," he continued. "Think of the places we can go an' the things we can do!"

In that way Rolf, who had barely left the village his entire life, came out into the world, with Ingemar as his guide. And through his old connections, they were even able to make a freighter trip to some of the ports Ingemar had long ago visited. They formed a good team, for Ingemar steered them, while Rolf kept him on an even keel. Neither could have made such journeys without the other.

They were like an old couple: Rolf with an apron tied around his middle, taking cinnamon buns out of the oven, Ingemar on his hands and knees weeding the garden. They spent long evenings talking in front of the open fire, surprised each other with Christmas and birthday presents, and went places in their little red Volvo. To outsiders, it seemed strange that Ingemar never moved in with Rolf. But neither wanted to take the risk of complicating what they had, for occasionally Ingemar still needed to isolate himself with his demons.

The years went by. Both were happier than they had ever expected to be in life, given their individual circumstances. Ingemar rarely felt the urge to drink, although when the demons occasionally knocked, he was drawn to their company.

And so it was one stormy evening.

"Why don't you stay the night?" Rolf suggested unexpectedly.

There was a power failure and they had been playing cards at the kitchen table by lantern light, listening to the wind howling down the chimney.

"Thanks, but I think I should be getting home," Ingemar replied. He could feel the demons sneaking up behind them.

"Don't be silly. It's icy as hell outside."

"It'll be OK with the stud tires." He scooped the cards together, evened their edges against the table top, and got to his feet. Rolf followed him to the door.

When he got home, his apartment was cold and dreary. The warmth from Rolf's wood stove had let him forget there was no electricity and, for him, no heat. He considered driving back up the hill again, but decided against it. The brännvin he had come home for would warm him up. He wrapped himself in a blanket and opened the screw top on the bottle.

Ingemar awoke with a start the next morning, stone sober. He felt strangely uneasy, nervous. Without stopping to wonder why, he got into the car and drove as fast as he could up to Rolf's. But he was too late.

Whether Rolf had slipped and fallen on the ice-covered path to the outhouse or had had a heart attack and fallen didn't matter: He wouldn't have frozen to death if Ingemar had spent the night there.

From that day on, Ingemar let the demons have their way with him, for only they could dull his guilt and grief. And in the end, suspect he willingly accepted their offer of permanent relief.

HILDA

Long rays from the setting sun slid under a layer of high, sandbar-ridged cirrocumulus clouds, reddening their undersides. The air was fragrant with newly warmed pine sap, mingled with the delicate hint of birch leaves about to unfold. On either side of the path fallow fields gave off their own special damp, almost swampy smell, and bits of new greenness were starting to sprout amongst the old raspberry canes and dried grass along their edges. Erin unzipped her jacket and let the gentle spring breeze open it while she walked toward the neighboring farm.

Half a century earlier this had been the road connecting her house to the farm where old Hilda now lived alone. In those days roads followed the twists and turns of the earth's contours, but as cars began to replace horses and wagons, they were straightened to accommodate faster traffic. But rather than straighten the many curves in this one, a completely new stretch of road had been built on the far side of the field, leaving the old road to fade back into the landscape. Already it was reduced to two parallel footpaths separated by a ridge of coarse grass and wild flowers.

Erin tried to imagine a horse and wagon coming along behind her on its way up to Hilda's, loaded with sacks of grain or perhaps empty ten gallon milk cans clanking together as it bumped over the uneven earth. She could almost hear it getting closer and closer, until she actually expected it to overtake her. But instead, the neighbor's junky old American car rattled up the road on the far side of the field, jolting her back to the present.

It wasn't the first time she had been sucked into the past while out walking in the Swedish countryside where she had been living for many years. Every one of the numerous of old houses decorating the landscape had its own story to tell of the past and the people who have lived in it. Together they created an atmosphere which pulls one back in time, for they have never really become a part of the 20th century. It wasn't like in America, where "the old days" were a couple of hundred years ago, when the pioneers were settling the country. Here the old way of life had existed close to its original form from medieval times all the way to the post war years. The Second World War, that is. Up until that time, the country was abundant with people who had no running water, no indoor toilets, no central heating, no telephones, no cars. But now, three decades later, those who were going to catch up with the modern world had caught up. Yet out in the countryside there were many elderly people who were content to live in the old way to which they were accustomed.

As she neared Hilda's house her dog barked from the back door porch.

"Hush, Lady." Erin yelled. "It's only me." But she was old and getting deaf, as well as more protective. She had tried to bite her once when she had cycled past, so Erin had respect for her. Hilda claimed it was because she had a thing about bicyclists, but Erin didn't trust her even when she was walking.

The back door opened and she heard Hilda's old lady voice order the dog into the house.

"Hello!" she called. "It's just me, out for a walk as usual."

"Oh, come in, come in! I was just going to have coffee. Surely you could drink a cup. I have freshly baked cinnamon buns. Still warm, they are. Lady, shut up and git in here!" A door slammed somewhere inside the house and Hilda stuck her head out the back door again. "Come on now. The beast is locked away," she laughed.

Although Erin was no great coffee drinker, it was impossible to say no to her cinnamon buns. Kicking off her boots in the hall, she went into the kitchen. A fire was burning in the wood stove and the oven door was open, letting the warm air drift out into the room. On the counter several hand woven dishtowels hid baking sheets of buns from view, but nothing could hide their enticing aroma. She sat down on the bench by the table and looked out the window. The sun was just pulling away from under the brilliant clouds and sinking below the black line of the horizon. Hilda placed cups and saucers on the oil cloth covered table, added a shot of cold water to the coffee boiling in the pot to settle the grounds, and filled their cups. Replacing the pot on the edge of the wood stove, she returned with a plate of cinnamon buns in crinkly paper baking forms.

"Var så god," she said, the inviting words one must wait for before taking that which has been set before one.

"Mmmmm!" Erin declared after the first bite. "These are wonderful!"

"Asch, they're too fresh!" Hilda scoffed. "You can't dunk 'em in your coffee without having 'em fall apart." She poured a bit of coffee into her saucer, placed a sugar cube between her front teeth, and sucked the rapidly cooling coffee through it. Erin had only seen men drink that way, but concluded that it was to compensate for not being able to dunk the bun.

Outside the window the sky had finished its show and was starting to darken, but Hilda made no move to turn on the light. Neither of them said anything for a long time.

"It's so nice to sit quietly in the twilight like this," she said finally. "We call it *kura skymning* [1] in Swedish. We always did

127

it in the old days. We never lit the lamp until it was absolutely dark."

"Tell me about life in the old days," Erin said. " Were you born here, or did the farm belong to your husband's family?"

"No, it belonged to my mother's aunt and uncle. I came to live with them 73 years ago, when I was seven."

"Hmmm," she mused, trying to put those facts together into some sense. "I don't understand. Did something happen to your parents?"

"Oh, no, not at all. Things like that were rather common back then."

"How so?"

Hilda leaned back in her chair and sighed slightly. Erin could see by the faint light from the window that her eyes were closed.

"I was born in the next village," she began. "I had three older brothers and a sister who was two years older than I was, and then a

---

[1] Sitting in the twilight

baby sister. We lived right in the middle of the village, across from

the school. My father worked for the railroad and my mother sometimes did odd jobs for people. She helped at weddings and funerals, or with the big laundries people did before Midsummer and Christmas. That sort of thing. One day when I was seven my mother's old aunt and uncle came to visit unexpectedly. That day changed my whole life.....

The summer sun had not yet reached the attic window when Hilda woke up that morning. Usually it was the warmth of it shining on the bed which woke her, but not today. Instead, it was the sound of voices coming from the kitchen below. She rolled onto her back, careful not to wake Dora who was sleeping head to foot with her. Outside the open window the wind was blowing the little propellers off the maple tree, making them fly through the air like dragonflies. Her big brother Harry said there were seeds for new trees in them. She couldn't quite figure out how such tall trees could come from those teeny little seeds, but if Harry said it was so, then it was so. He was 17 and knew things like that. Her other two brothers, Roland and Oskar, never told her interesting things. Mostly they teased her and acted stupid. As for her sister, she played with Hilda when no one else was around. But as soon as her school friends appeared, she treated Hilda like a baby.

She slipped out of bed, curious to find out who had come to visit so early in the day. Part way down the stairs she was able to see an old woman in a long black dress sitting at the kitchen table drinking coffee with her parents. Coming down one more step she saw a man on the far side of the table, also dressed in black. Something about them was familiar.

"I want to take Dora home with me," the woman was saying. "I'm getting old and I need a maid to help with all that has to be done on the farm."

Immediately Hilda recognized the voice of her mother's Aunt Amanda, who lived outside the next village. She had never liked her. In fact, she was afraid of her. Amanda was very proper and her mouth always seemed be pulled together as if she had eaten sour berries.

"Well, I don't know," her mother began slowly. "I need her myself."

"Take Hilda," she heard Harry say. "She's much nicer than Dora."

She snickered to herself, knowing he was joking. After all, she was only seven. Quietly she retreated back upstairs to wake Dora.

"No! No! They can't take me!" Dora cried when Hilda told her what she had heard. "Usch! I don't want to live with those awful old people!"

"Not me, either!"

Without bothering to get dressed, they hurried down to the kitchen.

"Good morning, Mamma and Papa," they said nervously, trying to ignore Aunt Amanda and Uncle Gustaf.

"Good morning, girls," their mother answered. "Where are your manners? Or haven't you noticed that we have guests?"

They curtseyed politely to the old people, then turned back to their mother, waiting for her to speak.

"Go upstairs and get dressed now," she told them. "It's not proper to go around half dressed like that. Then go out and feed the animals and leave us adults to ourselves."

"But..." Dora began, but her father cut her off.

"Do as you're told!" He motioned them away with his hand. Hilda was already considering the situation. Without her sister she would have the whole bed to herself and she wouldn't get punished for the things Dora did and blamed on her.

When they came back to the house after having fed the chickens and taken the cow out to the common grazing pasture, Amanda and Gustaf were getting ready to leave.

"Come along, Amanda," Gustaf prodded. "If we don't hurry we'll miss the train." They had walked the five miles from their farm to the train station and then would ride another five miles to attend a funeral in another parish.

"Have her things packed and ready by the time we get back from the service this afternoon," Amanda said in a tone close to an order.

"Yes, Auntie," their mother answered.

A train whistled in the distance. Gustaf steered his wife out the door and across the yard.

"Sit down and eat your breakfast," their mother told them. "Then we have to pack your things together, Hilda, so you can go with Aunt Amanda and Uncle Gustaf."

"Me?" Hilda cried. "I thought Dora was going."

"No, we decided that it would be better if you went. I need Dora to help me with the baby when I have to go and work. Besides, it's better if you start school there right from the beginning."

"School?" Ever since Dora had started school two years ago she had looked forward impatiently to the day when she could go to school with her.

130

"Of course."

"In the summer?"

"No. But Amanda needs help all year round. And she is going to need more and more help the older she gets. Eat up now, so we can gather your things."

Hilda shoved her porridge bowl into the middle of the table. "I'm not hungry," she said. "I don't want to go with them. I want to stay home!"

"Life is not a matter of doing what you want. If you're finished eating, let's get your things together."

Too proud to admit her hunger, Hilda left the table.

From her bride's chest where she kept the linen sheets, hand woven years ago for her trousseau, her mother took out a big piece of brown paper she had been saving. Smoothing it out on the kitchen table, she began laying Hilda's clothes on it: her other dress, her two pinafores, a sweater, and an old jacket that no longer fit Dora. When Hilda saw her long hand knit wool stockings and her shoes added to the pile, she knew she was going for a long time. She only wore shoes and stockings in the winter when there was a lot of snow. Otherwise she went bare foot.

By the time Amanda and Gustaf returned that afternoon, Hilda was washed and her hair brushed and pulled into tight braids. Her bundle of clothes lay on the table, wrapped in the brown paper and tied securely with a couple of rounds of thin string. Only her mother and brothers were there to say good-bye. Dora had gone off to tell her friends of her narrow escape and her father had gone to work.

Be good and do what Aunt Amanda and Uncle Gustaf tell you," her mother told her. "We'll come to see you as soon as we have a chance." She gave her a quick hug. Harry took a step toward her and stretched out his hand to pat her on the head, but she turned away and pulled her bundle from the table. Without looking at him, she stalked out the door and down the path after Amanda and Gustaf.

The first part of the way "home" was along the dirt road which wound up and over the ridge between the two villages. Once they reached the top of the ridge, they cut off onto a footpath through the forest. Here they had to walk single file, with Gustaf leading the way. Amanda followed, carefully holding up her long skirt so as not to tramp on it as she stepped over the many rocks and roots. Last came Hilda, clutching her bundle against her stomach while trying not to stub her bare toes. Not only were her strides short compared to those of the adults, but her legs were also bowed as the result of having had rickets. Nor was she used to walking long distances. Every once in a while one of them turned around to make sure she was coming. If she was too far behind, Amanda would stop and rest until she had almost caught up and then go on. Hilda never got a chance to stop and catch her breath even for a few seconds.

The bundle got heavier and heavier. She tried carrying it by the string, but it cut through her fingers, even though she switched it back and forth from one hand to the other. And her legs ached so that she could hardly lift them. Finally she sat down on a rock beside the path with the bundle on her knees. Amanda had disappeared from sight. The tears which she had held back all day suddenly overpowered her. If only one of them would come back and help her with the bundle, but neither of them appeared. Hilda rubbed her eyes with her clinched fists, smearing dirt across her face. Suddenly she was afraid. She had never been alone in the forest. Think if the wolves found her. She knew there were wolves, for she had heard a neighbor telling her father how they had killed one of his sheep.

Presently she heard a rustling sound beside her. Turning, she saw the hem of Amanda's black skirt brushing the pine needles in the path. Slowly she looked up. Amanda stood, hands on her hips, looking down at her. Her grey-streaked hair was pulled back to the knot at the nape of her neck so tightly that her face looked abnormally large and pasty.

"Get up," she said. "We haven't got all day."

Hilda turned around to pick up her bundle.

"Please can you carry this for a while?" she asked, but Amanda didn't hear her. She was already on her way down the path again.

It was evening by the time the three of them reached the farm.

Like all other farm houses of its time and size, Amanda's and Gustaf's house was just a cottage, consisting of a kitchen and "best room" downstairs and an unfinished attic upstairs. The best room was just that—a room which was only used on special occasions and otherwise closed off from the rest of the house. Daily life took place in the kitchen. Everyone washed at the wash stand just inside the door and at night the wooden seats of the two sofas were lifted and the box-like under portions pulled out into beds. When tramps came past on their wanderings, they slept on the kitchen floor. Privacy was not an aspect of peasant life.

"Leave your things there," Amanda instructed, pointing to the box sofa by the kitchen table. Hilda hoisted her bundle up onto the seat and climbed up beside it. Amanda and Gustaf stood, one at each end of the room, with their backs to each other and removed their church clothes piece by piece, replacing each garment with a similar, but well-worn, one.

"Come on," Amanda told her when she had finished changing her clothes. "This is no time to lie around. We have work to do."

Reluctantly Hilda slid off the sofa and followed her out to the barn. Without any introduction, she was handed a three-legged stool and a pail.

"This is how you milk a cow, "Amanda said simply. Placing her calloused hand over Hilda's tiny one, she demonstrated how to draw the milk down into the teat and squeeze it out. "This will be your job every morning and evening. My hands are too crippled to do it any longer."

Hilda looked more closely at the hands covering her own. The fingers were warped and bent at a strange angle. She shivered. They looked just like witch's claws.

By the time the five cows had been milked, the dung shoveled out, and the milk cooled in the well of cold water in the floor, Hilda was so exhausted that she could hardly eat the oatmeal which comprised their evening meal. As soon as their bowls and spoons had been washed, Amanda drew the curtains across the windows to shut out as much of the summer light as possible. She and Gustaf pulled on their night clothes over their heads and undressed underneath them. Then Gustaf tipped up the seat of the sofa by the window, set the peg in place to hold it up, and together they pulled out the box section.

"Where's my room?" Hilda asked timidly.

"Your room?" Amanda replied. "You sleep in the sofa bed by the table. You don't need to pull it out. For the time being you can keep your clothes at the foot end, since your feet don't reach that far."

Hilda understood that no one was going to help her lift the heavy wooden seat. It took all her strength to raise it enough so she could step into the box underneath and push it the rest of the way up against the back of the sofa. But before she managed to fit the peg into the hole to hold it in place it fell back down, knocking her out of the bed and against the table. She cried out from pain and surprise.

"Hush, child," she heard Gustaf say. "Let a person get a little sleep."

This time Hilda didn't try to lift the seat high enough to fasten it. Instead, she raised it just enough so she could squeeze underneath and fall onto the straw mattress inside. Gently she let it close above her head and cried herself to sleep.

And thus began Hilda's life as maidservant. Amanda schooled her meticulously as to how to make a fire in the kitchen stove without having it smoke, how to grind and boil coffee, bake, polish the copper pans, clean the silverware with sand, knit, sew her own clothes, take care of animals; in short, everything that a farm woman needed to know. And as soon as Hilda had mastered a job, it was added to her list of everyday tasks.

The first of these was to get up early every morning, make the fire, and have the coffee ready by the time the old people got out of bed. When she complained, it was pointed out that when Amanda and Gustaf were children, in the middle of the 1800's, most seven year olds had to go to work, usually for strangers. Often they had to live in the barn or a cold attic, get up at 3 am and work until 8 or 9 in the evening. If they were lucky they went to school every other day for a couple of months in the wintertime. Hilda had already heard the same thing from her grandmother, but it still didn't make her feel any better.

However, the times had changed in regards to school. One autumn day a boy from the neighboring farm knocked on the door.

"My-name's-Arvid-and-my-mother-sent-me-to-say-that-we-can-walk-to-school-together-tomorrow-so-that-I-can-show-you-the-way," he said as fast as he could. As the last word left his mouth he turned and ran down the hill towards home again.

Hilda's heart skipped a beat, not because of the boy, but because all summer she had feared that, with so many chores dealt out to her, she wouldn't have time to go to school.

It was a four mile walk along windy wagon tracks and forest paths to get to school. At first it seemed endlessly long, but after awhile Hilda became accustomed to it. Then came the dark cold rainy days of November when her leather boots were soaking wet long before they reached the school house, as was her thin woolen coat. Nor was the classroom particularly warm. Her feet were always freezing in her wet boots, and to take them off was not allowed. When winter came, she and Arvid often had to wade through hip-deep snow, taking turns forging a path. By the time they got home in the afternoons she was frozen clear through. But before she had a chance to get warm it was time to do the milking. Sitting on the milk stool sniffling against a warm soft cow flank, she longed to go home to her family. There she would simply have to cross the road to get to school and she only had a few simple chores to do. Why did she have to live with these old people? They never laughed or had fun. They just smelled bad and snored all night. And ordered her around.

The years passed and increasing responsibility fell onto Hilda's shoulders. Gustaf had a stroke which left him bedridden. Amanda's rheumatism became progressively more crippling. Although Sweden did not fight in the First World War, times were hard and food scarce. Their livelihood depended on what they could raise them- selves, their only source of income coming from milk and the cheese and butter they made and sold locally. Hilda's days were full to overflowing. Over the years she had rarely seen her parents or brothers and sisters, for they lived in a different parish and thus they did not meet at church or social events. Gradually they had taken on the guise of distant relatives and her longing had ceased. At the same time, daily life brought her into closer contact with Arvid and his family, until they replaced the one she had lost. She and Arvid were inseparable, even after they no longer walked to school together, so no one was surprised when, in their early 20's, they became engaged.

When they married Amanda sold the farm to them and she and Gustaf moved into an old people's home. At last Hilda was mistress of her own home and had a helpmate. The children came one after the other, five in a dozen years. She set out to create for them that which she had missed—a real family. She had never been so happy.

Then one day Arvid got sick. The local doctor was puzzled and sent him to the hospital for tests. There he was diagnosed with cancer and never returned home. Within a month he was dead. Hilda was left a widow at 39, her oldest child 15 and the youngest 3. And another world war on the horizon.

"How did you ever manage?" Erin asked in wonder. She knew all her children; they were a light-hearted bunch who were always ready to laugh. They certainly didn't give the impression of having had a deprived childhood. And Hilda herself was the most joyful of them all.

"When Arvid died I realized that you can either count your blessings and be happy or you can count your misfortunes and be miserable. Arvid and the kids were such a blessing in my life that they made my misfortunes insignificant. I already knew how to run this farm alone, but this time I had many small hands which helped me. We were a family and we were doing it for us—and for Arvid. It was as if he were always there watching over us and encouraging us when times got hard. The only other alternative was to put the kids in foster homes. But I had already lost my family once and I had vowed never to let it happen again."

She got up automatically to put more wood on the fire. Before she could close the firebox door it flared up, sending a flickering light dancing out into the otherwise dark kitchen. She lit a candle and picked up the coffee pot.

"How about some more coffee and another bun?" she said with a laugh.

TORA

The cold January wind swept down the mountainside and across the narrow valley, dumping its load of Arctic snow on the few homesteads scattered just below the tree line. Homesteading in northern Sweden during the first years of the 1900's was a hard life. Unlike pioneering in the New World, where settlers could either kill or drive out the enemy, here they were completely at its mercy. For here it was not human beings but, rather, the weather which was the unpredictable and uncontrollable enemy, sometimes aiding one's labors with both sun and rain, while other times destroying one's efforts with too much or not enough of one or the other. Either way, poverty was never far away. Even in the good years, it stood on the doorstep; in the bad years it moved inside and made itself an unwelcome guest.

Tora bent over the raised open hearth, stirring porridge in a three-legged iron pot standing in the fire. Outside, the wind howled eerily around the log cabin, rattling the door and demanding to be let in. Here and there snow flakes managed to force their way between the wall timbers and fell silently to the floor, building small drift-like piles which had no intention of melting in the chilly room. The insides of all three of the cabin's small windows were covered with a thick layer of ice, except for a tiny peep hole one of the smaller children had scraped on one of them out of boredom. It was already dark, even though it was only three o'clock, but the lamp wouldn't be lit for another couple of hours, when it was officially evening. Kerosene was not only expensive, but also difficult to carry home on one's back over the rough mountain paths. In the meantime, the flickering light from the fire sufficed.

Tora pulled her long baggy sweater more tightly around her thin body with her free hand. It had belonged to her grandmother, who wore it winter and summer. After she died, her mother cut off the too-long sleeves, unraveled them past the holes in the elbows, and sewed them back on again. There

138

must have been buttons on it at one time, for there were buttonholes down one edge of the front, but they had long since disappeared. Granny had always held it closed with a large safety pin, the only one Tora had ever seen. When she had learned that the sweater was to be hers, the prospect of inheriting that safety pin excited her even more than the sweater itself. But to her dismay when she finally got it, the pin was gone, replaced by one black button at the neck. Not wanting to seem ungrateful, she had said nothing. Under the sweater she wore one of her two dresses, the one her mother had re-made by "turning" a hand-me-down dress from a cousin, so that the less-faded inside of the material was on the outside. Over it she wore a pinafore-type apron made from a worn-out hand-woven sheet. And underneath she had on the long winter stockings of scratchy woolen yarn that her mother had spun and knitted. Every winter the toes were opened and knitted a bit longer and the heels re-darned. The leg sections never wore out, nor did their irritating scratchiness cease. On the floor by the door stood her brand-new shoes side by side, waiting for the next morning when she would wear them for the first time. She was nine years old and they were the only pair of new shoes she had ever owned; high leather ones with hooks instead of holes for the laces. She dared not even look at them for fear they weren't real. They had been a combination birthday and Christmas present, for after the holidays she was going to go to school in town, a two day journey from home. Not only that, she was to make the journey all on her own—she who had never even spent a night away from her family. She felt very grown-up, for not even her older brothers had left home on their own yet. At the same time, mixed with her joy was also anxiety, a fear of the unknown awaiting her.

Up until now, Tora's schooling had been rather sporadic. Since there was no school, or even village, within a day's walk, the young children in the area were taught by an ambulatory teacher who spent several weeks at each homestead, teaching those children who lived within walking distance of wherever he happened to be. In return, he was given room and board. Once his pupils were able to read and write and manage basic addition and subtraction, they had to move on to a school in a little settlement several hours' walk away. There they boarded at surrounding farms, only coming home on weekends. Tora's four older brothers had continued their required education in that manner and it was assumed that she would follow in their footsteps. But when her turn came, there was no place available for her to board. And thus it was decided that she should be sent to town. Town. She tried to imagine what it was like. The largest place she had been to was a village where an open market was held twice a year. Its only street was lined on both sides with small wooden shacks with large glassless windows on whose wide sills goods were laid out for sale. On market days it was crowded with people going from stand to stand, buying coffee, sugar, salt, flour, and other things they were unable to raise or make themselves. The one time she had been there with her father on a non-market day, the whole place had been devoid of people, the window shutters closed, and the doors pad-locked. Surely town wasn't like that—yet she wasn't at all sure.

"Tora," her mother called from across the room, "stop your day-dreaming and stir the porridge 'fore it burns to the pot! Otherwise the burned part will be your portion. There's hardly enough for all of us, as it is. And the rest of you, come to the table now. Your father and brothers will be in any minute."

From the dark corners of the room small feet approached the table. One after the other they climbed up onto the long bench on the far side; Tora's three younger sisters and two little brothers. One of them pulled open the drawer in the table, scooped out a dozen wooden spoons, and began passing them around. Each of them had a personalized spoon, carved by their father for his or her first birthday. When one finished eating, the spoon was licked off carefully, dried on one's shirt or skirt, and returned to the drawer.

There were stamping thuds on the porch and suddenly the door swung open, sucking in a cloud of snow, followed by her father and older brothers.

"Believe it or not, the wind is starting to die down. It will be calm and clear by morning," her father announced, looking at Tora. She began stirring more vigorously, not sure if she was glad or not.

She helped her mother ladle out the porridge into two large wooden bowls. To her surprise, she was told to fetch the syrup jar, whereupon her mother made an indentation in the middle of the porridge in each of the bowls and filled it with a spoonful of golden syrup. Everyone watched in awe. It was only on very special occasions that they had anything sweet with their evening porridge. Everyone looked at Tora. It was because she was going away. They began to eat, six of them from each communal bow, slowly and carefully, trying to get their spoons as close as possible to that delicious center without being accused of coming too near it. No one was allowed to take of the syrup until the soft walls of porridge enclosing it gave way, making it impossible not to. They chattered and laughed, hunching over the bowls, their shoulders pressed together. The icy chill had left the cabin and everyone seemed light-hearted in the midst of the storm. Everyone but Tora, whose lip quivered now and then at the thought of leaving the warmth of her large family.

That night when they covered the floor with the reindeer hides, that served as both their beds and bedding and on which they slept in pairs, all of the younger children begged to share Tora's with her. Long after everyone else had fallen asleep, she lay awake, surrounded by the small bodies pressed against her under the sheepskin, their light even breathing lulling her gently. As the oldest girl, she had helped with the younger ones all their lives, dressing, feeding, watching, and playing with them while her mother was busy with the spinning and weaving, milking and cheese-making, sewing, washing, and all the many household jobs which kept her constantly occupied. It was almost as though they were her own children, as much a part of her as her arms and legs. She wondered how they were going to get along without her.

The wind had abated completely by the time they awoke in the still-dark morning, and the sky was covered with millions of stars, giving the new snow a slightly bluish tint. It had been arranged that when the postman came on his weekly route, Tora would follow him down to the nearest village, some 20 miles away. He had arrived during the night after everyone had gone to bed and, as all travelers in the wilderness, had come in quietly, spread out his reindeer hide in a corner, and quickly fallen asleep. And now he was on his skis again, ready to set off, with the black leather mail pouch strapped to his back. Everyone gathered around Tora to help her push her new shoes through the leather toe straps on her homemade skis. She was bundled up in an old woolen coat, with a thick shawl wrapped around her head, neck, and upper body. On her back was a square pack basket made of woven strips of birch bark. In it were packed her other dress, another warm undershirt, an extra pair of underpants, a clean apron, Granny's sweater, and a nightgown made from her father's old shirt. She didn't understand why she needed such a thing, since she was used to sleeping in her underwear and long stockings, but her mother had been adamant when packing it the previous day.

"You are to sleep in this so that people won't think we are dirt poor," she explained. "The only time you can sleep in your underwear is when your nightgown is being washed. And you needn't say that these are all the clothes you own. Just say that these are all you had room for in your pack. That's not a lie."

And to make sure it was not a lie, her mother had loaded the space that was left with a Bible, a comb, Tora's pencil and eraser, and a little coin purse with a few coins in it with which to pay for her transportation and lodging on the way to school, as well as on her return trip at the end of the term. And now, just before lifting it onto Tora's back, she opened the flap and put in food for the trip; a small round loaf of bread and part of a leg of dried reindeer meat wrapped in a cloth.

"Ask Post-Anders politely if you can use his knife, when you need to cut off some meat," her mother told her.

"My spoon..." she began.

"You don't need that. They have real spoons at the school's boarding house. Maybe even forks and knives, too." She paused and reached into her pocket. "And one more thing," she continued, fumbling with the edge of Tora's shawl. "You shall have this, just in case you need it."

She backed away from her daughter stiffly, reluctant to show the unexpected flood of emotion which had suddenly overtaken her. Before Tora could look down, the small children rushed to fill her place, pulling at Tora's coat and ski poles, crying out for her to pick them up, to stay, to take them with her, to come home soon.

"Are you ready?" Post-Anders called over his shoulder.

Tora couldn't answer.

"Come on, line up!" her father commanded, loosening the youngest boy's grip on her leg. Automatically all nine of them fell into place according to age, leaving a hole where Tora usually stood. Her father stepped forward and placed his hand on her head. "Make us proud of you," he said simply.

Post-Anders pushed off down the gentle slope and Tora slid out from under her father's hand and followed in his tracks without looking back. As soon as she knew she was out of sight, her fingers sought the edge of her shawl and turned it over. There was the safety pin.

It was dark by the time they arrived at the little inn which had been their goal. Tora was exhausted. She had never skied so far before. Because Post-Anders was behind schedule, having been slowed by her pace, he knocked on the door without removing his skis. When Widow Lind, the proprietress, appeared he bid Tora a hasty good-bye and disappeared into the night. For the second time that day, she felt abandoned.

Even though she hardly knew him, he had been a familiar part of her life as long as she could remember.

As soon as she had warmed herself by the fire and eaten, Widow Lind took her to one of the upstairs rooms. Tora was horrified; there were four or five beds almost as high as tables sticking out into the otherwise empty room. She had never seen a real bed, let alone slept in one. Nor had she ever slept by herself. She clutched Widow Lind's hand pleadingly, afraid to say anything. She had been brought up to obey adults without arguing.

"Does Tora sleep on the floor at home?" Widow Lind asked.

Tora nodded.

"With lots of brothers an' sisters?"

Tora nodded again. "We're ten," she replied.

Without further questioning, Widow Lind led her down the hall to her own room. In one corner was a large cupboard with a curtain hanging across the front. She pulled the curtain aside to reveal a built-in bed with a high wooden edge to hold the straw-filled bolster in place.

"Tora won't fall out of this here bed," she said cheerfully. Tora's mood lightened at the sight of a bed in a cupboard. Suddenly she was so tired that she could hardly keep her eyes open. Widow Lind helped her undress and climb up into the bed, then sat beside her until she fell asleep.

Once in the middle of the night Tora woke up after a bad dream, not knowing where she was. Just as she began to cry, Widow Lind's arm pulled her close and she slept again.

The next morning Tora laid a couple of coins on the table after breakfast to pay for her room and board, as her mother had instructed. Widow Lind slid them back to her.

"Keep 'em and buy something for yourself in town," she said.

Tora looked up at her curiously, not sure she had heard right.

144

"If anyone asks, just say it is a present from Widow Lind. Hurry now, they're ready to go." She pressed the coins into Tora's hand.

In her excitement, Tora almost forgot to curtsey when she said thank you.

The first leg of that day's journey was made with a farmer who was taking his wife to see a doctor in a village at the far end of the long narrow lake. They put Tora between them in the sleigh, tucked reindeer hides around themselves, and set off over the ice. The sun shone in a cloudless sky, but the wind created by their speed stole all its warmth. By the time they got to the village, Tora was cold clear through. They left her at the little train station where she had an hour to wait for a bus. There the station master's wife took her into her kitchen and set her in front of the wood stove to thaw out, giving her a bowl of hot soup to speed the process. Just as she finished, there was a rumbling sound and then a toot. Going outside, she hesitated, not quite sure she wanted to ride on such a big bus.

"Climb on board, all who're goin' to Vilhelmina!" shouted the driver.

"Come on, little lassie. And don't forget your skis over there," called a voice from behind her. Turning around she saw an old Lapp man dressed in a bright red, blue, and yellow tunic and wearing a hat with a huge pom-pom on the top. She recognized him and his wife; they passed by her house every year on their way up into the mountains to help their two grown sons divide the reindeer herds. Both of them were tiny, not much taller than she herself, and their weather-beaten skin was brown and wrinkled. She was sure they were at least a hundred years old. She didn't like Lapps. They scared her. They were so different, living in teepees and tying their babies onto boards and hanging them up high to keep them out of the way. And they wore such strange clothes, especially the men who looked like they had on short skirts and tight leggings. And riding in little boat-like sleds pulled by reindeer, instead of ordinary horse-pulled sleighs. They never said much and when they talked to each other, people couldn't understand what they said. No, she preferred to keep her distance from them.

She handed her skis to the driver to tie onto the top of the bus, then climbed up the steps and sat down in the front seat, with her pack on the other seat to prevent anyone from sitting next to her. She had intended to watch every bit of the way from her front row seat, but they hadn't even reached the next village before she had fallen asleep. Several hours later the Lapp woman woke her. They were driving along Vilhelmina's main street.

"Does Missy know where she's goin' when she gets off the bus?" she asked.

"To the school," Tora replied, realizing as she said it that she had no idea where the school was.

"Has she been there before?"

Tora shook her head.

"We can show her. We're going that way," the Lapp man volunteered.

She didn't answer. When the bus stopped, the three of them got off and the man took her skis from the roof. He and his wife set off down the street on either side of her.

Tora was awestruck by all that she saw. Along the edge of the icy street was a raised walk way so that she didn't have to get her new shoes snowy. And on both sides of the street were real shops that one could walk into, with things she could never dream of lying in their windows. So this was what town was like. She could hardly believe it.

All too soon they reached the school, with its boarding house beside. The term had begun the previous day and the children were out for recess when they arrived. Tora tried to thank the Lapp couple for their help, in an effort to escape from them before entering the school grounds, but it was as if they didn't hear her. They took her into the building and to the headmaster's office.

"You must be Tora," he said. "We have been expecting you. And these are your parents, I assume." He held out his hand to the old man.

"No! They're not my parents!" she declared, embarrassed beyond belief. "They just showed me where the school was." She was almost in tears. How could he think that these old Lapp people were her parents! Lapps were considered by many people to be hardly more than animals. She was no Lapp girl! Such an insult!

There was a sharp knock on the door and a middle aged woman in a starched blue dress and white apron entered. Her hair was pulled back into a tight bun.

"Oh, this is the boarders' housemother, Fröken Sträng," the headmaster said.

Tora held out her hand and curtsied slightly, but Fröken Sträng ignored the gesture.

"It's about time you got here," she said. "Say good-bye to your parents now and follow me." She grasped Tora's hand and pulled her away from the Lapp couple. A door closed between them and it was over.

But it wasn't over. Not one child on the playground had missed Tora's arrival with her "Lapp parents." Before they had even met her they had something on her that they intended to not let her forget. And the more she would maintain that they had not been her parents and that she was not a Lapp, the more they would taunt her, adding for good measure that she was also a liar. Already her place in the social hierarchy was determined beyond recall.

Tora was the last one up to the nine year old girls' dormitory after dinner that first night. When she opened the door to the spartan sleeping room, fifteen girls were waiting for her. Iron beds lined both of the long walls, with identical wooden cupboards between them. On each side of the door stood a washstand with an enamel washbowl and pitcher on it and, on the wall beside it, a pegboard from which identical towels hung.

She stepped into the room hesitantly. One of the girls slipped behind her and closed the door. Silently they advanced on her from all directions until she was encircled by a tight ring of nightgown-clad bodies. She smiled, glad for such a welcome—until she realized they were chanting "Lapp-lassie, Lapp-lassie." Suddenly they looked like a pack of snarling dogs.

"I-I-I'm not a L-Lapp," she stammered. "Those people aren't my parents."

"Liar!" someone yelled. "Lyin' Lapp-lassie!"

"I don't even know those old people. They were on the bus only," she tried to explain.

"Little Lapp-liar! Little Lapp-liar!" sang a couple of the older girls, stepping closer to her.

Tora look around helplessly. She had always had her brothers to protect and defend her. For the first time in her life she was completely on her own.

"I'm not a Lapp! And I'm not lying!" she screamed.

The door opened behind her.

"What is all this racket about?" Fröken Sträng demanded angrily.

"I'm not a Lapp!" repeated Tora at the top of her lungs.

"Hush, child!" she snapped. "These girls have lived together in harmony until you came along and began making trouble."

"But they're calling me a Lapp and I'm not!"

"Don't talk back! Get into bed now, all of you," she ordered. "Lights out an' mouths closed."

That night Tora cried herself to sleep. Through her sniffling she could hear small voices whispering, "Cry baby! Little lying Lapp!"

The next day she resolved to never again let herself cry in school. And when her nickname became Lill-Lapp she withdrew behind a wall of indifference until she no longer heard their jeering.

Although, to outsiders' eyes, Fröken Sträng gave the appearance of being a substitute mother for those young girls who were away from home for the first time, she had a darker side which manifested itself in a sadistic manner. One of her standard rules was that, in spite of the fact that there was an indoor toilet, no one was allowed to use it. Instead, they were forced to go out to an outhouse in the corner of the school yard. Even at night. As if that weren't enough, they were only permitted to go one at a time. As a concession, they could take along a small kerosene lantern, but only on moonless nights. But for many of the girls, the shadows caused by the lantern light were almost as frightening as the darkness.

Her method of punishing a wrong-doer was to tell her, "I'll see you in my room tonight at bedtime," leaving the offender to spend the day in anticipation. When bedtime came, everyone in the dormitory had to gather to witness the punishment. The girl was laid across the housemother's lap, her nightgown pulled up, and she was beaten on her bare buttocks with a short-handled broom. The extent of the beating was not determined by the misdemeanor, but rather, by how long it took Fröken Sträng to work herself into a frenzy. The first time Tora was forced to witness such a scene, she was so upset that she ran directly up to bed as soon as she could escape from the room, without even going to the toilet or washing her face and hands. Consequently, she dreamed that she was sitting in the outhouse, only to be woken by wet sheets clinging to her legs. Terrified, she lay wide awake without moving for the rest of the night.

At 5:30 the next morning Fröken Sträng opened the double doors to the dormitory and clicked on the light.

"Everybody up!" she declared, clapping her hands.

All the girls stepped straight out of their sleep onto the floor beside their beds. Except for Tora.

"And what's wrong with Tora?" Fröken Sträng asked harshly, coming towards her.

"I don't feel well, Fröken," she answered.

Fröken Sträng stopped at the foot of the bed and sniffed the air like a horse. Without warning, she flung back the covers.

"Tora doesn't feel well," she mocked. "Well, you're about to feel worse. Get the switch!" she ordered the nearest girl.

Yanking Tora out of bed by the arm, she pulled her wet nightgown over her head, bent her over the edge of the bed, pressing her face into the wet sheet, and whipped her until the quickly raised welts began to bleed. For Tora, who had never in her life even been slapped, the shock and humiliation were as great as the pain. Her only consolation was that she had managed not to cry.

That was the first of many beatings, for the more Tora worried about wetting the bed, the more it happened. Nor did the others let her forget it. The first thing she heard when she woke up each morning was someone calling out, "Is Tora torr?"[2] while the others all laughed. Not one of them dared to befriend the girl from the mountains. To them she was only a lowly little Lapp girl trying to pass herself off as one of them. And a liar. The only attention they gave her was to tease her unmercifully.

So overpowering was Tora's misery that she was unable to separate herself from it. No other reality existed beyond the fear of wetting the bed, being beaten by Fröken Sträng, and the eternal teasing by the other girls. To let herself think of home and her family was too painful to endure. Yet without realizing it, she was careful to keep

---

[2] 'torr' means 'dry' in Swedish

her grandmother's safety pin pinned to whatever she was wearing, fingering it unconsciously when she felt most miserable. But even though they were required to write home once a month, she never considered telling her parents what her life was really like. They had sacrificed in order to send her to school and she must not complain. Then one day, just when she was on the verge of succumbing to tears, an invisible being seemed to spring out of her and place herself between Tora and the group of jeering girls, much in the same way her older brothers used to defend her. She called herself Tilda. From that day onwards she hid behind Tilda and let her take the brunt of the teasing, as well as the blame and punishment for her wet bed. With Tilda to protect her and absorb the pain, Tora lived like a clam, enclosed in her shell and unaware of what was going on around her. She neither heard nor spoke. The only thing she cared about was doing well in school, to make her parents proud her.

For every day that passed the sun climbed higher in the sky and bit by bit the world began to thaw. The snow in the streets turned to slush, then gathered into puddles that in turn overflowed into little rivulets, which ran toward the lake bordering the town. The first tiny wildflowers struggled to push aside last autumn's soggy leaves so they could dance in the mild winds from the south. Then one day the air was filled with birdsong and spring had arrived.

Tora began to anticipate the end of the school term when she could finally go home. May came and went, but she hardly noticed. Her life's clock was set for the end of the first week in June, when she would be free from the nightmare of the past months. As that day drew nearer, her mood lightened. Now and again she could let herself think about her family at home without tears coming. Along with everyone else, she began gathering together her few belongings.

The evening before the end of term ceremonies she was called in to Fröken Sträng's office. Wistfully she presented herself, wondering what she had done wrong this time.

"You needn't have all your things packed by tomorrow," Fröken Sträng said. "You won't be going home until next week."

For the first time in months someone's words penetrated her protective wall. Her eyes flared in anger. Although she said nothing, her look caused Fröken Sträng to explain defensively.

"I need help with all the washing and ironing and mending of bedding and cleaning of the dormitory rooms," she answered. "I've already written your mother and informed her that you will be home a week later than expected."

"Why me?" Tora screamed. "I want to go home!"

"Watch your mouth, young lady! It's already arranged."

Tora bit her lip to keep from crying as she stalked out of the housemother's office. Her fingers sought the safety pin fastened on the inside of her sweater pocket, opening and closing it over and over in her anger. This time Tilda had failed to come to her rescue.

The following day the sky was a deep cloudless blue and the air warm and summery. Everyone in the dormitory dressed in their finest clothes in preparation for the end of term ceremonies. The auditorium was decorated with birch branches whose first tiny leaves were just beginning to uncurl, giving off a delicious aroma. Everyone was in the highest of spirits—except for Tora. She put on the same dress she had worn for the last two weeks and didn't bother to re-braid her hair. Once everyone was seated below the stage, with the headmaster, Fröken Sträng, and all the teachers looking down on them, Tilda took over and Tora disappeared into herself completely. She never heard her name called out as the student in her class with the highest marks. One of the other girls poked her in the ribs to get her attention.

"Leave me alone!" Tilda screamed, slapping away the girl's hand.

Refusing to go up onto the stage to accept her award, Tora continued to sit with her arms crossed over her chest, staring vacantly into space. What should have been one of the proudest days of her young life was, instead, a day filled with hate and anger. Afterwards, while the students and their parents were having refreshments, she hid in the cellar of the boarding house, the only place where she couldn't hear the voices of the girls calling good-bye to each other as they left with their families. She longed to leave with them, to run away, but there was nowhere for her to go, no way for her to get home now. The bus which connected with the weekly boat had already gone.

During the week that followed, Tora and Fröken Sträng worked side-by-side, first washing and rinsing by hand the sheets from the 40 beds in the entire dormitory, hanging them up to dry, then cranking them through the huge mangle, and finally folding them into fourths and rolling them like fat sausages before putting them away in the storage cupboard. The same process was repeated with the pillow cases, but with one added procedure. Each one had three pairs of ties to keep the pillow from gliding out of the case. Not only must they be folded so that the ties all hung down over the edge of the pile when they were stacked in the cupboard, but the ties must all be crinkled with a gadget resembling a pair of scissors. Since there was only one of these devices, the task was left to Tora, with Fröken Sträng checking from time to time to make sure she was doing it properly. Any that didn't meet her approval were pulled out, often in such a way that the whole pile had to be restacked and arranged. Then the sleeping rooms had to be scrubbed from ceiling to floor, and the large windows washed.

Whatever Fröken Sträng's intention was in choosing Tora to help her—punishment, dislike, curiosity, sadistic pleasure—she failed to make any sort of contact with her whatsoever. Tora's eyes were glazed over and vacant and she responded to instructions mechanically. She never spoke, nor did the sharpest reprimand cause any reaction. She no longer even needed Tilda to hide behind. Nothing could touch her. At the end of the week, even though the cleaning was not finished, she took her pack basket with her few belongings, put her skis over her shoulder, and disappeared through the gate of the school yard.

This time when she made her way through the town, no one hurried her along. She had over an hour before the bus left. At the bottom of her apron pocket jingled the two coins Widow Lind had returned to her that long-ago morning. She had never had a chance to spend them, since school girls were not allowed to go into town. Nor had there been anything particular that she wanted. But now as she examined each shop window she passed, she was amazed at all the things there were to want. It was impossible to choose just one thing. And then suddenly she saw it—a sewing kit with pins and needles, a thimble, four small spools of different colored thread, and even a tiny pair of scissors, in a little cloth-covered box which was held closed with a snap. Never had she seen anything so grand! It was exactly what her mother needed! But as she stared more closely at it, she realized that it of course cost more than the 50 öre in her pocket. Sighing, she backed away from the window to continue down the street.

"Come in an' look at it," a voice called to her.

She had been so absorbed in the sewing kit that she hadn't noticed the clerk standing in the open doorway taking the breeze.

Tora obeyed like a robot.

The woman leaned over the low curtain at the back edge of the display window, picked up the sewing kit, blew a bit of dust off it, and handed it to her.

"Are you on your way home from boarding school?" she asked.

Tora nodded.

"Do you have far to go?"

"To Fatmomakke," she answered absently.

"Oh, you have a long journey ahead of you."

All the while Tora's small fingers ran gently back and forth over the contents of the sewing kit in the same way a blind person would "look" at a fragile bird's egg. Finally she closed the lid, snapped it, and turned the box over. The price was written on the bottom: 55 öre. She set it on the counter and started toward the door.

"Wait a minute!" the saleswoman called. "How much money do you have?"

Tora dug in her pocket and pulled out the two 25 öre coins.

"Give them to me," she said kindly.

Tora placed them on the counter obediently, while the woman tore off a piece of brown paper from the roll at the end of the counter and set about wrapping the sewing kit. Lastly, she tied a red ribbon around it.

"You can use this for a hair ribbon," she said, sliding it across the counter. "You have a good trip now."

Tora curtseyed. "Thank you, Ma'am," she said shyly. Her heart was thumping so wildly that she was sure the woman could hear it.

At last she was on her way home! The June sun, which barely dipped below the horizon during the daylight nights, had finally melted the last of the ice on Lake Malgomaj and the ferry was running again. Just buying a ticket and walking up the gangplank all by herself made Tora feel grown up, not to mention being able to sit out on the open deck without any adult to tell her to be careful.

As the ferry made its way northward, she felt as though she was waking up from a long sleep. Voices penetrated her wall of silence and she became aware of the people around her. Nor did she find them threatening, like the people at school. All at once she was overcome with an intense longing for her family; a longing which she had refused to let herself feel during the never-ending nightmare of school. Now she felt like she would burst into tears if she didn't get home soon.

"Oh, hello there!" Widow Lind cried when Tora appeared in the doorway of the inn. "Come in, come in. How was school?"

Tora was completely taken aback. She had long ago made up her mind that she was never going to tell anyone what it had been like. It had never occurred to her that people might ask.

"It was fine," she lied to avoid remembering.

"Tora's parents will certainly be glad to see her."

"I bought something for my mother with the money Widow Lind gave back to me," Tora offered quickly, seeing a chance to change the subject.

She began pulling things out of her pack basket until she came to the package. Carefully she unwrapped it, so as not to destroy the paper, and held up the sewing kit.

"I think she will like it." she said proudly.

"She will love it!" Widow Lind assured her.

"I hope so. She only has one needle an' some black thread, an' no scissors or thimble." It was the first normal conversation she had carried on in months.

While they admired it, Tora unpinned the safety pin from her dress and laid it inside the sewing kit beside the needles. Then she replaced the wrapping paper and Widow Lind re-tied the ribbon while she pressed her finger on the knot.

"What is this?" Widow Lind asked, picking up a paper which had fallen on the floor from amongst Tora's things. "Tora's report card?"

Tora nodded.

"May I look at it?"

She shrugged.

Widow Lind's eyes grew big when she opened it. "All A's!" she exclaimed. "Oh, Tora, your parents are going to be so proud of you! Congratulations!"

In that instant Tora understood that showing her report card would put an end to any questions about school.

"I can sleep in one of those regular beds now," Tora said on the way upstairs after supper.

"It's pretty lonely in this big room all by oneself," Widow Lind remarked when they came to the door of the big sleeping room. "Tora's more than welcome to sleep in my bed again, if she wishes. I thought it was nice and cozy last time."

Tora gladly accepted her offer. Widow Lind's presence made her feel secure in a way she hadn't felt since the first night she slept there. And she knew she would never wet the bed.

Then next morning Post-Anders was eating breakfast in the kitchen of the inn when Tora came downstairs.

"Well, here's the pupil from the big town!" he declared. "I hear she did all right by herself. Congratulations!"

Now that there was no snow, Post-Anders was able to do his postal route with a horse and two-wheeled cart. Several hours later Tora was home. He pulled to a stop by the outer gate and handed her the weekly newspaper, which was the only mail for her father that day.

"Run along now and show that report card to everyone," Post-Anders told her.

She jumped to the ground and he handed down her pack basket. She had barely gotten the gate closed behind her before she dropped her things and ran up the uneven path as fast as she could.

"Mamma! Mamma!" she yelled. "Mamma!"

The front door opened and she threw herself in her mother's arms.

"Little Tora, whatever is the matter? Are you OK?"

"Oh Mamma, it was awful! People were so cruel...." She could no longer hold back her tears, nor her resolve not to tell how she had been treated. The nightmare of the past five months exploded from inside of her in one long torrent, horrifying her parents.

Tora's report card was framed and hung on the wall under the picture of the Royal Family and she never went back to boarding school in Vilhelmina.

ELIN & TEO

The path up to the top of the ridge felt steeper than usual in the June heat. Elin held up the skirt of her ankle-length cotton dress so as not to tramp on the hem, oblivious to the basket bumping against her hip. She wished she had stayed home. Usually she traded her eggs and freshly churned butter for coffee and flour and perhaps a little sugar in the village store. But now, with wartime rationing, such things had disappeared from the shelves. All she came away with were the well-meant condolences over the death of her father from the villagers she had met. She felt like a hypocrite.

Her father had been a preacher in the fundamentalist chapel in the near-by mining village. As a young man he had broken away from the state church, which he found too lax, and gathered his own following. That he had never been ordained into the ministry was immaterial. His hellfire and damnation sermons, delivered with the aid of his fiery black Walloon eyes, hypnotized his congregation of miners, farmhands and common laborers and convinced them that their salvation lay in accepting his teachings. Although Elin was also one of them, they set her a bit above themselves, for she was the chapel's organist, a job she had inherited after her mother's death a decade earlier. The landowners and upper class mine officials, on the other hand, attended the Swedish State Church in town. Not only was fundamentalism too low-class for their tastes, but in their eyes Pastor Adamsson's self-righteousness showed a lack of respect towards his superiors. However, they themselves showed a certain respect for Elin, whose purity was equal to that of their own young women, by nodding when they passed her in the village.

At the top of the ridge she paused to breathe in the fragrance of the Queen Anne's lace, relieved to escape the villagers' sympathy. It only intensified her guilt. Those who had over the years observed her and her father walking to and from the chapel every Sunday, or had noted their interaction during the service, looked upon them as possessing a model father-daughter relationship. No one suspected the truth.

As a so-called 'afterthought,' Elin was born long after her four older sisters. Her father ruled over her with an iron hand, thanks to her oldest sister Amalia. One night, a year after Amalia had left home to work as a housemaid, she had re-appeared at the door with a bastard infant in her arms. Horrified, their father hid her and the child in the attic. As soon as darkness fell the following night he hurried her into the shed where he forced her to lie with the child on the floor of the farm wagon. In the event that they might meet someone, he tossed a couple of grain sacks over them. Then his whip snapped violently across the unsuspecting horse's rump, causing it to set off at a run with the wagon jerking behind it.

When he returned the next afternoon, both he and the horse were exhausted. His only comment was to forbid the rest of the family to ever mention Amalia again. At the same time, he commanded his wife to burn her belongings and to cut every trace of her from the photo album. He himself eradicated her name from the family Bible with a thick black line, placing a small cross and the year, 1910, after it.

To insure that his shame remained hidden, he took a job in the mining village several hundred miles to the north, where the family was unknown. There he gathered a flock of wayward miners in need of salvation. With the force of his voice and the power of his conviction, he inspired them to build a chapel and place him behind the pulpet and his wife behind the organ. His four daughters sang in the choir.

Amalia had ceased to exist. Never again would he permit such sinfulness to touch his family. Consequently, Elin grew up under the hand of his crushing control. Above all else, she was taught to fear the wrath of God and to unquestioningly obey His mouthpiece, her father.

Now as she walked along the heather-lined path, unwelcome thoughts floated to the surface. She began walking faster to escape them, but instead, they intensified. Her father was dead, a victim of the Spanish flu which had followed on the heals of the Great War. It had reaped a goodly number of lives in the village, including both the Methodist and Penticostal pastors. When the epidemic appeared to have abated, Pastor Adamsson maintained that he was spared because only he preached the true word of God. Shortly after that announcement he was stricken in the middle of the night and died two days later. Yet it wasn't his sudden death that upset her, but rather, the wave of relief that had washed over her in the instant she realized he was gone. Not only did she experience a deep shame over her relief, but she was frightened by the thought that both her father and God were watching her from afar and knew her innermost thoughts. She had grown up knowing that they were watching her day and night, but until now she had never had anything to hide. Suddenly she was shocked by the intense dislike that she felt towards her father.

"But I mustn't hate my father," she told herself.

"Why not?" replied an unfamiliar voice from within her.

"Because he's my father. One must love ones father and mother."

"But he has dominated you your whole life."

"It's a father's duty to protect his daughters," she reasoned.

"He hasn't protected you; he has stifled you. And since your mother died he has been a tyrant. 'Elin, do this!', 'Elin, bring me that!' 'Don't wear your blue dress!' 'Pull your hair back tighter!' 'You are not to associate with so-and-so!' 'Cast your eyes down in front of men! It is provocative to look at them!' And remember how he drove Holger away when he came courting. There was never a finer Christian than Holger. He has been a wonderful husband to Greta, even though he would rather have married you."

"Stop!" she cried aloud. "I never wanted to get married anyway!"

She could still hear her mother's warning words: "Marriage is like being in prison. One has no freedom. And then there is that disgusting business at night! Burning in hell can't be worse than that! And then having to go through the horrible process of giving birth to babies that you don't even want! Stay a way from men! They only want one thing!"

Sitting on the half-way-rock to rest in the heat, she pushed the ping-pong conversation from her mind, only to have the empty space filled with thoughts of enjoying life without her father. Sinful thoughts. How nice it was going to be not to have to tend to his needs. Selfish thoughts, full of guilt. She jumped to her feet and hurried towards home, but she could not out-distance the voices in her head.

As she neared the house she could make out a child sitting on her front step. Coming closer she recognized Little Sara, whose family worked on Ekbom's estate. Not only was Squire Ekbom Elin's landlord, but he was also the social welfare representative for the area. Little Sara often had to run unpleasant errands for him.

The child stood up and curtseyed to Elin.

"Did the squire send you?" Elin asked her.

"A-a-a, yes," she answered nervously.

"And?" Elin said.

"He said to tell Elin that he is sending a man to fetch Elin's two cows tomorrow," she said hurriedly.

"What is it you are saying, child?" Elin declared.

"He said to tell Elin that he needs his pastureland himself," Sara repeated importantly.

"And I need my two cows for my livelihood," Elin muttered.

"Shall I tell him that? " Sara asked.

"Tell him I shall pay him a visit tomorrow," she said.

"Yes, Ma'm," Sara promised.

Elin watched her skip down the path, barefoot and carefree.

"Watch out for snakes!" she couldn't help calling after her.

Her beloved cows! How could she live without them? The were her source of income; the milk, cream, butter and cheese that she sold. Together with her eggs it was all she had in the way of 'cash.' She must go to Squire Ekbom and plead, but she knew it would do no good. He had a reputation for being cruel and completely unsympathetic. And like all his renters sprinkled though his forest-land, she was afraid of him. And with good reason.

By the next morning her newly-acknowledged dislike for her father had been replaced by a child-like longing for the security of his presence. As a "hemmadotter", whose duty it had been to remain unmarried and care for her parents in their old age, her adult life had been centered around the running of the household. The workings of the world beyond her doorstep were as incom- prehensible to her as that of a foreign government. And now, after a sleepless night, she forced herself to lift the latch of Ekbom's iron gate and enter that unknown world surrounding the estate house. Alone. Although the sky was overcast, with a cool wind out of the north, Elin could feel small trickles of sweat running along her spine, sticking her cotton dress to her back.

A maid opened the servants' entrance with a slight nod of recognition. Elin followed her along a dark corridor to the back room which served as Squire Ekbom's office, keeping her eyes downcast out of nervousness rather than respect. After the maid's light knock on the door, she was ushered into the darkened room and the door closed behind her. In front of her sat Squire Ekbom behind a massive oak desk. He continued writing in a ledger, ignoring her presence. Elin fidgetted, shifting her weight from one foot to the other while waiting for him to take notice of her. It was well known that he enjoyed letting people stand before him and wait, increasing their anxiety and thus his power over them. But in spite of knowing that, she was unable to still her twisting hands under her apron.

At last he snapped the ledger shut and looked up.

"Well, if it isn't God's Holy Servant!" he remarked with a sardonic grin. "And what does she want?"

"I-I-I..." she stammered.

"Hurry up! I have other things to do today!" he barked.

Elin took a deep breath.

"I've come to ask Squire Ekbom to permit me to keep my cows," she replied, squeezing out the words as fast as she could as she exhaled.

"She has no need of cows in the poorhouse," he told her matter of factly.

"The poorhouse?" she gasped.

"Yes, the poorhouse," he mocked. "Has Elin forgotten that employment on the estate and the cottage go together, and that when the man of the house can no longer work due to illness, old age, or death, the family no longer has the right to remain in the cottage? That's how it's been since the beginning of time, wherever one goes. With no exceptions. Not even for one of God's Chosen Few."

"But the poorhouse...." Elin began.

"Has Elin anywhere else to go? To her sisters in America? Or to Amalia perhaps?"

At the mention of her oldest sister's name Elin understood that others than just God and her father were watching her. With-out so much as a good-bye, she ran from the room and along the back hall to the kitchen door. Once outside she forced herself to slow down to a walk until she was out of sight of the estate house. How had he known about Amalia? In all the years since moving to the mining village she had not once let herself think about her sister for fear that her very thoughts would somehow give away her family's secret. If Squire Ekbom knew about her, how many other

164

people knew? And what else did they know? She felt as though she had been cut wide open and her innards exposed to public view. For the first time in her life she was completely alone, with no one to turn to for comfort or advice.

The following afternoon while Elin was hanging up her washing on the line between the two apple trees she caught sight of an unfamiliar man coming along the path from the village. Her cows! He was coming to fetch her cows! As he neared the cottage, to her relief she saw that he was carrying a cardboard suitcase. Of course! He must be one of the tramps who went from cottage to cottage selling things: pins and needles, combs, small mirrors, buttons, shoelaces, soap, handkerchiefs, and such like. Without a word, he set his suitcase down between them. Fumbling in his jacket pocket, he pulled out a folded paper and handed it to her, motioning her to open it.

"This is Teo Stensson," it read. "He returned from many years at sea only to find that his parents are dead and the family farm sold, so he has no place to live. Since Elin does not want to move from her cottage, I am sending him to live with her. He can do odd jobs in exchange for food and lodging. Locally he is known as Döv-Teo because he is both deaf and dumb, although he can read and write. A. K. Ekbom."

She looked up from the letter to the tall thin figure in front of her. His suit was shiny and frayed around the edges from years of wear, but it was clean and had all its buttons. Under his coat his vest was buttoned up over a collarless white shirt. His clean-shaven face bore a friendly smile below a seaman's cap. But all that Elin saw was that he was a stranger and a man and thus dangerous. Instinctively she backed away.

"Herr Stensson cannot lodge here!" she declared. "Give me that pencil."

He looked at her and shrugged his shoulders.

With tears of frustration about to flow, she hurried into the cottage after her own pencil. But when she turned around to go out again he was blocking the door.

"Go away!" she screamed, but he remained standing in the doorway.

With shaking hands she smoothed Ekbom's letter face down on the table.

"He cannot live here!" she scribbled. "There is no place for him to sleep. And what will people say!"

She handed it to him and shooed him in the direction of the estate house.

Two hours later he was back with a new letter. He didn't bother to knock.

"He can sleep in the sofa-bed in the kitchen just as Elin does. People will say that it's about time Elin had a man in her bed. There is no room in the poorhouse for either Elin or Teo. A.K. Ekbom."

Her father had always maintained that Squire Ekbom was possessed by the devil, but this went beyond anything she could imagine. She crumpled the letter and let it fall to the floor, then covered her face with her hands. And all the while Döv-Teo stood in the middle of the room staring at her.

By now it was too late to send him back with another letter. She pointed to the box bed where her father had slept, then grudgingly divided the porridge she had saved from breakfast and shoved his portion across the table to him. Bowing her head over her plate, she mumble a prayer. Teo, too, bowed his head, but kept one eye on her so as to know when she was finished. They ate in silence, so unlike mealtimes with her father, who had bombarded her with his fanatical preachings as one of the meal's courses. As much as she had hated having to listen to him, she found herself longing to have him across the table from her now, rather than this deaf-mute stranger.

Once their meager meal was finished Teo pushed his chair away from the table noisily, crossed his legs, and lit his pipe. Billows of sharp-smelling smoke rose to the ceiling and floated out across the unpainted boards in search of an escape route. For Elin there was no escape route. She waved her arms at him wildly to indicate that he should go outside to smoke, but he was gazing out the window, lost in his own thoughts.

A helpless rage boiled up inside her, towards her father who had died and left her on her own, towards Squire Ekbom for having forced Teo on her, and towards Teo for having invaded her life. Quickly she set the copper dishpan on the wood stove, so violently that the water splashed over the edge onto the hot stove with an angry hiss. A cloud of steam rose to the ceiling, mixing with the tobacco smoke, but because he had his back to her, Teo was oblivious to her angry outburst.

She washed the dishes mechanically--two cups, two bowls, two spoons--just as she had done when her father lived. It wasn't having a stranger in the house that upset her. Like all country people, her family had often taken in passing travelers for the night. One was obliged by law to do so in the days when inns were few and far between, and the tradition had lived on. Such travelers arrived late in the evening and slept on the floor, rolled up in their own blankets, thankful for a roof over their heads against the weather and a door closed against the wolves. And they continued on their way at the break of dawn, leaving a few welcomed copper coins in payment for the night's floor space. Elin was used to that sort of lack of privacy. But her father had always been there, creating an air of respect. But now she was faced with being alone with a man--and a stranger at that.

As soon as Teo stepped outside to relieve himself "around the corner," Elin draped her long nightgown over herself and quickly pulled off her clothes under its protecting tent. Everyone, religious or not, knew it was sinful to cast their eyes on a naked body, including one's own. Even husbands and wives never saw each other naked, regardless of how many offspring they had created under the bedclothes. Elin's entire family had always slept together in the cottage's single room, having imbibed discretion with their mother's milk. As the only male in the family, her father had slept in his long underwear winter and summer which, like most men, he only changed when he bathed a couple of times a year.

167

But Teo seemed indifferent to such sinfulness. Without so much as turning his back, he stripped off his clothes and laid them neatly on a chair. Long underwear was not a part of his garb. Elin lay in bed on the far side of the room transfixed, unable to prevent her eyes from following him has he moved around the room. His pale skin glistened in the summer twilight. But it was the appendage which bounced gently between his legs that hypnotized her. Of course she had known that males were different from females. As a young girl she had seen a bull mount one of their cows and jab at it with what the local boys called his spear. But she had no idea what a human spear looked like. In the same instant, she realized she was staring at a naked man! Horrified, she pulled the covers over her head and prayed for forgiveness. Unaware of the drama playing itself out across the room from him, Teo slid into bed and fell asleep as soon as his head touched the pillow. Elin, on the other hand, lay awake until sunrise, weeping and chastising herself for her sinful behavior. What if her father were watching from up in heaven.

The next morning Elin was woken by the sound of wood being split. It couldn't have been more than four o'clock, for the sun was just riding on the treetops to the northeast. Pulling back the curtain, she saw Teo lift the ax above his head and bring it down on a piece of birch standing upright on the chopping block. His shirt was draped limply over the end of the nearby saw horse, giving the long rays of the rising sun the freedom to play across the sinewy ridges on his back, while rivulets of sweat glistened in the morning light. She could almost imagine how it would feel to run her hand over the smoothness of his skin.

"Dear Jesus," she whimpered, bowing her head, "deliver me from my sinfulness." But when she realized her eyes had remained open, still focused on the half-naked figure beyond the window, she was horrified. "Oh my God! I must be possessed by the devil!" she cried into the empty room.

She had to force herself to turn away from the window and light the stove. With fumbling hands, she dumped a spoonful of rye kernels, which served in place of real coffee, into the roaster and set it on the stove. Once they were browned, she ground them into a coarse powder with a small stone, then boiled them. Just as she set the ersatz coffee and a frying pan with potatoes and herring on the table, she caught sight of Teo buttoning his shirt while walking toward the cottage. With a brief nod, he sat down to his waiting breakfast. Elin remained standing by the stove, coffee cup in hand, staring at the floor. Her face burned at the memory of his naked body. Teo ate quickly, mouthed his thanks with a smile and went back out to work. Pulling back the curtain, Elin watched him begin chopping again, waiting for him to remove his shirt. But a cloud had covered the sun, chilling the air. After a few minutes she turned from the window and began the day's chores, fast resolved to ignore him as much as possible.

That evening, in spite of her best intentions, she once again found her eyes following Teo's movements as he undressed. The sight of his nakedness caused a tingling sensation in the pit of her stomach, yet she couldn't bring herself to look away. And thus the days and nights continued. One part of Elin wanted Teo out of her home and her life, while another part of her began to look forward to night time.

Teo, for his part, kept busy with the jobs that Elin's father had always taken care of outside: cutting trees, sawing and splitting wood for the coming winter, cutting hay for the two cows. Having grown up on a small farm, he knew, without being told, what needed to be done. Elin was thankful, realizing that she could never have gone on living there by herself. And because Teo apparently had never learned how to communicate, aside from a few practical signs, she was not bothered with having to converse with him. They lived in a silent harmony, neither knowing the other. Nor was she attracted to him during the daytime when he was fully clothed. It was when he undressed for bed that the devil took over her soul.

Soon she began dreaming about him, that she was sliding her hand over his back (the word caress was not part of her vocabulary). The next night her hand had moved to his chest and stomach. She could feel his skin under her fingertips. Then one night she dreamed that she held his spear cupped in her hand. It was soft and warm, nothing like the spear she had seen on the bull. She found herself wondering what to do with it, but before she reached any conclusion, she awoke with a start. Looking across the room, she noticed that he, too, had woken up. She watched as he threw back the covers and stepped onto the floor. To her horror, his spear no longer dangled loosely between his legs. It stood straight up, swaying slightly as it curved upwards towards his belly. It was huge! Elin's lower abdomen tightened automatically. Suddenly she was frightened. Think if he jabbed at her like the bull on the cow. She was too vulnerable in bed in her nightgown. As soon as he went out to relieve himself around the corner of the cottage she got up and dressed hastily.

Her hands were shaking. She was beginning to think that he was in cahoots with the devil, that he had been sent to test the strength of her religious conviction. Or perhaps he was the devil himself. She made up her mind to go back to Squire Ekbom and...and what? What would she say? She couldn't tell him about Teo's spear. No matter what she said, he would answer with his malicious laugh. Nor was there any other place Teo could sleep--no place where she would be safe. And on a practical level, she could not be without him.

He looked at her curiously when he came back in, obviously wondering why she was up so early. He shrugged and willingly sat down to an early breakfast before going outside to work.

Elin began having nightmares centered around his spear: that she was holding it, stroking it, squeezing it, that it was poking at her. Each time she awoke breathless, her lower abdomen thrusting rhythmically back and forth. Then one Sunday morning she woken by the sound of her own moaning and her

170

fingers playing between her legs. It was then that she knew the devil had taken possession of her. It was more than she could bear.

She put on her church clothes and taking her Bible from the shelf, hurried along the familiar path to the village. Because she was early, no one was yet in the chapel. Elin took her usual place on the organ bench and struck a loud, violent chord.

"Be gone!" she cried, in an attempt to drive away the devil. The chord was so powerful that the entire organ vibrated, and Elin with it. She screamed in horrified ecstasy, then banged her fists down on the keys, causing one long horrific discordant blast, before running from the building. The devil was at her heals.

"Get away! Leave me alone!" she cried over and over as she ran through the village crazily.

People on their way to chapel stepped aside to let her pass, too frightened by her screaming to stop her. Up on the railroad bridge a group of men stood waiting to watch the morning freight train pass under them, a Sunday morning tradition. They, too, automatically stepped aside as she ran toward them, obviously possessed. Just as she reached the middle of the bridge the whistle blew. As if on cue, Elin threw herself head first over the railing onto the passing box cars, breaking her neck instantly.

Afterward people began to speculate about Teo. Had he perhaps raped her? But when questioned, he wrote a statement saying he had never come anywhere near her. He laid the paper on the Bible, raised his right hand and, looking his interrogator in the eye, shook his head. The autopsy verified his statement. She was still a virgin.

Strangely, it was Squire Ekbom who came closest to the truth.

"She needed a man," he declared in his usual malicious way. "Teo's mere presence attracted her body, but contradicted her pious convictions. It wasn't Teo who was the devil; it was she herself."

Or was it he who was the devil?

Samuel

Holding the edges of her heavy shawl together with one hand, while her free hand clutched the letter, Emma plowed her way up the snow-covered hill from the village, driven by her excitement. At last! Impatiently she kicked the snow off her boots and, without bothering to shake off the hem of her ankle-length skirt, rushed into the house.

"Papa!" she shouted at the top of her voice, disregarding the families in the two downstairs flats as she hurried up the stairs noisily. "Papa has a letter from America!"

Samuel looked up from where he sat tailor-fashion on his cutting table, surrounded by pins and needles, scissors, tissue paper pattern pieces, and scraps of cloth. Although he was just over fifty, his full beard was pure white. Otherwise his body gave no indication of his age, aside from a few tiny crows' feet fanning out from the corners of his somewhat sad blue eyes.

He took the letter, turning it over slowly. It bore no return address; only a black postmark stamped across George Washington's face. Squinting, he could barely make out the words "Groton, S. D. Nov. 16, 1909." The handwriting below was definitely Walter's! Like others of his generation, Samuel was not a man to show emotion. But his shaking hand betrayed him. It had been over a year since he had heard from his only son and he had begun to fear the worst. It was not uncommon that young men who went to America "to seek their fortune" were swallowed up by that huge continent and never heard of again. Seeing Walter's handwriting now was as if he had suddenly come home again. Emma backed out of the room and closed the door quietly, leaving her father alone with her brother's long awaited letter.

Samuel cleared a pathway across the cutting table and dropped nimbly to the floor. In the desk drawer amongst buttons and spools of thread he found the letter-opener that had once belonged to his father. Sliding its ivory tip under the corner of the flap, he slit open the envelope. Carefully he pulled out the single sheet of paper, unfolded it and smoothed the creases against the table top. It was written in pencil, with the last sentences trailing like ivy around the edges of the page. After some searching through the tangle of words, he finally found the beginning.

"Beloved Father," it began. "God's peace and grace be with thee. I hope this letter finds thee in good health. I apologize for my long silence. I have just returned from many months of prospecting out west in Indian Territory. I was shot in the leg during a raid and lay for weeks in a make-shift hospital, but now I am finally back home in South Dakota. I was greatly shocked and saddened to hear of Mother's death. I had no idea she was ill. I understand that Father is going to be very lonely without her, especially once Emma is married. Could he think to come and live with me in America? I am in the process of obtaining a small farm under the Homestead Act. I can receive the land for free as long as I build a house and farm it. It would be nice to have a little company...."

Samuel let the letter fall to the table without reading further. Unlike his daughters, who were occupied with their husbands, children, and homes in Chicago, Walter was alone and understood lonliness. His words touched him in a place he had avoided going to since his wife's death. True, Emma was still at home. She was only seventeen, but already engaged. He couldn't bring himself to ask her to give up her future with Fritz and stay home to become a traditional "hemmadotter" in order to care for him for the rest of his life. Nor could he imagine re-marrying and sharing his life with another woman. At the same time, he couldn't help wondering how he would manage once Emma moved away. It was she who cooked and cleaned and washed his clothes. Men did not do such work; they didn't even know how. Of course many widowers or unmarried men had housekeepers, but all too often such situations became complicated, resulting in illigitimate children and some- times forced marriages. But most of all, he missed not having Matilda close by, for he had grown very fond of her.

Samuel sat down by the window and gazed out at the snow-covered forest, remembering when he and Matilda had met in a neighboring village over a quarter of a century earlier......

....The day was sunny and warm, even though it was the middle of October. Golden birch leaves dotted the path through the forest, while the last yellowing aspen leaves twisted on their stems, seemingly anxious to detatch themselves and experience the once in a lifetime free fall to the ground below. Samuel and his father Torbjörn, better known as Tailor-Tor, were making their annual round through the parish, measuring, cutting, and sewing winter clothes for the members of each household. Because most country folk wore the same clothes day after day they needed to be replaced at least once a year. As was the custom, the local tailor lived with each family while he sewed for them, enabling him to make the necessary fittings and adjustments as he worked.

After having spent several weeks sewing in poor peasant homes, where the fare was the usual porridge, "blue" milk , salted herring, and potatoes, and the mattresses were bags filled with straw, they were now on their way to the richest estate in the parish. Samuel had passed it many times, but he had never been through the gate. As a child he had been afraid to go near the place, for it was rumored that anyone caught trespassing was beaten. Even now that he was an adult, having been confirmed in the state church when he had turned thirteen, he felt uneasy following his father through the iron gate and along the gravel driveway to the side door.

"I'm tailor Nordström and this is my son Samuel," his father informed the maid who opened the door.

"Madame Sahlin is waiting in the drawing room," they were told. "Follow me."

She led them along a hall and opened the door to a large room filled with heavy furniture. A middle-aged woman was sitting beside a round table, a coffee cup in her hand.

"I have been awaiting Nordström since yesterday," she remarked coldly as soon as the door was closed behind them.

"My humble apologizies," Torbjörn answered, bowing. "It is not always possible to know ahead of time how long a job will take."

"It can't take so much time to throw together something for those good-for-nothings in the shacks down the road," she snorted.

As much as Torbjörn detested the attitude of the rich towards the poor, who were poor because the rich refused to pay them decent wages, he looked at the floor and said nothing. Sewing for the people on the estate was his biggest job and he couldn't afford to lose it.

"Next time Nordström will start his rounds here at the estate," she told him.

"Yes, Madame," Torbjörn replied meekly.

It took them several weeks to cut and sew for the Sahlins and their hired help. Each person was called in individually and measured for the clothes he or she was to receive. They started with the squire and his wife and children, all of whom required everything from church clothes to everyday clothes to outdoor clothes. Once that was finished, it was just a shirt or a pair of pants for each of the farm-hands as part of their yearly pay. And for the maids, who were also paid in kind, it would be a blouse or a skirt. (A new apron was an extra bonus.)

One day when Samuel had gone out to relieve himself behind the woodshed he heard laughter coming from the barn.

Suddenly the heavy door swung open and one of the milkmaids ran out across the yard toward him in tears. Nervously he stepped closer to the building and finished his business. But she ran past without seeing him and disappeared into the wash house, slamming the door behind her. The next day he once again saw her run from the barn weeping, followed by the same jeering laughter. Yet another day he watched her pick up a crying child when it slipped and fell in the muddy barnyard. He could hear her cooing soothingly as she cradled it in her arms for a few short seconds, until one of the house maids came running across the yard towards her waving a stick.

"Put that child down, you slut! How many times have you been told not to touch the children. We don't want them covered with lice!"

The milkmaid set the child on the ground gently just as the stick struck the back of her legs. She winced involuntarily.

"Who is that?" Samuel asked a farmhand who had also witnessed the incident.

The young man looked at him incredulously.

"Has Samuel never heard of Crazy-Matilda?"

"Yes, of course I have but...."

"That's her who runs from the barn an' gives folks lice." He wrinkled his nose in disgust.

"But what's wrong with her?"

"She's a bastard. Her mother's a bastard, too. She lyed inna hay with any man who wanted her. An' Matilda's the same."

"How does one know that?"

"'Cause she has a bastard kid."

"Does she still lie with men?" Samuel wondered.

"Once a whore, always a whore. Samuel can try 'er his self."

The thought disgusted him. He had been brought up in a God-fearing family, where men only lay with their wives, and that only for the purpose of procreation.

"But why's she called Crazy Matilda?"

"'Cause she's stupid. She can't read or write an' she can barely count. She has to make a chalk mark on the wall for every liter of milk the cows give."

"But that doesn't make her crazy," Samuel persisted.

"See for yourself. Go and talk to 'er."

That evening after supper Samuel waited outside for Matilda to finish eating. She never ate with the others. Instead, she was made to wait until everyone had finished, whereupon she sat on the floor in a corner of the kitchen and ate left-over scraps from a bowl. She hesitated when she came out onto the porch and saw him waiting.

"Hello," he said. "I'm Nordström's son Samuel."

"What does Herr Nordström want with me?" she asked with a sigh of resignation.

"I wondered if I may walk a little ways with Matilda."

"Jus' like all the others," she remarked sarcastically.

"What does Matilda mean?"

"You men're all the same. You get me by myself and force yourselves on me, then say I'm a whore."

"I am not like the others," he answered her. "I want nothing from Matilda, I promise. Just to walk and chat with her."

"People'll make fun of Herr Nordström--or worse--if they see 'im with me," she warned.

"Let them," he declared, walking beside her.

"But why's Herr Nordström want to walk with me?" she asked.

Samuel thought for a moment, unsure as to what his motive had actually been.

"I don't think anyone should be treated the way Mathilda is treated by people here," he said finally.

She shrugged. "I'm used to it. It began when I was born. My mother's treated the same way. It is the fate of folk like us."

They continued walking for a while. Samuel was at a loss for what to say.

178

"Matilda hasn't been measured for her new clothes," he remarked finally, glancing at her ragged blouse and patched skirt.

"I'm not to get new clothes," she said simply.

"But why not?"

"They say I don't need 'em 'cause no one ever sees me."

"Is that really true?"

"Yes, 'tis so."

Samuel had often heard rumors about how badly the Sahlins treated those who worked for them, but he had always assumed such tales were over-exaggerted. But obviously not.

By now they had reached the barn.

"I must go in an' clean up behind the cows before the foreman comes an' beats me for bein' lazy," she told him.

Samuel gasped. "Maybe we can talk another day then," he offered.

"Maybe."

Matilda filled his thoughts for the rest of the evening. In spite of the harshness of her life, she seemed to be rather light-hearted. And he had been deeply touched by the way she had picked up the crying child and comforted it, even though she knew she would be punished for doing so.

During their few remaining days on the Sahlin's estate he went out of his way to cross paths with Matilda. There was a goodness about her that attracted him. A motherliness. Whether the attraction was for the person she was or out of pity was not something he troubled himself over. Quite simply, he liked to be with her and he felt he could give her a better life than what she had hitherto experienced.

When he mentioned this to his father, Torbjörn was taken aback.

"My son, she is ten years older than you. And she has an illegitimate child, not to mention a reputation."

"Her reputation is put on her by the men who use her against her will," Samuel replied. "She is treated worse than an animal."

Torbjörn was silent for a minute, considering the situation.

"Perhaps you are right. I, too, have seen that she is ill-treated. But remember, marriage is a life-long commitment. At the same time, if you are going to begin sewing on your own you are going to need a wife to take care of the household tasks. What does Matilda think about it?"

"I don't know. I haven't asked her yet. But under the circumstances, she can hardly refuse."

Torbjörn patted him on the shoulder.

"True. You have my blessing, my son," he concluded somewhat reluctantly.

Samuel continued to seek out Matilda as discreetly as possible. But the evening before they were to leave the estate he approached her more openly.

"Can we go for a walk?" he asked straight out.

"Of course."

They walked along the road a few minutes without speaking.

"I understand that the Nordströms are finished here and will be leaving tomorrow," she remarked finally, to break the silence. There was an unmistakable sadness in her voice. "It's been pleasant to talk together."

"Yes, I think so, too," he replied.

"Perhaps we can talk again next time Herr Nordström comes," she suggested.

"I'm not coming again," he told her. "I'm going to begin sewing on my own this winter."

"Oh," she replied simply.

"But I have a little problem. I am going to need someone to keep house for me while I work and earn money."

Matilda stopped and looked at him.

"They say I'm a good worker," she offered. "Soon 'tis free week. Maybe I could stop working for the Sahlins and work for Herr Nordström instead."

"That isn't what I had in mind. I would like Matilda to marry me and we could have a family."

"But Herr Nordström cannot marry me!" she cried. "I am too old. Besides, he certainly has heard that I have a fatherless girl-child what lives with my sister. He knows what people says 'bout me."

"None of that matters. I have seen that Matilda is hard-working and kind. I don't want a paid housekeeper. I want a wife."

Matilda shook her head.

"What'll people say?"

"They can say what they want. I'm going to set up shop in another village where people don't know either me or you. Come with me as my wife."

"But what about my child?"

"I can be a father to her."

Matilda left the Sahlins during the free week at the end of October, when all farm workers had the right to seek new employment elsewhere if they wished. Madame Sahlin protested her decision, maintaining that Matilda belonged to the estate since she had no family.

"She is not entitled to move during free week because she is not considered to be hired help, since we don't pay her," she declared, realizing too late what she had said. And thus Matilda was free to marry Samuel.

They made their home outside a near-by village, where they rented the upstairs in a three-family house. Like in other working class families, the kitchen was the focal point, where they ate, slept, and spent their time. But unlike other working class families, the other room was not kept as a "best room" for special occasions. Instead, Samuel set up his cutting and sewing table, an ironing board, and his treddle Singer sewing machine there. A desk served as his office and a large cupboard held bolts of cloth.

At first Matilda's ten year old daughter Marie lived with them. But with the arrival of her half sister, she begged to go back to living with her aunt and uncle, where she was the only child.

Matilda was deeply grateful to Samuel for having seen beyond her reputation and given her a new life. Even though she never man- aged to learn to read or write, she did everything within her power to show him that he had not made a mistake by marrying her. She bore him two daughters and a son during their first six years of marriage, followed five years later by another daughter when she was forty-two. And five years later, at the age of forty-seven, she gave birth to Emma.

Unfortunately, her illiteracy had prevented her from being confirmed, yet Matilda was deeply religious in her own way. She went to church to listen to the music, finding the sermons boring. She believed that all one needed to do to be a good Christian was to live according to The Golden Rule. That single directive made all the rest of Christianity, including the Ten Commandments, and even the Bible itself, redundant. Such views she kept to herself, however, only hinting of them now and then to Samuel. And true to her beliefs, she did her best to do unto others as she would have them do unto her. She kept their home neat and clean, was economical, a loving mother, a true companion to Samuel, and was known in the community for her kindness.

Although Samuel found it difficult to put his emotions into words, he went out of his way to show Matilda how much she meant to him. In his spare time he sewed clothes for her from his nicest cloth, adding bits of lace he had saved for the collars. During the summer small bouquets of wild flowers appeared on the kitchen table. He borrowed books he thought she might enjoy from one of his well-to-do customers and read aloud to her on winter evenings while she knitted or mended clothes. And while he welcomed the birth of each new child, they were all secondary to Matilda. A few days after each birth, when she was safely out of danger, he held her hand and silently thanked God for having watched over her.

There were other signals of love which passed between them, unreadable to outsiders: A light touch when they moved around each other in the crowded kitchen, her small tug at his tie to straighten it before he went out, a look. And every night, unbeknownst to each other, they each thanked God for having let their paths cross that day long ago.

The children grew up without any serious illnesses or mishaps. One by one they emigrated to America in search of better economic possibilities, for at that time Sweden had nothing to offer people of their class. Both Samuel and Matilda were filled with sorrow each time one of them left, uncertain as to whether they would ever see them again. At the same time, they looked forward to growing old together, just the two of them. At last only Emma was still at home. She was seventeen and engaged to Fritz, a young man in the next village.

One Saturday afternoon when Samuel had taken a pause from his work and gone into the kitchen to see if there was any coffee left, he came upon Matilda sitting with her head resting on the the kitchen table.

"Whatever is the matter?" he asked? "Is Matilda not feeling well?"

"I have pain in my stomach," she replied.

Samuel laid his hand on her forehead. It was burning.

"Come and lie down," he said, helping her to her feet. "How long has it been going on?"

"Since this morning."

"Shall I send for the doctor?" he wondered.

"No, no. It'll pass."

But it didn't pass. Samuel sat beside her all night, soothing her forehead with cold wet towels. She was was worse on Sunday, now and then losing consciousness. He sat beside her all day, visibly worried. She had never been sick in all the years they had been married. The only thing that had put her in bed was giving birth.

"If Matilda is not better by tomorrow morning I'm going to send to town for the doctor," he told her.

He sat up beside her that night also. At daybreak on Monday morning Emma went down to the telephone station in the village and placed a call to Dr. Hagström.

But when he arrived an hour later it was already too late. Matilda had died while clutching Samuel's hand. The autopsy revealed a burst appendix.

Samuel was unconsolable.

"Why, God, have you let it end like this? What did we do wrong?" he cried over and over silently.

He was to ask the same questions hundreds of times in the twenty-nine years he had left to him, but he never received an answer.

Samuel picked up Walter's letter and continued reading it half-heartedly. He appreciated his offer to go and live with him in America, but he knew he would never do it. For one thing, he couldn't leave Emma, nor would she go with him. Both she and Fritz had many times remarked that they had no desire emigrate. But most of all, he couldn't imagine abandoning the world that he and Matilda had shared. He felt her presence in the rooms and surroundings where they had lived together for thirty years. Every Sunday he walked several miles to church in the next village. It wasn't because of the service or the fact that they had worshipped there together their entire married life. Nor was it because of the proximity of her grave just outside the wooden building. It wasn't in these places that he felt her spirit. It was when he walked home on the path through the forest which they had always taken. Because it was too narrow to walk side by side, Samuel always went first "to scare away the vipers" which sometimes sunned on the rocks. The path climbed upwards through the trees to a ridge, on top of which the landscape suddenly opened up to the east. One could see so far that the horizon became just a dark line against the sky fifty miles away. The first time they saw the view they were overwhelmed. Simultaneously they sank down side by side onto a large flat stone and gazed out in awe over the endless forest below them. Neither of them spoke, for there were no words for what they both felt. They simply sat like Siamese twins, joined where their shoulders touched, and let their feelings flow freely between them.

Finally Samuel laid his hand over Albertins's where it rested on her lap and they stood up.

"Now I know why I never find God inside the church," he said. "He's not there. He's out here in nature."

The experience had joined them in a silent bond which was to last the rest of their lives. Every Sunday on their way home they rested on the stone without speaking, as if to renew that bond.

Even after her death Samuel continued to visit the ridge to marvel at the view, sitting on the stone alone, yet not alone. Matilda's spirit was so strong that he could almost feel the pressure of her shoulder and the warmth of her hand under his. At first Emma tried to convince him to go with her to Fritz's church in another village, but he excused himself by saying that he felt more at home in his own parish church. His real reason was too private, too unmanly.

When Emma and Fritz married a few years later Walter repeated his offer. This time Samuel was forced to consider it. Emma was moving to Fritz's family's farm, which he had taken over when his parents retired. In keeping with farming tradition, they had moved into the little cottage on the edge of the land which existed solely for that purpose. Consequently, there was no place for Samuel to live. Just when he was about to write and accept Walter's offer, Beda, an old family friend, came to his rescue by offering to rent out her upstairs to him. This was no love affair. She was a widow and, like Samuel, couldn't imagine sharing her life with anyone else after her Jakob. But she liked the security of knowing that she was not alone in the house, especially at night. And because she had spent her younger years in America and had become quite fashion-conscious, she often went to Samuel with a piece of material she had come across and asked that he sew something according to her own design. In return, she saw to it that he had at least one warm meal a day, as well as taking care of his washing and ironing.

When Fritz's parents died it was natural that Samuel moved into the little cottage on their land. Once again Emma cooked for her father and took care of his household needs. She tried to convince him to go to church with them, but he argued that he preferred to continue attending his old parish church where he felt at home, even though he now had further to walk. He couldn't bring himself to speak of his meetings with Matilda.

By the time Fritz and Emma eventually bought a larger farm even further from his parish church, Samuel was in his early eighties. Not only was there no cottage for him there, which meant that he would have to live in the main house with them, but it was too far for him to walk to the ridge. For twenty-nine years he had communed with his Matilda on their ridge every Sunday, except when the deep snow made it impossible, and he couldn't bring himself to stop. It was his life-line. Reluctantly, he chose to move to the old people's home in his native village. Emma found his decision strange, but knew her father well enough to understand that it was useless to argue with him.

The first Sunday after he had moved into the old people's home he set out as usual for the ridge after church. He hadn't reached the beginning of the path on the far side of the villge before a nurse from the home caught up with him. She grabbed him by the arm, jerking him to halt.

"Just where does Herr Nordström think he is going?" she demanded.

"I'm going to visit my wife," he replied innocently.

"Herr Nordström is not allowed to go home," she told him, ignoring his answer.

"I'm not going home, I'm going to visit my wife," he repeated.

"No one is allowed to go out walking without being accompanied by one of our nurses."

He jerked free of her grasp.

"Leave me alone! I do not need an escort when I visit my wife!" he declared.

Just then one of the men who worked at the home caught up with them and, in spite of his angry struggles to free himself from their grasps, they marched Samuel back to his room.

The next day he was diagnosed as being out of contact with reality and potentially dangerous. He was sent to a near-by mental hospital. A few days later he was discharged and returned to the old people's home.

The following Sunday he once again set off for the ridge. This time he was brought back by two strong men. When he protested that he was only going to meet his wife, he was told that she had been dead for thirty years.

"I know that," he wept in frustration, but no one appeared to hear him.

From then on he was kept under close scrutiny. But when he failed to show up for dinner one day a search party was sent out to find him. They returned empty-handed. He wasn't found until several days later when one of the maids went up into the attic to hang up the washing out of the rain. The first thing she saw when she reached the top of the stairs was his feet swaying gently above the floor as the wind passed through the attic window.

PART FOUR
FICTION

"Alulf"

This story was inspired by a photograph of a man lying on his bed looking at the photos on his wall. But once I had created him, I had no idea where he was going. I simply watched his life unfold as my pen moved across the paper, often finding myself curious or surprised by his actions.

"'The Bridge"

When I drove to the far north of Scandinavia in 1965, the roads along the rugged coast of Norway were connected by ferries that crossed the numerous fjords. The majority of their passengers were local people, who chatted together like children on a school bus as they floated from one landing to the other. And for outsiders, the ferries offered a view of some of the world's most spectacular scenery, which could only be seen from the water. But as the years passed, the ferries began to disappear, replaced by long dark tunnels burrowing deep beneath the majestic landscape. It was as if the scenery and the ferries had never existed. But when I drove the same route forty years later, I discovered that, rather than tunnels, the ferries in the Lofoten Islands, in the far north, had been replaced by gracefully arched bridges connecting the islands that trail out into the North Atlantic from the Norwegian mainland, while many abandoned ferry landings still

ALULF

The summer sun had already disappeared behind the slum's grimy tenement buildings, but the stifling heat remained like a curse over the city. A typical New York July. The half-melted asphalt oozed through the worn-out soles of Alulf's shoes. It wouldn't have burned more if he had been barefoot. He paused outside the door of the shabby bachelors' hotel that had been his home for so many years, pushed his hat back off his forehead and wiped the streams of sweat from his face with his coat sleeve.

Out of habit he turned and looked behind him before lifting the sandwich board, which he had carried all day, from his shoulders. Then, with a sigh, he pulled open the door and went inside. After leaning the board in a corner of the hallway, he made his way slowly up the stairs to the fourth floor and his room. His legs were weak and he felt much older than his 60 years. He had long ago tired of that sandwich board which was his livelihood.

Life had been better before the Depression, when he was still working in the garment factory. In those days he still had a few dollars left over for himself after he had sent money home to his family in Sweden. But since having lost his job a few years back, life was hard. Carrying a sandwich board didn't pay much. But luckily, as the hotel's handyman, he didn't have to pay rent and even got his dinner for free. So, life wasn't completely unbearable.

He kicked off his shoes and stretched out on the iron bedstead's lumpy mattress, causing the naked springs to squeak like small mice. Outside the sooty half-open window the red hotel sign was already lit and the sound of a passing freight train forced its way in over the windowsill. Alulf's eyes wandered around the little room, pausing over each of the few pieces of furniture: a wooden orange crate that served as a bedside table, a washstand holding an enameled washbasin and pitcher of water with a shaving mirror hanging on the wall above it, a bureau with three drawers and a table with two spindle-backed chairs. The linoleum was threadbare and the water-stained wallpaper had loosened in a number of places. Actually, it was unnecessary to have two chairs, since Alulf didn't know anyone well enough to invite them up. But the back of the extra one made an excellent hanger for his Sunday suit. He liked to look at it hanging there; it reminded him of a better life then that of everyday. He closed his eyes with a sigh. Saturday evening, that little bridge between two realities, was always hard. And likewise Sunday evening, when the bridge went in the other direction.

His thoughts wandered back to the 1890's, the Sweden of his childhood, when the whole family—his parents, his twin brother Ulf, and his six younger sisters—slept together in a kitchen that wasn't much larger than his present room. He wondered how life had gone for them, if they had put to good use the money he had sent home every Christmas and Midsummer for almost 40 years. Never had he gotten even the smallest thank you. At the same time, he was convinced that they had received his letters with the enclosed money; he had always written his return address on the back of the envelope and none had ever been returned to him. Deep inside, he knew that his father lay behind the silence. He

190

could still feel his wrath marching up his spine when he remembered that day....

The twins, Alf, as he was then called, [which means "elf" in Swedish] and Ulf [which means "wolf"] were the oldest of the family's eight children. As fraternal twins, they were two distinct individuals. Ulf grew up to be big-boned and strong, but Alf didn't grow along with him. Instead, he remained small and rather frail. They were, in fact, like an elf and a wolf, a fact that their father had constantly assailed them with since early childhood. It didn't matter what Alf did, it was never good enough in his father's eyes. He only saw Ulf; Ulf who was bigger and stronger and best at everything, just as he himself was. Alf idolized Ulf for his strength but hated him as a brother; a brother who enjoyed belittling him cruelly whenever he had the chance. And, although he knew he would never succeed, he never gave up trying to win their father's attention away from his brother. Until that March day just after they had turned twenty.

On their way home from town that day they had decided to take a shortcut across the little lake bordering the farm. They checked the ice by the dock. Since it still seemed to be thick under the previous day's snowfall, they set out walking straight across. After a couple hundred yards Alf began to get nervous, both afraid to say something and afraid not to. Finally he took courage.

"Wait, Ulf," he said cautiously. "I think we should go a little more to the right in order to avoid the spring in the middle of the lake. The ice can be thin right there."

"Don't worry. I know what I'm doing, Baby Brother," Ulf answered, cocky as usual.

Alf knotted his fists in his jacket pockets. He detested that demeaning nick-name everyone in the family used whenever he asserted himself. In protest, he fell a good bit behind Ulf.

Half way across the lake the sound of a dull crack echoed through the silence and Ulf disappeared from sight. The first time he came to the surface he screamed. The second time he splashed hysterically, gasping for breath. Alf ran towards him, while yelling for help at the top of his lungs. Just as he had thought, there was a large hole in the ice where the somewhat warmer spring water flowed straight up through the lake. The ice around the edge of it was thick, as if having been cut by an ice fisherman. Alf got down on all fours and crawled towards his brother. But when he was finally able to grasp Ulf's wildly waving hands, he realized he was powerless to pull him up in his water-drenched clothes. Worse, he realized that Ulf would drag him down into the hole if he didn't let go of him. Neither of them could swim. Paralyzed with fear, they looked at each other in the midst of their tug-of-war. What happened next remained forever between the two of them. When help finally came, it was too late. Ulf was gone, his fully-clothed body having vanished under the ice.

Their father was in a frenzy.

"You drowned him!" he screamed when he finally caught up with Alf in the woodshed. He pulled off his leather belt, forced Alf into a corner, and beat him with all his strength.

"You drowned him on purpose! You've always hated him! You've always been jealous of him because he was bigger and stronger—more clever—a better person than you'll ever be! I'll never forgive you! Never! You're nothing but a worthless good-for-nothing! I wish you had drowned instead!"

He continued to beat Alf wildly, unable to burn up his anger. He would gladly have beaten him to death, but Alf's thick homespun clothes protected him from the knife-like lashes, which only further inflamed his father's fury. He continued swinging his belt, striking blows wherever he could, until he was exhausted. Shaking and out of breath at last, he sank down onto the chopping block.

"Get out of here and don't ever come back!" he growled. "I never want to see your evil face again! If I do, I'll kill you!"

When his father closed his eyes to wipe the sweat from his face with his mitten, Alf ran past him and out the door.

Without looking back, he kept on running along the path that led towards the road.

When Ulf's body came to the surface in the spring, Alf was already in America.

The first years in America were hard. New York had many immigrants who never got further than the city's various ethnic districts, where every language except for English was spoken. As a farm boy, Alf felt alone in the city, even though everyone in the neighborhood spoke Swedish. He longed for home. Most of all, he longed for the gentle encouragement his mother had always offered him. It had given him a tiny spark of faith in himself, in spite of his father's efforts to undermine any self-confidence he might have had. But now, away from them both, the words that rang loudest in his head were the demeaning words his father had constantly shouted at him, words that had always been much louder than his mother's. Nor could he imagine what she would have found to say to him after that day on the ice. More and more he had understood that his father was right; he was a worthless good-for-nothing. He would never strike it rich and be able to return home with pockets full of dollars. Ulf could have done it, but not he. No, he would be glad if he didn't starve to death in the Promised Land.

At night Ulf appeared in his dreams, glaring at him accusingly and mouthing the word 'murderer' over and over. And even though he hadn't actually forced Ulf under the water, he knew in his heart that he was guilty of murder. But while it was true that they had had their conflicts, at the same time, they were twins. The only thing which could have drawn them closer to each other would have been if they had been identical twins. As a means of honoring his brother and at the same time attempting to inherit a bit of his strength, he decided to put their names, and consequently their characters, together and call himself Alulf.

After a few lean years, Alulf finally got a steady job as a janitor in a large garment factory and, by living frugally, he was able to save a few dollars which he sent home with his first letter. He was determined to make his father proud of him.

> *Beloved parents and sisters,*
>
> *I am just sending these lines to let it be known that I am in good health and hope everyone at home is the same. I like it here in New York and have gotten a job in a factory that produces machine-made clothes. I'm enclosing a little money for Christmas, which can surely be of use, and will send more at Midsummer. I promise to continue to send money twice a year in the future to try to make up for the loss of the only two sons in the family.*
>
> *I deeply regret what happened to Ulf. I did my best, but I couldn't pull him up. He was too heavy in his wet clothes. What is done cannot be undone. Can Father forgive me? Can God forgive me?*
>
> *Please, Father, I beg for thy forgiveness.*
> *Your son,*
> *A. Erlingsson*

On the back of the envelope he wrote simply, A. Erlingsson so as to avoid revealing that he had changed his name, and the address to the tenement house where he rented a room from a Swedish family. He waited for weeks, then months, for an answer, but no sign of life came from Sweden.

At Midsummer he once again sent money and wrote that he was in good health and that everything was fine with him. And once again he begged his father fervently to forgive him. No answer came back.

The next Christmas he sent a little more money than before, to show that he had become even more successful. It wasn't actually the case, but he was desperate to win his father's forgiveness and acceptance. He had already understood that it wasn't possible to win him with words, but money should speak for itself. There was never any money at home and he was prepared to sacrifice himself for their sakes. If he could just send enough money his father would be forced to acknowledge his capability and see that he wasn't the good-for-nothing he had accused him of being. Or so he thought. But no response came from Sweden.

When his Midsummer letter failed to soften his father, he began to scrimp and save in order to send even more money home the next time. Winning his father's forgiveness and praise had become an obsession.

The following Christmas he wrote that he had been promoted to a job with more responsibility and thus was able to send home a greater sum of money, thinking his father would be proud of him. In truth, he had simply scrimped and saved all autumn in order to be able to increase the size of the money order. But to no avail.

Eventually he was able to move to a residential bachelor's hotel in another part of the city. But although he was glad to be on his own at last, he missed the connection with the old country that he had felt in the Swedish neighborhood. Most of all, he missed his native language, for he felt like a stranger was using his mouth when he tried to speak English. Nevertheless, at first he did his best to learn from the people around him, but after being laughed at a number of times for his efforts, he gave up. He was by nature shy and withdrawn and soon became even more so. Nor had he any friends. Each day after work he came back to his bachelor's room and lay on his bed day dreaming about the nice Swedish girl he would one day meet. In his loneliness she began to take form. He named her Rose-Marie. Some days she seemed so near that he could almost see her. Before long they were holding mental conversations in Swedish. He told her about his father and mother and Ulf and she reciprocated with tales of her own family. Soon they were planning their future; where they would live, how many children they would have, what they would name them. They had no secrets from each other. He no longer felt lonely.

At first he left her in his room when he went out. Thus he lived in two worlds; one outside his room when he went to work and the other inside his head when he was in his room. Both were equally real. Then gradually he began to take her with him when he went out and his worlds slowly lost their individual contours and eventually merged into one. And because she had been brought up in the old country and knew her place, Rose-Marie always kept herself in the background when around other people.

One day on his way home from the garment factory he paused to look at some pictures of people and street scenes displayed in the window of a photographer's studio. Down in one corner of the window were a couple of box cameras for sale. The thought that a person could create such pictures with one of those little boxes fascinated him.

Every day for the next few weeks he studied the photos on his way home. Finally one day he plucked up his courage and went inside.

"The little box," he began in his broken English. He pointed towards the window. "How much cost it?"

"Prata du svenska?" the man asked.

"Ja!" Alulf exclaimed excitedly.

It was the first time he had heard his own language spoken since he'd moved away from the Swedish quarter. He held out his hand.

"Alulf Nykvist from Bjurtjärn Parish."

"Isaksson. Hugo Isaksson. Kalv Parish," the man reciprocated, shaking his hand.

They chatted in Swedish, drawn to each other by the soft, sing-songy melody of their native language. It was the beginning of a friendship which would last many years, albeit governed by the formal reserve they had both brought with them from the old country.

"So Nykvist is interested in the box cameras?" Isaksson said finally.

Alulf nodded.

"They cost two dollars and thirty-seven cents. And then one needs film, of course, which costs a dime."

"Oh," Alulf replied. He had no idea how a camera functioned. He just knew that he wanted to capture people and places on paper.

Isaksson lifted one of the cameras out of the display window and set it on the counter in front of Alulf.

"Does Nykvist know how a camera functions?" he asked him.

Alulf shook his head.

"One holds it like this and looks through this little window," he instructed. "When the picture is centered, one must hold very still and gently push this button."

He went on to explain how to load the film, wind it, and take it out when it was finished.

Alulf stood spell-bound, not uttering a word. When the man had finished his demonstration he looked at him questioningly.

"I buy it," he said.

He dug in his pocket and pulled out a handful of loose change which he lay on the counter. Slowly he slid all the nickels into one group, all the dimes into another, and left the pennies in between them. There were no quarters. When he had counted it all, it only came to a dollar ninety-eight. He shrugged and scooped the coins into his hand again and was about to drop them back into his pocket.

"Wait," Isaksson said, putting out his hand to stop him. "How long would it take to save the other forty-nine cents?"

Alulf shrugged again. He had already taken from the money he had put aside to send home come Midsummer.

"I'll tell you what," he continued. "I've seen Nykvist standing outside my window every day for the past month, so I know this is important to him. I will set the camera aside until Nykvist can get together forty cents more and then he can have it with the film included."

"Oh, many thanks, sir!" Alulf said happily. He held out his hand and they shook on the deal.

When Alulf awoke on Sunday morning the July sun was already beating down on the city. The previous day he had made the final payment on the camera and now it stood on the table across from his bed, its lens aimed at him expectantly. He picked it up carefully, measuring its weight in his hand. Isaksson had helped him load the film, so it was ready to go. Quickly he put on his Sunday suit, slid his fingers under the strap on the top of the box, and went downstairs to the street. He had long ago decided that he would take his first pictures at Coney Island.'

The trolley was filled with families bearing picnic hampers and umbrellas, seeking to escape the heat of the city, and the beach was already crowded when they arrived. Alulf wandered aimlessly amongst the sunbathers and children, camera poised against his stomach, trying to decide what to photograph first. Then he saw it; an organ grinder with a monkey on a leash collecting coins in a tin cup. He looked down into the view-finder, but just as he placed his finger on the shutter button a young woman stepped between him and the organ grinder.

"Oh, sorry," she laughed, stepping back quickly when she realized her mistake.

But too late. His finger had already pressed the shutter to capture the monkey with its cup.

"It does nothing," he replied shrugging his shoulders.

The girl continued on her way and Alulf took a picture of the organ grinder and the monkey, this time making sure no one was about to walk between them. He took a couple more pictures, then spent the rest of the day sitting on the beach watching people and enjoying the cooling sea breeze.

198

The following Saturday Alulf stopped by the photography studio to see if his pictures were ready.

"Oh yes, they were finished a couple of days ago. I develop them myself right here," Isaksson told him, ducking into the room behind the curtain and returning with an envelope. "So if Nykvist ever wants extra copies or enlargements made, just let me know."

Alulf unfastened the little clip holding the envelope closed and slid the photos out onto the counter. There was the girl from Coney Island smiling up at him from the top of the pile!

"Oh!" he gasped.

"I say, she's quite a beauty," Isaksson commented. "I take it she's Nykvist's girl friend," he added.

Alulf nodded, unable to take his eyes off the photo.

"What is her name, if I may ask?" he continued.

"Rose-Marie," Alulf heard himself say.

"That certainly suits her! Lucky man!"

"Thanks," Alulf replied, not daring to look up in his confusion.

"How much do they cost?" he continued quickly.

Isaksson quoted the price, adding that he also needed a new roll of film.

Alulf laid the money on the counter, collected his photos and film, and said a hasty good-bye. Once out on the sidewalk he realized that he hadn't even looked at the rest of his pictures.

When he got back to his room he emptied the envelope onto the table and stared at the girl.

"Rose-Marie," he murmured. "Rose-Marie."

He pulled out one of the thumbtacks holding up the peeling wallpaper and pinned the photo on the wall beside his bed, then lay back, hands behind his head, and gazed at it longingly.

Every Sunday for the rest of the summer he returned to Coney Island and combed the beach for Rose-Marie. But he never found her. Come autumn she continued to fill his Sundays, even though he no longer went to the beach. He began exploring various parts of the city, often with her by his side. He always walked with his head slightly turned, so that Rose-Marie was just out of range of his peripheral vision. Sometimes he photographed a café where they had sat and drunk coffee or somewhere they went on an outing or a house that they would like to buy.

One Sunday he saw a young woman dressed in a housemaid's uniform walking a little dog in Central Park. Rose-Marie! As she came nearer, he lifted his camera and clicked the shutter. When he looked up he realized his mistake. Although she had blond hair and blue eyes and was pretty, she was not Rose-Marie. Hugo Isaksson, however, did not notice the difference when he printed the picture, for he had not spent hours studying her face.

"So how is Rose-Marie?" he asked, with a nod towards the envelope of new photos as he handed it to Alulf.

"Oh, she's fine," he replied, emptying the contents of the envelope out onto the counter as usual. When he came to the picture of the woman he paused. She actually did look a lot like Rose-Marie. He could feel Isaksson's silent questions.

"She's Swedish," Alulf told him, "and works as a housemaid for some rich people—cleans, irons, walks their dog. His name is Fritz." His voice began to tremble when he realized that he had no control over the words coming from his mouth.

Once again he said a hasty good-bye and left the shop.

Back in his room he pinned the two photos side by side on the wall and gazed at them, comparing what features he could discern in the tiny snapshots. Although they were two different women, for him they soon became simply two different aspects of Rose-Marie.

As Christmas neared, he asked Isaksson if he could make a slightly larger copy of the Coney Island photo of Rose-Marie to send home to Sweden.

Keep this one," Isaksson told him when Alulf came to pick it up, "and give the smaller one to Nykvist's family. It's cheaper to send and besides, she is more important to him than to them."

He took Isaksson's advice. The larger photo was much nicer to look at when he lay in bed.

Along with the little picture and the Christmas money order to his family, he wrote:

Beloved Parents,

As you see, I am sending a little more money than usual. I have gotten another promotion. And I have met a wonderful girl. She works as a housemaid for some rich people here. Her name is Rose-Marie and she comes from Bosebo Parish in Småland. I hope that soon I will have enough money so that we can get married.

I beg for your forgiveness for that which happened to Ulf. Please write soon.

Your son,

A. Erlingsson

In reality, there wasn't much hope that he would ever rise above the position of janitor at the garment factory. They hardly knew he existed. But surely his father would be impressed. Once again he waited for an answer. In vain.

Undaunted, he continued to send money home twice a year, often accompanied by a photo of some place he had gone with Rose-Marie.

One Sunday in June he awoke earlier than usual, full of excitement. As usual, his gaze fell on his good suit hanging over the back of the chair expectantly, having been thoroughly brushed the previous evening. Hanging over the back of the other chair was his only white shirt, with his tie draped over it. He got up and folded back the mattress to where his suit pants lay on newspapers to protect them from the naked bed springs while being pressed under his nightly weight. He dressed quickly, grabbed his camera on his way out of the room, and let the door slam behind him. At the bottom of the stairs he pulled his Sunday hat down low over his forehead, hunched his shoulders, and stepped out onto the sidewalk. But as soon as he had rounded the corner at the end of the block he straightened up, pushed his hat back, and walked as if he owned the world. Rose-Marie walked by his side. They had recently gotten married and were going to look for a flat in a better neighborhood.

A few weeks earlier he had photographed a newly married couple coming out of a church holding hands, with a crowd of people visible behind them. When Isaksson had printed it he confronted Alulf half-jokingly.

"Has Nykvist lent his camera to someone else?"

"What does Isaksson mean?" Alulf asked innocently.

"That looks like Nykvist and his Rose-Marie coming out of church as man and wife," he said, indicating the tiny figures in the photo. "The photographer should have stood a little closer."

"I know. It's a shame. We got married a couple of weeks ago. Just a small wedding." He examined the photo more closely. "There are Rose-Marie's relatives behind us. My father thought it was a pity that they couldn't be here, but they can't afford such a journey. But he sent his blessing."

Alulf sighed as he remembered the conversation. Perhaps his father had given him his blessing and the letter had just gotten lost in the mail. Surely he was pleased that his eldest son had found a nice Swedish girl.

He spent most of the day walking around in Brooklyn with Rose-Marie, searching for a house in a quiet neighborhood. At last they found what they were looking for; a well-kept brownstone for rent with a flower garden in the little front yard and shady trees lining the street.

"What does Rose-Marie think?" he asked.

"It's lovely," she answered. "It will feel like being back home when I can dig in the earth and plant flowers once again."

He raised his camera and snapped a picture.

"Let's see what shops there are in the next block," he suggested.

They crossed the street and as they ambled along the sidewalk looking in the various shop windows, he could feel her hand resting in the crook of his elbow. It felt good to have her by his side.

They walked for several more blocks, past a school, several churches, and a park with a little duck pond in the middle.

"It's a nice place to raise children," Rose-Marie remarked.

"Yes, and it seems to be a mixed area instead of being solely Italian or Irish or Greek," he observed.

"I wonder if there are any Swedes or Norwegians here," Rose-Marie said.

"It doesn't matter," he told her. "We have each other to talk to and we will speak Swedish with our children."

The following Saturday, dressed properly in his Sunday suit, he returned to Brooklyn and rented a mail box in the post office. In his next letter home he informed his father that he and Rose-Marie had moved to a nicer neighborhood, giving the post office box number as his mailing address. Included with the letter and money order was a copy of the wedding photo, along with one of the brownstone.

"We live on the ground floor," he informed both Isaksson and his parents. "There is a little yard behind the building where we can grow potatoes."

"It looks nice," Isaksson commented enthusiastically when he saw the picture.

"Yes, it's a quiet neighborhood," Alulf told him. "And there are a couple of grocery stores, a butcher shop, a post office, and a church on the same street. And even a park. Rose-Marie loves it."

"Nykvist seems to be doing well for himself," Isaksson said. "Not everyone from the old country is so successful."

"My boss seems pleased with my work and already I've had a couple of promotions," Alulf told him. In English he added, "I try to keep my nose clean and work hard."

He wasn't quite sure what keeping his nose clean had to do with anything, but it made him feel important to be able to use such clichés in his limited English.

Every Sunday Alulf performed the same ritual. He put on his good suit which he periodically replaced with a newer one from the Salvation Army, took his camera, and went out with his hat pulled down low on his forehead. By the time he turned the corner at the end of the block, however, he had straightened up, pushed his hat back on his head, and held out his arm to Rose-Marie. Together they walked around their new neighborhood, first stopping to check his post office box to see if he had gotten a letter from home. And each time he could see thorough the little window above the combination dial that the box was empty. Nevertheless, he opened it and stuck his hand in all the way to the back, just to make sure.

"It looks like Father's letter has gone astray," he commented to Rose-Marie. "I thought for sure it would be here today."

Then they continued their walk, pausing now and then so he could photograph street scenes and neighbors.

One Sunday a year or so after they were married, they saw a baby buggy outside a drugstore. It was summer and the baby was clad in only a diaper. He raised his camera and clicked the shutter.   "Wait till Isaksson sees what's on this roll of film," Alulf said when he left it to be developed the following Saturday.

Isaksson gave him a curious look.

"We have become a family," Alulf told him proudly. "Isaksson is the first person to see a photo of little Samuel. And, of course, I need a copy to send home. My parents were so excited when I told them we were expecting a baby! He's their first grandchild. I promised them a photo as soon as he was born."

And so the years passed. Those Saturdays that Alulf went to Isaksson's photo shop to leave his film or pick up the finished pictures were almost as special as his Sundays. He always dressed in his best suit and made sure his shoes were shined. As soon as he put on his suit coat he felt different. Even though he never took Rose-Marie the photo shop with him on those Saturdays, he walked with his head high, as though she were by his side. Even his step was lighter.
In time there were more children. Dora. Fredrik. Alice. He photographed them all. There were moves to a larger flat and finally to a house on the outskirts of the city, with a new post office address. And because Alulf spent his Sundays in his new neighborhood, people there began to recognize him. They called him Camera Man, for although he smiled and waved, he never spoke. No one knew anything about him. They assumed he was a deaf-mute. The children, especially, liked him, for he often brought them small presents—a bag of candy or a ball or jump rope—to share. They willingly posed for him and sometimes he gave them copies of the pictures he had taken of them. He was accepted as part of the neighborhood and they became his children. And his camera followed their progress as they grew up.

One Sunday a motor car drove up the street and stopped across from the vacant lot where the children were playing. As soon as the driver disappeared into the drugstore on the corner, they ran over to have a look. Alulf raised his camera. Just as the oldest boy stroked the shiny black paint on the hood, he clicked the shutter.

"Wait till you see what I've bought!" he told Isaksson when he left the film to be developed. "Samuel was so excited when he saw it! Can you print a copy for me to send home to Sweden, please." Isaksson was certainly impressed by the shiny new automobile.   "She's a real beauty!" he remarked when Alulf came to pick up his photos. "Nykvist has certainly been successful over the years. His father must be extremely proud."

"Oh, yes, he is!" Alulf assured him. "And he is so glad for the money I have sent home twice a year. Life is not so easy in the old country, as Isaksson knows. It would have been easier if the whole family had emigrated with me, but my father's parents refused to leave Sweden and he didn't feel he could go without them. But it feels good to be able to help them."

He scooped together his pictures, with the two copies of the automobile on top, and bid Isaksson good-bye.

Back in his room, he added one of the copies to the collection of photos tacked on the wall beside his bed. Lying back against the pillow, hands behind his head, he gazed at them: Rose-Marie on the beach, Rose-Marie walking the dog, their wedding, their first apartment, Samuel in the baby buggy, the house in the suburbs, the other children, numerous outings, and now the new car. He closed his eyes and could feel the steering wheel in his hands and hear the excited chatter of the children as he took them for a spin. Even Rose-Marie loved the new car and was so proud to sit by his side as they went for Sunday drives in the country.

He sat up, took out pen and paper, and began to write.

> *Beloved Parents,*
>
> *Once again it's time to write and send a little money. I have my health, thanks to God, and I hope that everyone at home is also well. As Father and Mother can see from the enclosed photo, I have taken one more step upward in life and have gotten myself a brand new motor car. The children were so excited when I brought it home, especially Samuel who is standing there with such a big smile on his face. In sunny weather we often take a Sunday drive out into the countryside, as is the custom in this country.*

Father, please forgive me for Ulf's death and write soon. Rose-Marie sends her warmest greetings to my entire family.

Your son,

A. Erlingsson

He took out the money order he had bought the previous day and folded it into the letter. In the 35 years that he had been sending money home, he had never really considered whether his parents were still living or not, nor what their economic circumstances might have become. In his relationship to them time stood still. He was forever the son who had let his twin brother drown; the son begging his father to forgive him, the son begging his father to see him as someone worthwhile.

When America was hit by the Depression, like everyone else, Alulf's life changed overnight. The clothing factory came to a halt and he lost his janitor's job. But because he had served the bachelors' hotel as handyman for so many years, he was the only person there who understood the intricacies of its heating and electrical systems. Thus he was allowed to keep his room, even though he could not pay the rent. However, his dinner was no longer included. Instead, he was forced to join the long soup kitchen lines outside various charitable organizations. The little money he earned from occasional odd jobs he saved and sent home to his family in Sweden. Having empty pockets didn't bother him much; he had been nurtured on poverty.

Life got better when he eventually got the sandwich board job. Once more he could pay his rent at the hotel and receive free dinners, which were much more nutritious than soup kitchen food. But the years of walking the sidewalks in every kind of weather, with the heavy wooden boards hanging over his shoulders, had taken their toll on his back and feet, as well as his general health. Nevertheless, he continued to live for Sundays, when he could put on his suit and step into another world, where sandwich boards didn't exist. He and Rose-Marie had long ago settled into middle class life, with no more upward moves or new cars. He continued to follow the children with his camera. Gradually they grew up, graduated from school, and moved out into the world. He kept Isaksson informed as to their progress, although he took fewer pictures nowadays.

One summer day he rushed into the camera shop full of excitement.

"Guess what!" he exclaimed. "I have become a grandfather!"

He set a roll of film on the counter with a proud bang.

"Be prepared to meet Samuel's son Joseph."

"Congratulations!" Isaksson replied cheerfully, shaking his hand. "Has Nykvist written the good news to his parents?"

"Not yet. I'm waiting until I have a picture to send. Can Isaksson make two copies of the best one, please?"

"Of course. Come back in the middle of next week, Grandpa."

That Sunday Alulf had a surprise waiting for him when he stuck his hand into his post office box. Lying flat on the bottom of the box was a slip of paper informing him that he had a package, but that he would have to pick it up on a week day when the window was open. Since no one but his father knew his post office address, it could only be from him. He was both curious and excited.

Monday afternoon he stopped parading a little earlier than usual and, leaving the sandwich board in a safe hiding place, took the subway out to the post office. He handed in the slip of paper at the window and was given a package the size of a shoe box. Despite the hot humid weather, he ran to catch the next train back into town. Once he had retrieved the boards and adjusted their weight on his shoulders, he hurried towards the hotel, anxious to discover what his father had sent him after all these years. But he wasn't used to being out with his boards during rush hour and he found it difficult to manouvre his way through the crowds, especially with his hat pulled down almost over his eyes as usual. Finally he had to push it back wipe his brow. As he did so, a man across the street thought he looked familiar and began to follow him, unable to believe his eyes.

When Alulf got to the hotel he paused, took his hat off, and wiped the sweat from his face with his sleeve. Then, as always before starting to free himself from the boards, he glanced behind him. There stood Isaksson!

"I thought I recognized Nykvist..." he began, but Alulf had already crumpled to the ground between the boards. Hastily Isaksson lifted them away and knelt beside him.

"It doesn't matter," he said, having instantly understood the past 40 years. "I'm still Nykvist's friend. Let me help him up to his room."

He pulled the key from Alulf's pocket, took the package which he was still clutching, and started to lift him into a sitting position. But it was too late.

"It looks like a heart attack," the medic said when the ambulance arrived. "Do you know him?"

"Yes, I'm his cousin," Isaksson said instinctively. "I'm all he has."

He gave them his name and address, saying he would notify his relatives in Sweden and make other necessary arrangements.

When they had gone, he let himself into Alulf's room. He switched on the light and looked around. The wall beside the bed was covered with photos, all of them familiar to him. For a long time he just sat and stared at it, letting all those years fall into a completely different pattern than the one he had been led to believe.

Finally he decided he might as well open the package. Lifting the lid of the box, he saw that it was crammed with letters. On top of them was an envelope with the word "Alf" written on it. After a bit of hesitation, he tore it open and began reading.

Dear Alf,

I regret to tell you that Father passed away a few weeks ago at the great age of 91. When going through his things, we came across this box of letters that you had written. Father never mentioned having ever heard from you. Since they were just addressed to him, we felt it was better to return them to you. As you see, he never opened any of them. Sadly, as far as he was concerned, you were as dead as Ulf. Why he bothered to save your letters instead of burning them, I will never know. We always wondered what happened to you, but we were forbidden to mention either you or Ulf. Nor do we know any more now, aside from the fact that you are still alive and living in New York. Our mother died some years ago, but I can tell you that she never forgot you in her prayers.

I hope that you will write and let us know how your life has been all these years.

Your oldest sister,

Emma

By now the sky was dark and the neon hotel sign outside the window had come on, casting an unreal light into the room. A train rumbled by outside the window and disappeared into the night. Isaksson found a piece of paper and pen in the drawer of the table and began to write:

Dear Emma,

My name is Hugo Isaksson. I was a friend of your brother's. I regret to tell you that he passed away today from a heart attack on his way home with the package of letters, which he had not yet opened. I am returning them to you because I suspect they can tell you more about his life in New York than I could, even though I have known him for many years. Also, I believe they contain the money that he always sent home to your family at Christmas and Midsummer.

I didn't know Alf socially, so to speak. We only met when he came into my camera shop to leave a film or pick up his prints. At those times he told me about his wife and children (whose photographs he included in his letters to your family), but I never had the opportunity to meet them. Unfortunately, I do not know where they are living. Alf's post office box was just a business address.

Alf was a fine man and I always enjoyed his visits to my shop. I am going to miss him.

> *Sincerely,*
> *Hugo Isaksson*

The next day Isaksson mailed the shoe box of letters back to Sweden, without a return address. It was the only act of friendship left to him.

THE BRIDGE

The grandfather clock in the corner of the room struck six, its last tone stretching out in a long echo through the stillness of the cabin. The world beyond the window was pitch black, save for the aurora borealis shooting up into the silent sky, outshining the stars and casting a gentle sheen over the snow-covered Norwegian landscape. It would be several more hours before the sky lightened to the usual twilight which passed for daylight above the Arctic Circle in the dead of winter. It had been over a month since the sun had shown its face above the horizon. And now at last, around noon on this ordinary weekday, it would rise shyly out of the sea far to the south, exposing its upper edge for a few moments before sinking into oblivion once more. But for those who lived along the rugged coast, with the often cruel Atlantic as a neighbor, those few moments were enough. The sun still existed, and it was on its way back to them. In a few months it would stay with them day and night, circling overhead without ever sinking into the sea. Today was the beginning of it's re-birth.

Enok sat up, swinging his legs over the side of the bed while making sure to keep his feet above the icy-cold floor as they searched blindly for his slippers. The fire had gone out during the night and his breath came in great white clouds. Going to the window, he held his finger against the pane until it had melted a hole in the frost large enough for him to shine his flashlight through to the thermometer outside. The mercury had shrunk almost down to the bulb.

After breakfast, he pulled his heavy sweater over his head, followed by his padded corduroy vest, and then over that, his coarsely woven coat. Next, he drew up his woolen stockings over his pant legs and stuck his feet into a pair of torn fisherman's boots. Lastly, he lifted his fur hat from its peg by the door and pulled it down over his still thick snow-white hair, with the earflaps hanging loose over his ears. No sooner had he stepped outside and closed the door behind him than the freezing north wind lifted the earflaps like bird wings, trying to make off with it. With a sigh of resignation he fumbled with the strings hanging from the flaps and tied them in a bow under his chin. It made him feel like a child, but he had no desire to lose his hat in such weather.

He walked a little stiffly along the path towards the ferry landing. Most likely the water had frozen sufficiently during the night to have imprisoned the ferry at the landing on the other side of the fjord, but it was best to check just in case. Odd always brought it over from the mainland in the mornings when he came with the school bus, leaving Enok to make the first run back and forth the while he himself picked up the island's school children. He strained his eyes towards the water, but it was too dark to make out the ferry. He continued down to the landing, his feet recognizing every little stone and root they stepped on through the snow. He had walked the same way almost every day for over eighty years. Furthermore, his father had walked the same path ever since he began working as a ferryman long before Enok was born, just as his father's father Edvin had done before him....

In the beginning, in the last half of the 1800's, Edvin went down to the primitive landing only when a traveler came and asked to be ferried over to the mainland. In those days, the means of transport was a raft which was big enough that it could, with the help of the guiding cable, carry a horse and wagon or carriage over the fjord. Life had been simpler then. Edvin had built a little cottage well out of reach of the sea's worst rages and, with the combination of a potato patch, fishing, and the few coins he received from travelers, the family could live a life that was equally as tolerable as that of those around them. No one had more than the absolute necessities. His wife had given him eight children, but only four had survived the dangerous childhood years to become adults. But instead of grieving over the young lives that had been lost, they thanked God for those who had survived.

The eldest of them was Enok's father Vidar. As a boy he had often accompanied his father on the ferry. To him, there was nothing more wonderful than to stand beside the cable house in the wind and look up at the clouds, while listening to the water slapping rhythmically against the side of the hull. It went without saying that he would one day take over after his father. But that was many years away. First there was his confirmation—the rite of passage into adulthood—after which he would serve as his father's assistant. But he dreamed of the day he would be a grown man and have sole command over the ferry. Unfortunately, that day arrived much sooner than he could ever have imagined.

It had begun like any other day. All morning Edvin had ferried the islanders to the spring market on the mainland. The majority of those on board had something with them—dried fish, hand-woven cloth, newly spun yarn, a few chickens, eggs or butter, as well as animals—which they planned to sell or trade for flour, coffee, sugar, salt, and other necessities they could not produce themselves. Those lucky enough to have a little money would perhaps come home with a calf, or a goat, or even a horse—and definitely a young piglet to fatten up for Christmas. For the women, market day meant a chance to meet friends and exchange a bit of gossip. For many of the men, the market was a chance to get drunk and fight with anyone over anything. For Edvin, market day meant double the number of trips back and forth, and thus, double the amount of cash at the end of the day. Already his pockets felt pleasantly heavy. As he steered the ferry toward the mainland dock on one of the last afternoon runs, he pulled a few coins from his pocket and pressed them into Vidar's hand.

"Buy a couple of meters of pretty material for your mother," Edvin told him. "You have plenty of time to look around before I get back. And buy some candy for yourself and your brother and sisters with the money that is left over."

Vidar clasped the still-warm coins in his fist. Never had he had so much money to spend as he chose.

"Thank you, sir," he said, shaking his father's hand and bowing formally.

Before the raft had tied up at the landing he hopped ashore and, running past the throng of waiting homeward bound islanders, disappeared along the dirt road toward the marketplace. Edvin watched him go while he collected the fares from his friends and neighbors as they clambered onto the raft with their bundles. The women were tired and nearly all the men were more or less inebriated. The animals on board became nervous as soon as they felt the raft roll a little under their feet. Everyone wanted to get home as quickly as possible.

Edvin closed the gate after the last passenger and let the raft move out into the current of the ebb tide. He could feel how the cable, with its small rhythmic jerks, passed like clockwork through the wheel in the cable house. But when they came out into open water the wind suddenly came up and the outgoing tide tried to pull the raft with it as though it were a toy. Edvin became anxious. Dear God, he prayed silently, take us safely over the fjord. Suddenly he felt a jerk and the cable slackened and the raft swung out into the open sea. Edvin rushed to the cable house, followed by the majority of the curious passengers. The raft tipped from their weight and two newly purchased cows lost their footing and slid down towards the crowd, causing it to capsize. Men, women and children screamed hysterically as they tried to keep themselves from sliding into the water. In vain. The entire raft was cleared as though by an avalanche. Most of the people had never had any reason to learn to swim, since the water in the fjord was uninvitingly cold, even in the middle of the summer. And even if they had been able to swim, there was no chance to keep oneself afloat in the rough sea. The women's long skirts and heavy shawls stuck to their bodies and quickly pulled them under, as though they had been in a sack full of stones. The men who were drunk didn't grasp what had happened and were too confused to save themselves. The few who were sober survived a bit longer, but in the end they also became victims of their inability to swim. A couple of them, however, succeeded in grabbing a rope hanging from the raft before it was swept away by the maelstrom. After a harrowing journey they were cast up on a stony beach when the raft finally went aground on a little island. Things went quickly for the children on board, for they knew nothing of the dangers of the sea. After a little splashing, they sank like small pebbles. Although Edvin tried to rescue a neighbor woman and her two children who landed in the water beside him, he drowned with the others. Not even he could swim. Within ten minutes all the cries and screams and thrashing about came to an end. Then the sea smoothed over the scene of the disaster and pretended that nothing had happened there. If it hadn't been for the two men who had hung on to the rope, no one would have ever known what had actually taken place.

Like the others at the market, Vidar was unaware of what was going on out on the fjord. The marketplace was located a couple hundred yards inland from the landing, protected from the sea by a wooded area. That, together with the wind, prevented the desperate calls for help from reaching folk at the market. Nor had there been anyone down at the landing when the accident occurred, since the ferry had just left and wasn't expected back for more than an hour.

Time passed. People made their last purchases and finally began to wander in small groups down towards the landing. Soon sacks of grain and flour were piled up along the causeway, together with potato baskets, wood baskets, farm tools, fishing equipment, boxes of nails, grindstones, and other materials. Women stood in small groups and chatted, with baskets filled with coffee, sugar, flour and salt over their arms, while groups of men, many of them drunk, bragged about their various successes during the day. The newly purchased cattle and horses, the majority of them young and inexperienced, stamped anxiously in the strange surroundings, while their new owners tried unsuccessfully to control them. A pair of small pigs didn't realize that they were tied together by their back legs and tried in vain to run away, while chickens flapped their worthless wings in small handmade cages. It was the usual the end of a market day atmosphere.

Vidar stood a little apart from the others, a package of flowered material wrapped in brown paper under his arm and a bag of candy in his pocket. Out of habit his dream-like gaze wandered out across the water, unconsciously seeking the raft which should have been back some time ago. Suddenly he realized that it was nowhere in sight; neither on its way towards the mainland nor at the island's landing. He ran back up the ramp to get a better look, while at the same time he knew it was gone.

"The raft has disappeared!" he yelled down to those on the landing. "It's nowhere in sight!"

People stopped talking and turned at once to look out over the water towards the island. The next second chaos broke out. Everyone knew that the raft went back and forth on a cable and was always in sight, wherever it was between the mainland and the island. It could only mean one thing. A couple of men ran to where the cable was connected to the landing. It hung straight down in the water instead of stretching out a couple of feet above the surface as usual.

Vidar ran to the village to find his uncle who was a fisherman, afraid to believe what he knew to be true.

"Uncle Erik!" he gasped. "The worst has happened. The cable has broken and the raft is gone!"

"Calm down, boy," his uncle told him. "That the raft has sailed away on the tide isn't the worst that can happen. It will go aground on one of the islands."

"But my father is gone!" Vidar screamed.

"Ah, I don't believe that."

"He's dead! I can feel it inside me.!" Vidar persisted, without realizing what he had said.

"Come, we'll take the boat and have a look," Erik said.

They rowed out in the fjord to where his fishing boat was anchored. Uncle Erik was convinced that the raft could sail free with no problem and thus wasn't worried about his brother's fate. He hoisted the sail and set course towards the island. By now the tide had turned and the maelstrom was slowly on it way back into the fjord again. As soon as they came out into open water they met a terrifying scene. Here and there floated various articles of clothing: a man's hat, a black shawl, gloves, a child's cap, amongst them. Further away a woman's basket bobbed on the waves. Erik's face turned grey. He swung the boat around and sailed out towards a group of tiny islands a mile or two away, where the current cast up rubbish it had taken with it from inside the fjord.

As they approached the tiny islands they could see two men waving their arms wildly. Beside them on the stony beach lay the raft, waiting for the high tide which would free it again. Vidar cast anchor while Erik pulled the rowboat up along side them. Together they rowed ashore to the two men who told them of the accident and of Edvin's attempt to rescue his neighbors, which lead to his death.

And so it was that at the age of 16 Vidar became the breadwinner for his mother and younger siblings. But the fact that the sea he had always loved could be so grim had frightened him. For a long time he was afraid to even go on board the new raft the islanders had built, even though it was much safer than the old one. But with time his fear matured to a profound respect for the sea's unpredictable humor. Finally, when people asked him to take over in his father's footsteps, after a little hesitation he agreed. He had sailed on the raft since he was a child and people depended on his inbred knowledge of the sea. At the same time, he discovered that his dream of having sole command of the ferry, and thus feel like a full-grown man, had lost its charm. He would gladly have been his father's apprentice for the rest of his life if he could only have him back.

The years passed. The wooden raft was exchanged for a steam-driven ferry. Vidar was no longer afraid, but he missed his father and mourned the loss of his ability to feel the same joy in the sea and the ferry that he had felt as a child. But he worked hard to support his family. In time his siblings grew up and moved away from home. Not long afterwards his mother died. Suddenly life seemed empty. Slowly he withdrew into his loneliness. It was as if he were ensnared in a spiderweb-like curse from which he could not disentangle himself. The thought of looking for a wife was too overwhelming to consider. Then when he was nearing forty, a fisherman in the village killed himself, leaving a wife and two daughters to survive as best they could. Vidar felt sorry for them and went to the woman and asked her to marry him. In her gratitude she bore him a son whom they named Enok. For Vidar, it was as if he were given his life back after so many years. When Enok was barely a year old he began taking him with him on the ferry. He pointed out things and explained how they worked and let the child's delicate fingers hold the rudder so he could feel the ferry's vibrations. When Enok turned two, Vidar let him carry the leather purse with its brass clasp and collect fares from the passengers. Even though he couldn't count, it would never have occurred to anyone to cheat him. Everyone loved little Enok. In some way he was like a part of the ferry and belonged to everyone on the island.

And thus, life carried on up until the First World War. There had never been a real village on the island and the widespread farms and fishing hamlets had, for the most part, been self-sufficient. People lived rather isolated from each other, as well as from life on the mainland. The only times they met were on the occasional church Sundays and at markets. But with the war's end, island life had changed forever. People began to move about more widely and the ferry became a more important part of their existence. All the news and gossip sailed back and forth with it like a permanent passenger, transforming it into the island's central meeting place. Enok grew up in the center of this universe. Even as a child he knew that he would one day follow his father and grandfather as ferryman. School seemed unnecessary and he quit after the required six years. The year after that he was confirmed and entered adulthood, whereupon he became a full-time ferryman's apprentice, then assistant.

When he was a bit over thirty the Second World War began, followed by the devastating German invasion along the Norwegian coast. And once again a son lost his father to the sea, a victim of his inability to swim. But this time it was the German bombs that sank the ferry with all on board. After that his mother fled to her married daughters in Sweden.

Life was hard during the war years. It was impossible to build a new ferry and people had to use whatever small boats were available to get to the mainland. When he no longer had a job, Enok joined the underground resistance movement, determined to avenge his father's death, even if it meant sacrificing his own life. But he was somehow shielded by his wrath and returned home unharmed, only to find the entire coast nothing but charred skeletons of the buildings were people had once lived and worked. Not even the chimney was left from his own cottage. The first thing he did was to build himself a new cottage on the old foundation, but it felt empty without his parents. A house but not a home.

After a while the islanders got a larger ferry, which could carry the cars people had begun to buy, and once again Enok worked as ferryman. Often at the end of the day he stayed on board, preparing his food on a hotplate and sleeping on a bench. He maintained to himself and others that he did so in case someone needed to cross to the mainland in the middle of the night, but in truth, it was boring to sit at home alone. The ferry became his home. Sometimes a few fishermen would come by in the evenings and they played cards. And on the light summer Saturday evenings there was always someone who turned up with an accordion or fiddle and people gathered on the landing, where they danced the night away under the undying sun. But many people had disappeared during the war, either as homeless refugees or in fear of losing their lives. Others had simply been victims of the countryside's eternal fate, forced to move into town to look for work. Those who were left all knew each other and any sparks which were going to flame up between them had already done so. Those who hadn't experienced this spark with the opposite sex had no choice but to look for a partner elsewhere or remain single. In Enok's case, his love for the island and the ferry was greater than his love for an unknown woman who perhaps didn't even exist. His real sorrow was over the fact that he had no son who would follow in his footsteps.

One day the district nurse, Sister Jensen, knocked lightly on the machine room window after the others had disembarked. Enok opened the door.

"Does Sister want something?" he asked.

"Yes, she does," answered Sister Jensen. "Does Enok know a little seven-year-old boy named Odd Halvorsen?"

Enok nodded. He had noticed the boy a number of times because he always looked like a scared dog.

"He has a hard time at home," she continued. "His father is an alcoholic and beats the boy when he is drunk. His mother says that Odd won't come home after school and that he can't sleep because he's so afraid of his father. He must be taken from that dreadful situation before it's too late. I promised her that I would try to find a foster home for him. I thought that perhaps Enok could take him."

"Me?" he said, looking around as if there might be another Enok standing behind him. "Why just me? I don't know anything about children."

"Because Odd needs a positive father-figure, someone who doesn't have his own children that he must compete with. Someone who has time for him."

"But what is his father going to say about it?"

"To be honest, I don't think Halvor cares about the boy. According to the mother, he denies that he is his father, since Odd isn't big and strong like the other boys in the family. She is afraid that he is going to beat him to death."

Enok stood quietly a moment, considering the matter.

"It could be nice with a little company also," Sister Jensen added. "I have the feeling that Enok could be the perfect father-figure for Odd. Think about it."

Enok thought about it during the rest of the day's trips back and forth across the fjord. He remembered the thrill of going on the ferry with his father, of their comradeship as Vidar showed him things and taught him about the sea, and about life. He could still feel the warmth of his father's big hands over his little child's hands when he got to hold the rudder, and how he grew to love the wind and the sea's many moods. Perhaps he could get Odd to love the sea and the ferry as he himself did. Think if he could be transformed into a happy little boy instead of a scared dog.

The next day Enok was waiting for the district nurse when she came aboard.

"I'll take the boy," he said simply.

"Wonderful! Enok will never regret it."

That afternoon she came to the machine room with Odd. His short pants were dirty and his jacket had a hole in the elbow. He carried a pair of boots tied-together over his shoulder and a cardboard box with his clothes under his arm.

"I assume Enok and Odd already know each other," Sister Jensen half-questioned.

Both nodded shyly.

"I'm sorry that his clothes aren't clean," she said. "We had to hurry. And now I have to go ashore again."

"That doesn't matter. We'll manage, won't we Odd?"

Odd didn't answer. He just looked down at his bare feet.

"You can leave your box here in the machine room," Enok said when Sister Jensen had gone. "It's almost time to cast off. You can unhook the chain and let people on board. There aren't so many, so we can sell tickets once we're under way."

Odd opened the gate as though he had been doing it his whole life. Then, without being told, he closed it again after the last passenger had come on board. Afterwards he stood by the railing and gazed out across the water.

"Odd! Come!" Enok called from the machine room. He saw how the boy jumped nervously and regretted his choice of words. He tried again. "Odd, can you please sell tickets for me? The purse is here."

The boy came slowly and stood in front of him, his eyes downcast. Enok held out the leather purse.

"Odd," he said gently, "look at me."

The boy didn't move.

Enok hunkered down and looked him straight in the face.

"Listen to me, Odd. I promise that I will never hit you, no matter what you do."

Odd looked up at him for a moment, then looked down again.

"I promise," Enok repeated.

Without a word, Odd took the purse and ran off to sell tickets. Watching him, Enok wondered if he ran out of joy or simply to get away from him.

Towards evening, when they were about to make the last trip to the mainland, Odd came running to the machine room, terrified. Before Enok had time to ask him what had happened he saw Halvor's huge figure marching along the quay towards the ferry. It was obvious that he was both drunk and angry. Without a word, Enok went to meet him, blocking his way just as he was about to climb on board.

"Where is the boy?" Halvor yelled.

Enok glared at him, his clinched fists hanging like dead weights from his sleeves. Both men were the same height, but Enok was much more powerfully built. Alcohol had long ago taken its toll with Halvor's once-strong body.

"He's here and here he's going to stay!" declared Enok, loud enough for everyone on the ferry and the landing to hear. "If Halvor ever dares to come near the boy, now or in the future, he will be met with these here," he continued, lifting his fists slightly. "Now get out of here! Halvor is no longer welcome on the ferry."

He swung around and went back to the machine room while the passengers stood and stared at Halvor, ready to defend both Enok and Odd if necessary. Wisely Halvor accepted defeat and left the landing. For Odd, who had witnessed the scene, it was a turning point. It was the first time anyone had ever defended him. He could hardly believe it was true.

The same evening, they built a box bed against the wall opposite Enok's. Odd didn't say anything while they worked and Enok saw that he was on his guard, making sure to keep a good distance between them. Enok acted as if he didn't notice. He talked a bit about the actual building process and showed Odd how to hold the hammer and pound in nails. Finally, the boy began to relax a little.

In the middle of the night he was woken by hysterical cries.

"No! No! Please don't hit me! I haven't done anything!"

"Wake up, Odd," Enok called gently from across the room. "It's only a dream."

When Odd continued screaming he crept under the blanket beside him and slowly encircled him with his arm.

"Wake up, Odd. It's just a dream. You're with Uncle Enok now. Nothing can hurt you here."

He repeated the same words over and over until Odd was completely awake. Then he got up and brought him a glass of water.

"Sit up now and drink this," he told him. "You have to be awake for a little while in order to get rid of the dream."

He sat beside him until he was sure the dream had passed, then he stood up to go back to bed.

"Don't go," Odd sniffed, holding up his arms beseechingly.

Suddenly Enok remembered how it felt to be a little child and wake up from an ordinary nightmare. How it felt to wake up from a nightmare which was also reality was beyond his ability to comprehend. He crept under the blanket again and held Odd in the curve of his body.

"I won't leave you. I promise," he whispered.

And at last they both fell asleep.

Even though the picture of Enok standing up to his father was etched in his memory, Odd dared not believe it. Halvor could also be nice to him and then suddenly light into him with his fists when he least expected it. Certainly, Enok could do the same. But in the middle of the night, when the nightmare attacked in the darkness, he was so helpless that he had no choice. He was forced to call out for Enok and risk being beaten, rather than being comforted. But Enok was never angry when he was woken from a sound sleep. After a while Odd began to trust him and to find pleasure in the security he felt in that big man's arms, a security he had never before experienced. Not even his mother had been able to protect him from his father. Slowly the intensity of the nightmare began to fade as his trust in Enok grew.

The hours that Odd wasn't in school he spent with Enok, following him like a shadow, afraid that his father might appear if he let him disappear from sight. At the same time, like Vidar, Enok taught him everything he knew about the ferry, the sea, and about life. And with his father's unquenchable thirst, Odd drank in all the knowledge Enok offered him.

When he was ten years old, Halvor drank himself to death. For the first time in his life, Odd experienced an unlimited feeling of freedom. But his relief was dampened by the thought that he would soon have to move back to his family. Enok and Odd and grown together like father and son and people had long referred to the boy as Enok's-Odd. And more than anything, he wanted to continue to be Enok's-Odd. He lived in dread of the day the district nurse would come and fetch him. But she didn't come. Finally, he couldn't stand it any longer.

"When is Sister Jensen coming?" he asked one evening while Enok stood with his back to him frying fish for dinner.

"Sister Jensen?" repeated Enok. "Why should she come?"

Odd's throat was so tight with the tears he tried to hold back that he couldn't answer.

Enok turned around and looked at him.

"What's wrong?" he asked. "Has something happened?"

"I don't want to leave here," he blurted.

"What do you mean?"

"Even if my father can't beat me anymore...."

Enok set the frying pan on the cooler side of the wood stove and put his arms around the boy.

"You aren't going to move away from here," he reassured him. "You're Enok's-Odd and this is always going to be your home."

Odd's body relaxed, as if he had let out an enormous sigh of relief.

When Odd turned 13, like Enok, he quit school and was confirmed. Afterwards he worked full-time on the ferry. To celebrate his 18th birthday he changed his last name from Halvorsen to Enoksen. It was hard to know who was most proud, Odd or Enok.

In the years that followed they took in other boys who needed to get away from their home environments. Yet it was Odd who remained closest to Enok's heart, while Odd looked upon Enok as his beloved father. But the day Mari entered his life, Odd felt himself pulled in two directions. It had never occurred to him that he might one day abandon the man who meant so much to him. Sensing his dilemma, Enok gave him his blessing.

"Mari is a wonderful girl," he remarked one evening over dinner.

Odd looked up, startled. They had never mentioned Mari, even though it was no secret that they often spent their free time together.

"I don't mean to sound pushy, but I would love to have her as my daughter-in-law," he continued. "The two of you could take over the empty lighthouse keeper's house up on the hill. You have to admit that this cabin gets pretty crowded when other boys are living here. I wouldn't consider it a loss if you had your own place, but, rather, as a gain if you brought Mari into the family..."

"What do you mean, we could take over the old lighthouse keeper's house?" Odd interrupted. "How do you know that's possible?"

Enok just shrugged his shoulders innocently.

"Why you sly old fox!" Odd declared laughingly. "So, you've been sneaking around planning my future behind my back!"

"I'm sorry," Enok replied a little sheepishly. "I'm not trying to get rid of you. It was just an idea I had."

"And a great one! Is it really possible?"

Enok nodded.

Odd gulped down the rest of his dinner, excused himself, and hurried out to find Mari. It was as if a stone had been lifted from his heart.

"Is it really true?" Mari asked excitedly. "How wonderful!"

And so, it was decided.

Without telling anyone, Odd and Mari decided to get married in a simple ceremony, with just Enok and her parents present. It was a warm summer day. The church stood silhouetted against a deep blue cloud-dotted sky on the hill above the fjord, from which the view stretched past the outer islands and disappeared into the sea beyond the curve of the earth. It couldn't have been more beautiful. Only the harbor, which lay straight down below the hill, was out of sight. When they came out of the church, Enok suggested that they go to the mainland and eat lunch at the Grand Hotel. They could easily be back before he had to make the next run. They all agreed.

When they reached the ferry, Odd noticed immediately that something was wrong. The gate was open. He looked at Enok, who looked just as puzzled. They rushed on board, dragging Mari with them. The car deck was empty. Odd jerked open the door to the lounge, ready to catch the thief in action. Instead, they were greeted by a crowd of joyful islanders. Spel-Kalle pulled out a long note on his accordion.

"Congratulations! Congratulations!" everyone cried. "Welcome Mr. and Mrs. Enoksen!"

The room was decorated with red, white, and blue streamers. Along one wall was a long table covered with all sorts of food that people had brought with them, as well as coffee and a huge wedding cake.

Odd and Mari stood hand in hand, dumbfounded in front of these people they had known their whole lives.

"I thought we were going to get married secretly," remarked Odd and looked at Enok.

"Don't blame me," Enok answered. "I'm just as surprised as you are. I had no idea whatsoever."

"Oh, it's wonderful!" sighed Mari. "Thank you all so much!"

The rest of the day was a party on board. The islanders, together with others who happened to be crossing, ate and danced through many runs back and forth while Spel-Kalle's accordion breathed in and out.

That evening Odd and Mari went to their new home just up the hill from the cottage which had been Odd's home so many years. Enok went home to his two foster boys, happy for Odd's happiness, but with a little empty hole inside.

For a quarter of a century Enok and Odd continued to work together on the ferry, while Odd also drove the school bus in order to better support his growing family. Enok thoroughly enjoyed Odd's three sons and impatiently awaited the day that each of them was big enough to go with him on the ferry.

There he showed them how everything functioned and let them help him, while at the same time passing on his knowledge of the sea and of life. On summer days the other children on the island made their way down to the ferry to partake in what became known as Enok's School, where they got to listen, learn, and help out. Nor was it only the children who enjoyed the atmosphere. Enok was just as happy to teach as they were to learn. As adults, many felt a deep gratitude for the great contribution he had made toward enriching their lives, a gift their parents had neither the time nor the knowledge to give them.

As time went on, the population of the island dwindled, the houses and farms being bought up by city people for summer homes. When the island's school finally had to close, Enok suggested that Odd move to the mainland with his family. By now the boys were in gymnasium, which meant that they would have to go to school in town, some distance inland from the village where the ferry docked.

"We'll see each other just as often," he maintained, "and it will be better for the boys to be able to live at home, rather than have to board with people in town. Then, when they have moved away from home, you can move back to the island if you want to, or when I retire, I can move to the mainland myself."

Odd laughed. "First of all, you are never going to retire, nor will you ever move from the island."

Enok laughed, a bit embarrassed at the truth. "But think about it," he concluded.

Odd thought about it the whole summer. Enok was right, but it felt wrong to move so far away from him. The deciding factor was when Mari got a job in town. Then they had to live on the other side of the fjord. They tried to get Enok to move with them, but even though he no longer had anyone living with him, there were a couple of boys he felt he wanted to keep close contact with. The truth was, he couldn't imagine leaving the island. But as he had maintained, they met just as often as before. Or almost, at least.

In the beginning of the 1990's the rumor that a bridge was to be built reached the island. Everyone was enthusiastic. Rather than crossing the large expanse of water as the ferry did, it would be built further to the south, where the distance was shorter.

"Think," someone said, "then we can go back and forth to the mainland whenever we wish, without having to plan according to the ferry schedule."

"And poor Enok can finally retire and take it easy," remarked someone else.

But Enok had never dreamed of retiring. The ferry was his life. At the same time, he understood that people had no idea of what it meant to him. They simply saw it as his job. Nor could he deny that a bridge would be practical. People were becoming more and more stressed and unable to enjoy a relaxing half hour ferry ride across the fjord with their friends and acquaintances, surrounded by weather and wind, sea and sky. Everyone was in a hurry. With a bridge, one could cross in a couple of minutes, each alone in his or her own car, without having to pay any attention to the weather and wind or sea and sky outside the closed car window. Only Odd realized what all this meant to Enok. Once more he tried to get him to move over to them on the mainland, but Enok refused. Nor did he partake in the bridge's opening ceremony that autumn.

"Why should I celebrate something that I don't want, some- thing which not only takes away my job, but also my life!" he told Odd.

Odd had no answer.

The thing that no one knew was that Enok had refused to look at the bridge, even when it was being built. It was only visible from the very end of the landing and he was able to maneuver the ferry in such a way that he did not need to look in its direction when docking. Consequently, the bridge did not exist for him.

The day before the ferry was to be towed off and junked, he cleared away everything that was his or had any meaning for him, then went ashore without looking back and locked himself in his cottage. For two days he refused to let anyone in. On the third day Odd forced the door open. Enok was so hung-over that he could barely stand up.

"Don't worry," he said reassuringly. "I'm not going to drink myself to death. All the bottles are empty now and I have no way to go into town and buy more."

"Come home with me," Odd begged. "You need to get away from here for a while."

"No, I don't want to. Leave me alone to handle this myself. You can come back in a couple of days."

He wasn't angry, but Odd could see that he was very upset and really wanted to be left alone. It wasn't Enok's style to show his feelings in front of others.

Odd continued to try to persuade Enok to move to the mainland near him and Marit. In vain.

"Don't worry about me," Enok said. "I'm fine. I have things to do to pass the time."

"What kind of things?" Odd asked challengingly.

"Well, everything that is necessary in order to stay alive. Cut firewood, make food, wash clothes, and such. And then I have a whole pile of un-read books."

All that was true, but how Enok actually spent his days was another story. He got up at the same time as he always had, carried out his morning routines, and then went down to the landing. There he sat for hours, looking out over the fjord towards the landing on the other side. The longer he looked, the more it was as if he were on his way there with the ferry. He could feel the motor's vibrations and even hear the familiar sound of the water when the bow cut through the

231

waves. It was his life's symphony, like a mother's voice. He closed his eyes and listened longingly.

On weekdays Odd came past at three o'clock, after having left off the younger children who now went to school in the village on the mainland. By that time, Enok had already gone home to make coffee for them. Then, after Odd left, he made another trip down to the landing before evening fell. And thus his days passed. In spite of the fact that he loved Odd and his family, he couldn't bring himself to leave the island.

When Enok reached the landing that morning he saw that the ice wasn't as thick as he had thought. With a little effort the ferry could cut through it. He sat down on an old girder at the end of the dock and leaned against a couple of posts to wait for Odd to bring the ferry from the mainland when he came with the school bus. By now the northern lights danced weakly in the north, like a soundless orchestra. Slowly they faded and Enok closed his eyes in order to fully enjoy the silence surrounding him. He must have fallen asleep, for suddenly he was awakened by hundreds of familiar children's voices behind him. He turned around, prepared to welcome them. But instead of the children, for the first time he saw the new bridge stretching across the fjord to the south, long and thin and graceful like a leaping antelope. He was shaken! He had never imagined that men could create something so beautiful! And behind it the sun had just begun to rise, huge and red, out of the sea. It was too much for him.

At three o'clock Odd drove past the old landing, longing for coffee as usual. He was surprised when he saw Enok sitting down by the water and even more surprised that he didn't wave when he tooted. Suddenly he felt as though an arrow had pierced his heart. He swung out onto the landing, but even before he could jump out of the bus he knew.

Whether it had been his heart or the cold didn't matter...